中译经典文库·中
Chinese Classical Treasury – The Traditional Chinese Culture Classical Series
(Chinese–English)

禅宗语录

Excerpts From Zen Buddhist Texts

江蓝生 编选　黎翠珍 张佩瑶 英译

中国出版集团
中国对外翻译出版公司

图书在版编目（CIP）数据

禅宗语录：汉英对照/江蓝生编；黎翠珍，张佩瑶译. —北京：中国对外翻译出版公司，2008.1

(中译经典文库. 中华传统文化精粹)

ISBN 978-7-5001-1827-5

Ⅰ. 禅… Ⅱ. ①江…②黎…③张… Ⅲ. ①汉语—英语—对照读物②禅宗—语录—中国 Ⅳ. H319.4：B

中国版本图书馆 CIP 数据核字（2007）第 181935 号

出版发行 / 中国对外翻译出版公司
地　　址 / 北京市西城区车公庄大街甲 4 号物华大厦六层
电　　话 / (010) 68359376　68359303　68359101　68357937
邮　　编 / 100044
传　　真 / (010) 68357870
电子邮箱 / book@ctpc.com.cn
网　　址 / http://www.ctpc.com.cn

出版策划 / 张高里
策划编辑 / 李　虹　宗　颖
责任编辑 / 韩建荣
封面设计 / 大象设计工作室

排　　版 / 艾林视觉·陈默　ailincc@yahoo.com.cn
印　　刷 / 保定市中画美凯印刷有限公司
经　　销 / 新华书店

规　　格 / 880×1230 毫米　1/32
印　　张 / 12.75
字　　数 / 202 千字
版　　次 / 2008 年 1 月第一版
印　　次 / 2012 年 1 月第二次

ISBN 978-7-5001-1827-5　　　定价：22.00 元

版权所有　侵权必究
中国对外翻译出版公司

世界丛书中认识中国
中国通过书走向世界

出版说明

"中华传统文化精粹"丛书脱胎于我公司出版的 20 世纪八九十年代中国最富盛名的双语读物"英汉汉英对照一百丛书"。这套丛书曾经影响了几代英语和中华文化学习者、爱好者,深受读者的喜爱,以至今天还有许多翻译界、外交界、教育界等各界取得卓越成就的人士,对这套书籍仍怀有浓重的情结。这套书不仅仅是当初他们学习英语的课外启蒙读本,亦是他们的良师益友,是他们追求知识、拼搏向上的青春记忆。

这套丛书最初由中国对外翻译出版公司于 20 世纪八九十年代同香港商务印书馆合作陆续推出,丛书的编者和译者都是在各自领域做出贡献的学者、教授,使得该套丛书在读者中获得了很好的口碑,创造了良好的社会效益和经济效益。

为了将这一品牌发扬光大,我公司对"英汉汉英对照一百丛书"进行了修订、重组,聘请了享誉海内外的中国翻译界专家组成阵容强大的顾问团,在题材、选篇、译文、栏目设置等方面进行了严谨的论证、精心的编辑,打造出适应新时代读者需求以及提升中国文化新形象的精品图书——"中华传统文化精粹"。

"中华传统文化精粹"丛书内容丰富。秉承以中外读者为本的宗旨,我们增加了白话翻译、中文注释、汉语拼音、经典名句等栏目,删除了晦涩、冗长的篇目,使丛书更加通俗、实用。

"中华传统文化精粹"丛书整体性强、版式精致且与内容和谐统一,相信必将受到中外读者的喜爱。

The Classics Bring a
Modern China to the World

Publication Note

The Traditional Chinese Culture Classical Series originated from the Chinese-English 100 Bilingual Series, the most popular one in the last two decades of the 20th century in China. The series had so impressed generations of English learners and admirers of Chinese culture that still leaves a deep impression in readers' mind. The books were their primary reading materials of English language, resourceful teacher and intimate friend, witnessing a perennial youth in pursuit of knowledge and success.

The series gradually came into being through the cooperation between China Translation and Publication Corporation (CTPC) and Hong Kong Commercial Press in 1980s and 1990s. The series was compiled and translated together by a group of outstanding scholars and professors.

To bring the superb quality of the previous series into full play, CTPC has put enormous effort in revising and reorganizing it, drawing from the contributions by renowned translation scholars and experts in China. Their critical assessment and compilation with regards to topics, original selections, English translations, and overall layouts will surely stand to the reader's demand and create a new image of Chinese culture, that is, in "The Traditional Chinese Culture Classical Series".

The Traditional Chinese Culture Classical Series enjoys rich content and realizes our reader-oriented principle. To these ends, we add modern Chinese renditions, annotations, pronunciations, and highlighted classical sentences while removing those obscure and tedious sections, in an effort to make the series both popular and pragmatic.

Characteristic of holistic configuration and harmonious unity between the fine format and the excellent content, the Traditional Chinese Culture Classical Series will certainly be cherished by readers from both home and abroad.

禅宗语录 中华传统文化精粹

CONTENTS

目录

01　前　言 Preface

02　不立文字(初祖菩提达摩语录)
　　Not through the written word
　　(Recorded Dialogues of the First Patriarch Bodhidharmna)

06　法佛无二(二祖慧可语录)
　　Buddha and the Way of Buddha are the same
　　(Recorded Dialogues of the Second Patriarch Huike)

10　无人缚汝(三祖僧璨语录)
　　Nobody has tied you down
　　(Recorded Dialogues of the Third Patriarch Sengcan)

12　非心不问佛,问佛不非心(四祖道信语录)
　　The heart is Buddha, and Buddha is the heart
　　(Recorded Dialogues of the Fourth Patriarch Daoxin)

16　大厦之材,本出幽谷(五祖弘忍语录)
　　Timbers for buildings come from secluded valleys
　　(Recorded Dialogues of the Fifth Patriarch Hongren)

18　佛性无南北(六祖慧能语录)
　　No regional differences
　　(Recorded Dialogues of the Sixth Patriarch Huineng)

22　仁者自心动(六祖慧能语录)

目录
CONTENTS

Your minds are wavering
(Recorded Dialogues of the Sixth Patriarch Huineng)

26 诸佛妙理,非关文字(六祖慧能语录)
The wonderful mysteries of Buddhist enlightenment have nothing to do with the written word
(Recorded Dialogues of the Sixth Patriarch Huineng)

28 何名禅定(六祖慧能语录)
Zen meditation (Recorded Dialogues of the Sixth Patriarch Huineng)

32 清净法身(六祖慧能语录)
The nature of man is pure
(Recorded Dialogues of the Sixth Patriarch Huineng)

36 一灯能除千年暗(六祖慧能语录)
One bright lamp can clear away the darkness of ages
(Recorded Dialogues of the Sixth Patriarch Huineng)

38 无别之性(六祖慧能语录)
No qualitative difference
(Recorded Dialogues of the Sixth Patriarch Huineng)

40 识心见性(六祖慧能语录)
Know your own mind, discover your own nature
(Recorded Dialogues of the Sixth Patriarch Huineng)

42 顿悟见佛(六祖慧能语录)

目录 CONTENTS

In the moment of enlightenment you see Buddha
(Recorded Dialogues of the Sixth Patriarch Huineng)

46　法地若动，一切不安（善慧语录）
If the foundations of dharma stir, all will be upset
(Recorded Dialogues of Shanhui)

50　本无所断，亦无所得（法融语录）
Nothing to give up, and nothing to acquire
(Recorded Dialogues of Farong)

52　无心恰恰用（法融语录）
When you are not concentrating, you are concentrating
(Recorded Dialogues of Farong)

54　一切自看（崇慧语录）
You have to work things out for yourself
(Recorded Dialogues of Chonghui)

58　八十老人行不得（道林语录）
Not even an eighty-year-old can do it
(Recorded Dialogues of Daolin)

62　吾不如也（神秀语录）
I am not as good as he is (Recorded Dialogues of Shenxiu)

64　不见不闻（道树语录）
See nothing, hear nothing (Recorded Dialogues of Daoshu)

目录 CONTENTS

68 不记年岁(慧安语录)
I remember not my age (Recorded Dialogues of Huian)

70 如人饮水,冷暖自知(道明语录)
When you drink water, you know if it is hot or cold
(Recorded Dialogues of Daoming)

72 善恶如浮云(峻极语录)
Good and evil are like floating clouds (Recorded Dialogues of Junji)

76 磨砖作镜(怀让语录)
Polishing a brick to make a mirror (Recorded Dialogues of Huairang)

80 小乘是大乘(神会语录)
Hinayana is Mahayana (Recorded Dialogues of Shenhui)

82 是法平等(慧忠语录)
All creatures are equal (Recorded Dialogues of Huizhong)

86 佛还曾迷也无(慧忠语录)
Was Buddha ever deluded? (Recorded Dialogues of Huizhong)

90 何不自看自静(崛多语录)
Why not keep peace in your own mind
(Recorded Dialogues of Jueduo)

94 但看弄傀儡,线断一时休(本净语录)
Watch the Puppeteer (Recorded Dialogues of Benjing)

98 一宿觉(玄觉语录)

CONTENTS
目录

The one-night enlightenment (Recorded Dialogues of Xuanjue)

104 常定无出入(玄策语录)
Mindless in meditation (Recorded Dialogues of Xuance)

108 石头路滑(道一语录)
That stone is a slippery one (Recorded Dialogues of Daoyi)

112 莫道我解佛法(道悟语录)
Don't think that I can explain Buddha's Way
(Recorded Dialogues of Daowu)

116 一切不为(惟俨语录)
Doing nothing (Recorded Dialogues of Weiyan)

118 龙生龙子,凤生凤儿(天然语录)
Dragons beget dragons, Phoenixes beget phoenixes
(Recorded Dialogues of Tianran)

122 丹霞烧木佛(天然语录)
Danxia burnt a buddha carved in wood
(Recorded Dialogues of Tianran)

126 洪炉上一点雪(旷禅师语录)
A snowflake on the stove
(Recorded Dialogues of Zen Master Kuang)

130 汝无佛性(慧朗语录)
You have no Buddha-nature (Recorded Dialogues of Huilang)

目录

CONTENTS

134 野鸭子什处去也(怀海语录)
Where are the ducks going? (Recorded Dialogues of Huaihai)

138 自家宝藏(慧海语录)
Your own treasure (Recorded Dialogues of Huihai)

142 饥来吃饭,困来即眠(慧海语录)
Eat when I'm hungry, sleep when I'm sleepy (Recorded Dialogues of Huihai)

146 师子身中虫,自食师子肉(智藏语录)
The fleas on the lion eat of the lion's flesh (Recorded Dialogues of Zhicang)

150 有与无(智藏语录)
Yes and no (Recorded Dialogues of Zhicang)

154 梅子熟也(法常语录)
The plum is ripe (Recorded Dialogues of Fachang)

158 亲者不问,问者不亲(法常语录)
He who is closer does not ask (Recorded Dialogues of Fachang)

160 万灵归一(灵默语录)
An return to the One (Recorded Dialogues of Lingmo)

164 捉虚空(慧藏语录)
Grasping the intangible (Recorded Dialogues of Huicang)

166 不可思议(惟宽语录)

CONTENTS 目录

170 Beyond comprehension (Recorded Dialogues of Weikuan)
金屑虽珍宝，在眼亦为病（惟宽语录）
Gold dust may be valuable, but it can hurt the eyes
(Recorded Dialogues of Weikuan)

174 事怕有心人（希运语录）
With will and perseverance (Recorded Dialogues of Xiyun)

178 义学沙门（希运语录）
A stickler for dogma (Recorded Dialogues of Xiyun)

182 自了汉（黄檗语录）
A man who only looks after himself
(Recorded Dialogues of Xiyun Huangbo)

186 拽出死尸著（性空语录）
Take this corpse out of here (Recorded Dialogues of Xingkong)

190 见无左右（常观语录）
The left horn or the right? (Recorded Dialogues of Changguan)

192 发言异常（神赞语录）
Unusual way of talking (Recorded Dialogues of Shenzan)

196 道在粪中（从谂语录）
The Way is in the dung (Recorded Dialogues of Congshen)

200 我大悟也（智通语录）
I'm enlightened (Recorded Dialogues of Zhitong)

目录 CONTENTS

204 禅门本无南北(弘辩语录)
There is no division into North and South in Zen itself
(Recorded Dialogues of Hongbian)

208 指示心要(崇信语录)
Show me the way of the mind (Recorded Dialogues of Chongxin)

212 棹拨清波,金鳞罕遇(德诚语录)
When the oar stirs the waves (Recorded Dialogues of Decheng)

216 我国晏然(高沙弥语录)
My country is at peace
(Recorded Dialogues of the Religious Novice Gao)

220 切不得错用心(义忠语录)
Do not attend to the wrong things
(Recorded Dialogues of Yizhong)

224 半肯半不肯(良价语录)
I half affirm him, and half do not (Recorded Dialogues of Liangjia)

228 柱杖子(芭蕉语录)
If you have a staff (Recorded Dialogues of Bajiao)

230 出门便是草(庆诸语录)
There is grass when you step outside
(Recorded Dialogues of Qingzhu)

234 呵佛骂祖(宣鉴语录)

CONTENTS

目录

Abusing the buddhas and the patriarchs
(Recorded Dialogues of Xuanjian)

238　定取生死（善会语录）
Know life and death (Recorded Dialogues of Shanhui)

242　黄檗佛法无多子（义玄语录）
Huangbo's teaching is as simple as can be
(Recorded Dialogues of Yixuan)

248　佛今何在（义玄语录）
Where is Buddha now? (Recorded Dialogues of Yixuan)

252　真佛无形（义玄语录）
The real buddha has no shape or body
(Recorded Dialogues of Yixuan)

256　佛法无用功处（临济语录）
No special effort is needed (Recorded Dialogues of Linji)

258　何汩没于此（裴休语录）
Why do you hide your light here? (Recorded Dialogues of Peixiu)

264　眼里耳里鼻里（仰山语录）
In the eyes, in the ears and in the nose
(Recorded Dialogues of Yangshan)

268　和尚何似驴（仰山语录）
Do I look like an ass? (Recorded Dialogues of Yangshan)

目录

CONTENTS

270 智闲省悟(智闲语录)
The enlightenment of Zhixian (Recorded Dialogues of Zhixian)

274 不较多(澡先语录)
Almost ready (Recorded Dialogues of Zaoxian)

278 鳌山成道(义存语录)
Enlightenment at Aoshan (Recorded Dialogues of Yicun)

284 透过祖佛(居遁语录)
To see through the buddhas and the patriarchs
(Recorded Dialogues of Judun)

288 禅师不看经(休静语录)
Zen masters don't read sutras (Recorded Dialogues of Xiujing)

290 神前酒台盘(蚬子语录)
The tray of wine offerings (Recorded Dialogues of Xianzi)

294 文偃契旨(文偃语录)
Wenyan in harmony with Zen (Recorded Dialogues of Wenyan)

298 莫趁口乱问(文偃语录)
Don't ask without thinking (Recorded Dialogues of Wenyan)

302 各在当人分上(文偃语录)
Do your own work (Recorded Dialogues of Wenyan)

306 莫空过时(文偃语录)
Do not waste your time (Recorded Dialogues of Wenyan)

CONTENTS

310 自幻自怕(师备语录)
Scaring yourself with your own delusions
(Recorded Dialogues of Shibei)

314 休从他觅(幼璋语录)
Do not seek it outside yourself (Recorded Dialogues of Youzhang)

318 竹密岂妨流水过(善静语录)
A thick bamboo grove does not block the water-flow
(Recorded Dialogues of Shanjing)

322 一时抛与诸人(道匡语录)
I will toss it all to you (Recorded Dialogues of Daokuang)

326 赚杀人(道匡语录)
Split a joke with the dead (Recorded Dialogues of Daokuang)

330 元本契书(澄远语录)
The deeds of the land (Recorded Dialogues of Chengyuan)

334 做个无事衲僧(守初语录)
Be carefree monks (Recorded Dialogues of Shouchu)

338 知音即不恁么问(匡果语录)
The enlightened would not have asked this question
(Recorded Dialogues of Kuangguo)

342 亲见作家来(延沼语录)
You've met a veteran (Recorded Dialogues of Yanzhao)

目录 / CONTENTS

348 佛法见成（文益语录）
Buddhism is about what is here (Recorded Dialogues of Wenyi)

352 长连床上稳坐地（道钦语录）
Go sit on the bench (Recorded Dialogues of Daoqin)

356 不惧生死和尚（缘德语录）
The monk who fears not death (Recorded Dialogues of Yuande)

360 夜放乌鸡带雪飞（警玄语录）
A blackbird flying in snow in the dark of night
(Recorded Dialogues of Jingxuan)

364 美食不中饱人吃（义青语录）
Food has no attraction for a man who is full
(Recorded Dialogues of Yiqing)

368 为汝正之（楚圆语录）
Look, I'll straighten it (Recorded Dialogues of Chuyuan)

372 主要梵语词汇表
375 A Glossary of Selected Sanskrit Terms

前言 PrEFACE

禅宗是佛教中国化的最终产物,在历史上曾对我国及邻国(如日本、朝鲜等)的哲学、伦理、文学、艺术的发展产生过广泛而深刻的影响;在现今世界里,禅宗又以其东方文化的独特魅力,向西方文化渗透。作为人类的一种精神遗产,禅宗一直吸引人们去了解它、研究它,并从其中汲取营养。

禅宗是佛教宗派名,尊奉印度的菩提达摩为师祖。不过禅宗这一名称是到了唐代才出现的。从禅宗的始祖达摩到二祖慧可、三祖僧璨、四祖道信、五祖弘忍,弘忍的门下分成南北两宗,北宗神秀持渐悟说,南宗慧能持顿悟说,后世只盛行南宗顿悟说,并尊慧能为六祖。慧能的弟子神会在慧能去世后挑起对北宗的论战,使得南宗教义大大显扬,并在社会各阶层中广泛盛行开来。

禅宗一方面保持着与原始印度佛教的血缘关系,另一方面又对原始佛教和传统禅学进行了最彻底的变革。在内容上,禅宗提出自心自性即佛心佛性,佛性人人都有,人人都可以"即凡成圣"。在形式上,顿悟说革除了坐禅修行的方式,认为人的觉悟可以不靠坐禅和读经,甚至也不必采取出家当和尚的方式,心本身、平常心就是觉悟之源,"一念若悟,众生是佛"。禅宗在人性与佛性之间建立的直接等同关系,禅宗的顿悟方式,对探求解脱门径的芸

前言 PREFACE

芸众生产生了极大的吸引力，这正是禅宗得以盛行且长久地保持其生命力的主要原因。

禅宗的宗教观，禅宗的思维模式，集中地反映在历代编辑整理的禅宗语录集中（如五代的《祖堂集》、宋代的《景德传灯录》、《五灯会元》等）。语录是门徒对禅师口头说法的记录，是以书面形态反映口头形态的佛教典籍。禅宗语录里记录了许许多多的祖师问答、对众说法和自我内省的故事（禅家称之为"公案"）。这些记录字面上明白如话，但读起来却往往义理难通。这一方面固然由于对禅宗教义不甚了然，另一方面也由于对禅师的特殊思维方式、表达方式缺乏了解所致。比如，在禅问答中，禅师往往不正面回答提问，不是问东答西，就是就所问反施一问，甚而不假言语，仅以动作回答。禅问答中充满了违背常理的悖论，充满了含蓄隐晦的讽喻和形象生动的类比，充满了耐人寻味的机锋和理趣……。禅宗倡导的领悟方法是超概念、超逻辑的，只能凭借心求意解的感受和体验来实现，这是它素称难读的主要原因，读者诸君只能各依悟性来领会其中旨意了。

禅宗思想最活跃的时代是晚唐五代，宋代以后已基本上停滞，元代禅宗遭到统治者的压抑，明代以后与净土宗合为一体，逐渐失去了原有的风貌。因此，本书所选收的一百段语录，全都采自唐、五代禅师的语录；既考虑内容的代表性，又兼顾文字的可读性。

为了帮助读者理解，每段选文之后一般都有白话译文及简单的注释，必要时还加上了提示。在这里我要特别感谢黎翠珍女士及张佩瑶女士，她们不仅把本书的内容翻译成准确精美的英文，

前言 PREFACE

而且在某些提示中还加上了她们自己的独到见解。本书还附设一个梵语词汇表，列出书中常见的梵语词语。这不仅给一些初涉禅学者提供了很大的方便，而且也使本书避免了某些词语多次出现而重复注释的烦琐。

可以说，本书是兼纳了译者的见解、创意而编写出来的，而这正好体现了禅宗容纳不同意见的特色。俗语说："既来佛会下，都是有缘人"，这本禅宗小书成全了我与黎女士及张女士的一段缘分，我还希望通过它广结善缘，跟读者诸君共同体会禅的精神、禅的韵味。禅宗语录浩如烟海，限于水平和能力，拣沙遗金之处在所难免，还望方家指正。

江蓝生
一九九七年七月于北京听雨斋

PREFACE

Zen Buddhism is the product of the sinicization of Buddhism. Historically, Zen Buddhism has made a wide and lasting impact on the development of philosophy, ethics. literature and arts in China and its neighbouring countries such as Japan and Korea. In the present-day world, Zen Buddhism, as a form of oriental culture with a unique attraction of its own, is extending its influence on Western culture. Being part of the spiritual heritage of human civilisation, Zen Buddhism has always attracted people to understand it, to study it, and to gain nourishment from it.

Zen Buddhism is a Buddhist sect that acknowledges as its founder the Indian saint Bodhidharma. But the term Zen Buddhism* did not come into existence until the Tang Dynasty. The line of patriarchs for Zen Buddhism started with Bodhidharma and went on through the Second Patriarch Huike, the Third Patriarch Sengcan, the Fourth Patriarch Daoxin, and the Fifth Patriarch Hongren. After Hongren, Zen Buddhism split into two branches: the Northern School was headed by

---

* Zen Buddhism: See Translators' Notes 1 on Page 8.

PREFACE
前言

Shenxiu who emphasised a gradual process of enlightenment, and the Southern School was headed by Huineng who emphasised the process of sudden enlightenment. Subsequently the Southern School gained more popularity and Huineng was venerated as the Sixth Patriarch. After the death of Huineng, his disciple Shenhui started a major debate with the Northern School. This helped to spread the teachings of the Southern School, the fame of which soon pervaded all strata of society.

While Zen Buddhism maintained its link with its origin in primitive Buddhism in India, it also brought about a most thorough transformation of the earliest Buddhist tradition to which it belongs. In substance, Zen Buddhism advocates that the nature of the self is the nature of Buddha, and the heart of the self is the heart of Buddha, that Buddha nature is there in everyone, and everyone can attain Buddhahood. In terms of form, the emphasis on sudden enlightenment makes the formal practice of Zen meditation redundant, since it is asserted that revelation can be attained not necessarily through Zen meditation and the study of the scriptures, or even the formal process of ordination as monks, and since harmony of heart and body and natural ease are regarded as the sources of enlightenment. In short, "One sudden awareness would make a man a buddha." The equating of human nature with Buddha-nature and the emphasis on sudden enlightenment have proved very attractive to the many who seek liberation from the troubles of the world, and these are some of the reasons for the prolonged popularity of Zen Buddhism far and wide.

PREFACE

前言

The religious outlook, mind-set and ways of thinking of Zen Buddhism are seen in their many manifestations in the edited records of Zen dialogues over the centuries, e.g. in *A Collection from the Halls of Patriarchs of the Five Dynasties*, or in *Jingde Record of the Transmission of the Lamp and Amalgamation of the Sources of the Five Lamps* of the Song Dynasty etc. These records, known as "koans", preserve in written form what the Zen masters said to their disciples orally, and they make up a special genre of Buddhist texts. In these koans, there are records of many question-and-answer sessions between the masters and their disciples, there are also records of the masters' lectures, and stories for self reflection. These records have an apparent simplicity, but they often present a lot of difficulties to the reader, partly because the reader may not be familiar with the doctrines of Zen Buddhism, and partly because of the unconventional ways of thinking and of ex pressions practised by the masters. For instance, in question-and-answer sessions, the master often does not answer the questions di rectly, preferring instead to give what appears to be an irrelevant answer, or simply to counter with another question, or even to dispense with verbal answer and reply with a physical gesture. Zen dialogue is full of apparent illogicalities or irreverence, of opaque commentaries and ironies, and of lively metaphors and analogies which challenge the intellect and the curious mind. Zen Buddhism inspires one to enlightenment by transcending accepted concepts, by going beyond logic, and by appealing to feelings and to the intuitive faculties.

PREFACE
前言

Therein lie the difficulties for the reader. And the reader has to meet the challenge with his own intuitive powers.

Zen Buddhism was at its most dynamic in late Tang Dynasty and the Five Dynasties. By the Song Dynasty, its development had come to a standstill. In the Yuan Dynasty, it fell into obscurity under the oppression of the ruling regime. By the Ming Dynasty, it had lost most of its distinctive characteristics and it merged with the Pure Land sect of Buddhism. The 100 excerpts selected for inclusion in this book have all been culled from records of the Zen masters in the Tang and the Five Dynasties, and they are chosen for their representative qualities as well as their readability.

As an aid to fuller understanding, each excerpt is provided with simple annotations, and a translation into contemporary Chinese; observations on the stories are also included to help interpretation where necessary. The translators, Martha Cheung and Jane Lai, have not only rendered the excerpts into English, but have also offered their own observations on some of the excerpts. Also provided is a simple glossary of terms which have their origins in Sanskrit, for ease of reference for those new to Zen discourse and to obviate the need for repeated annotations.

In a way, this book is the product of the joint effort of the editor and the translators, and the multiple perspectives rightly reflect the multiplicity of Zen perceptions. As the saying goes, "Those who in Buddha's name do meet, destiny has made them each other to greet."

PREFACE

前言

With this little book, Martha, Jane, and I have found a meeting point, and I hope that through its circulation, we will have an opportunity to share with our readers the vital spirit of Zen.

Among the numerous volumes of records of Zen discourse, I have selected excerpts from only a few volumes to share with our readers. In view of this limitation, and of the imperfections of my choice, I crave the indulgence of the erudite and the wise.

Jiang Lansheng
Tingyu Study
July, 1997

Translators' Notes

1. The translators had originally intended to translate by its pinyin — i.e. as "Chan" — and 禅宗 as "Chan Buddhism". However, "Chan" happens to coincide with the spelling of a surname of many Cantonese in China, and an expression like "the teachings of Chan" or "the appeal of Chan" might lead to considerable confusion in meaning. In view of this, and in view of the fact that Western readers are in any case much more familiar with "Zen" — the Japanese rendering of 禅 — the translators finally decided to translate 禅 as "Zen" and 禅宗 as "Zen Buddhism".

2. In the Chinese texts, some of the Zen masters have two names each, and can be referred to by either one of the two names. For instance, Zen Master Liangjia of Dongshan (洞山良价禅师) is

PREFACE

前言

referred to as Zen Master Liangjia (良价禅师) in some stories and as Zen Master Dongshan (洞山禅师) in others. To make reading easier for the common reader, if a Zen Master has two names, both names will be provided in the translation when the Master first appears in the text of a story. In the rest of the story, the Master will be referred to by the name he received on ordination (as Zen Master Liangjia, for example). The bilingual reader will therefore find that the names of the Zen masters as they appear in the translation sometimes differ from those as they appear in the Chinese texts.

3. The footnotes provided by the compiler of the Chinese texts have sometimes been incorporated into the translated texts and therefore will not appear as footnotes.

4. The compiler of the Chinese texts has sometimes made some observations on the stories to help the reader in interpretation. These observations are indicated by the sign "☆". Most of these observations are translated, the rare exceptions being those on stories the meaning of which is already quite clear in the translation. For stories which are more intriguing, the translators have sometimes offered their own observations, which are indicated by the sign "★" and placed below the compiler's observation on that story. Zen stories are well known for being rich in interpretive possibilities, and therefore provocative to the mind. By offering their own observations alongside those of the compiler, the translators hope to heighten the pleasure of the text for the reader and invite them to come up with their own

PREFACE

interpretations.

5. A Glossary of Selected Sanskrit Terms used in the translated texts (printed in italics) is provided at the end of the book to avoid duplication of footnotes. "Buddha" and "buddha", however, are not printed in italics as they have long acquired currency in the English language. But an explanation of the different ways in which "Buddha" and "buddha" are used in the translated texts is provided in the Glossary.

6. The translators would like to thank Jiang Lansheng for her patience in answering our questions about the source text. We are also grateful to the Centre for Translation of the Hong Kong Baptist University, in particular Chow Pul Sze, Hui Wan Yin, Kwok Ho Sze, Lau Ming Pul, and Wong Kim Fan for their assistance in the preparation of the manuscript.

禅宗语录　中华传统文化精粹

EXCERPTS FROM
ZEN BUDDHIST TEXTS

不立文字

神光闻是语已，则取利刀，自断左臂，置于师前。师语神光云："诸佛菩萨求法，不以身为身，不以命为命。汝虽断求法，亦可在。"遂改神光名惠可。又问："请和尚安心。"师曰："将心来，与汝安心。"进曰："觅心了不可得。"师曰："觅得岂是汝心？与汝安心竟。"达摩语惠可曰："为汝安心竟，汝今见不？"惠可言下大悟。惠可白和尚："今日乃知，一切诸法，本来空寂。今日乃知，菩提不远。是故菩萨不动念而至萨般若①海，不动念而登涅槃岸。"师云："如是，如是。"惠可进曰："和尚此法有文字记录不？"达摩曰："我法以心传心，不立文字。"

——初祖菩提达摩语录，引自《祖堂集》卷二

Excerpts from
Zen Buddhist Texts

Not through the written word

When Shenguang heard what was said, he took a sword and cut off his left arm and placed it before the great Zen Master Damo①. The Zen Master said to Shenguang, "In their search for the Way of Enlightenment, *buddhas* and *bodhisattvas* thought nothing of their bodies or their lives. Since you would give up your arm in your determination to embark on your search for Enlightenment, you should do." So he accepted Shenguang for a disciple and named him Huike. Huike said, "Please, Master, put my heart at ease." The Master replied, "Hand me that heart, and I will put it at ease." Huike said, "Search as I will, I cannot find my heart to give you." The Master replied, "If it can be found, it is not your heart. I have now put it at ease." Then he added, "Now that I have put it at ease, do you see?" Huike had a sudden realisation, so he said to the Master, "Now I see. All things are ultimately nonsubstantial, and the Way to *Bodhi*, to Wisdom, is not a matter of distance. That is why it does not take the *bodhisattvas* any time to reach the sea of wisdom, and it does not take them any time to reach the shores of *nirvana*." The Master said, "That is so. Just so." Huike then asked, "Master,

不用文字记录

　　神光听完这话,就取出利刀,砍断自己的左臂,放在达摩大师的面前。大师对神光说:"诸佛和菩萨追求佛法,不把身体看作身体,不把生命看作生命。你虽然是断臂求法,也算可以了。"于是把神光改名为惠可。惠可说:"请和尚安定我心。"大师说:"把心拿来,帮你安定。"惠可又说:"寻找我心,怎么也找不到。"大师说:"如能找到,岂是你心?已经帮你安好了心啦。"达摩又对惠可说:"已经帮你安好了心,你现在看到了吗?"惠可立即大悟,对和尚说:"今天才知道,一切事物本来空寂。今天才知道,菩提并不远。所以菩萨不费时间便到达萨般若之海,不费时间便登上涅槃之岸。"大师说:"是这样的,是这样的。"惠可又问:"和尚的这种道法有文字记录吗?"达摩说:"我法以心传心,不立文字。"

① 萨般若:梵语音译,意为无所不晓的佛智。

 Excerpts from Zen Buddhist Texts

your way of teaching ... is it recorded in written words?" Damo replied, "My way is taught through the mind, not through the written word."

— Recorded Dialogues of the First Patriarch Bodhidharma, from *A Collection from the Halls of the Patriarchs*, vol. 2

① Damo: Damo is the popular name for *Bodhidharma*, reputed as the founder of Zen Buddhism.

5

法佛无二

有一居士①，不说年几，唯有十四②，及至礼师，不称姓名，云："弟子身患风疾，请和尚为弟子忏悔。"师云："汝将罪来，为汝忏悔。"居士曰："觅罪不可见。"师云："我今为汝忏悔竟，汝今宜依佛法僧宝③。"居士问："但见和尚，则知是僧，未审世间何者是佛？云何为法？"师云："是心是佛，是心是法，法佛无二，汝知之乎？"居士曰："今日始知，罪性不在内外中间，如其心然，法佛无二也。"师知是法器④，而与剃发，云："汝是僧宝，宜名僧璨。"

——二祖慧可语录，引自《祖堂集》卷二

Excerpts from Zen Buddhist Texts

Buddha and the Way of Buddha are the same

A forty-year-old lay brother[①] came before Zen Master Huike. Without giving his name or his age, he bowed before the Zen Master and said, "Master, I am afflicted with an illness. Please help me repent and cleanse me from my sins." The Master said, "Give me your sins, and I will help you repent and cleanse you from your sins." The lay brother said, "I have searched for them but cannot find them to give you." The Master said, "I have helped you repent and cleansed you from your sins. You should now follow the three gems[②] — the Buddha, the Way of Buddha and the monastic order founded by Buddha." The lay brother said, "Now that I've seen you, I know what a monk is like. But I do not know, from my experience in the world, what is Buddha or the Way of Buddha." The Master said, "The spiritually enlightened heart is Buddha, and it is also the Way of Buddha. Buddha and the Way of Buddha are the same. Do you understand?" The lay brother replied, "Now I know, Sin is not something with its own nature within us, or outside us, or in our midst. In the same way there is no difference between Buddha and the Way of Buddha. A thing and its nature are one." Seeing that the lay brother was

法和佛没有区别

有一位居士，不说自己多大年纪，估计年过四十，他向慧可禅师行礼时也不报出自己的姓名，说："弟子身患风疾，请和尚为弟子忏悔罪过。"师说："把罪过拿来，我为你忏悔。"居士说："我寻找罪过，无法找到。"师说："现在我已经为你忏悔了罪过，你如今应该皈依佛、法、僧三宝。"居士问："见到和尚，才知道什么是僧。不知道世间什么是佛，什么是法？"师答："心就是佛，心就是法，法和佛并无区别，你懂了吗？"居士说："今天才知道，罪性本不在内、不在外，也不在中间，如同心就是佛，心就是法那样，物性之间并无区别。"禅师知道他是具有领悟、传承佛法才智的人，为他剃除头发，说："你是僧中之宝，应改名为僧璨。"

① 居士：指在家修习的佛教徒。
② 唯有十四：此句疑有误。《五灯会元》卷一作"年逾四十"。
③ 佛法僧宝：佛教称佛、法、僧为三宝。
④ 法器：指具有领悟和传承佛法才智的人。

 Excerpts from Zen Buddhist Texts

quick of understanding and had a capacity to learn, the Master accepted him as a disciple, shaved his head in the ordination ceremony, and said, "You are a gem amongst Buddhist monks, you shall be known as Sengcan — Monk Brilliance."

— Recorded Dialogues of the Second Patriarch Huike, from *A Collection from the Halls of the Patriarchs*, vol. 2

 Notes

① lay brother: one not ordained as a monk but practises the Buddhist religion.
② the three gems: Buddha, the *dharma* (the Way, or the doctrine, of Buddha), and the sangha (the monastic order founded by Buddha). They are sometimes also called the "three jewels", or "the trinity" in Buddhism.

无人缚汝

（僧璨）大集群品，普雨正法。会中有一沙弥，年始十四，名道信，来礼师，而问师曰："如何是佛心？"师答曰："汝今是什么心？"对曰："我今无心。"师曰："汝既无心，佛岂有心耶？"又问："唯愿和尚教某甲解脱法门。"师云："谁人缚汝？"对曰："无人缚。"师云："既无人缚汝，即是解脱，何须更求解脱？"道信言下大悟。

——三祖僧璨语录，引自《祖堂集》卷二

没人束缚你

僧璨召集各种品级的僧众，向他们宣讲正宗佛法。法会中有一个小和尚，才十四岁，名叫道信，来礼拜僧璨禅师，并问禅师："什么是佛心？"禅师答道："你如今是什么心？"小和尚说："我如今没有心。"禅师说："既然你没有心，难道佛就有心吗？"小和尚又问："请求你教给我解脱束缚的方法。"禅师说："谁束缚着你？"小和尚说："没人束缚我。"禅师说："既然没有人束缚你，这就是解脱，何必再求什么解脱！"道信立刻大悟。

Excerpts from Zen Buddhist Texts

Nobody has tied you down

Sengcan (Monk Brilliance) summoned monks of all ranks to a lecture on orthodox Buddhist teachings. In the assembly, a young novice called Daoxin, aged fourteen, came forward to pay his respects to the Zen Master and asked, "What is the heart of Buddha like?" The Master asked him, "What is your heart like?" He replied, "I have no heart." The Master said, "If you have no heart, do you think Buddha has a heart?" The young novice asked again, "Please teach me how to free myself from bondage." The Master asked, "Who has tied you down?" The young novice said, "Nobody has tied me down." The Master then said, "If nobody has tied you down, you are free. Why do you have to free yourself?" Daoxin was enlightened.

— Recorded Dialogues of the Third Patriarch Sengcan, from *A Collection from the Halls of the Patriarchs*, vol. 2

非心不问佛，问佛不非心

祖曰："夫百千法门，同归方寸，河沙妙德，总在心源。一切戒门、定门、慧门①，神通变化，悉自具足，不离汝心。一切烦恼业障，本来空寂。一切因果，皆如梦幻。无三界②可出，无菩提可求。人与非人，性相③平等。大道虚旷，绝思绝虑。如是之法，汝今已得。更无阙少，与佛何殊？更无别法，汝但任心自在，莫作观行，亦莫澄心，莫起贪嗔，莫怀愁虑，荡荡无碍，任意纵横，不作诸善，不作诸恶，行住坐卧，触目遇缘，总是佛之妙用。快乐无忧，故名为佛。"师曰："心既具足，何者是佛？何者是心？"祖曰："非心不问佛，问佛不非心。"

——四祖道信语录，引自《祖堂集》卷二

Excerpts from
Zen Buddhist Texts

The heart is Buddha, and Buddha is the heart

The Fourth Patriarch, Daoxin, said to the monk, Farong, "All the myriad ways and approaches to Buddhist enlightenment are in the heart. Innumerable beautiful virtues also have their source in the heart. All the disciplines, the state of Zen enlightenment, ways to wisdom and power for miraculous changes lie ready in the heart. There, vexation and evil do not exist. There, all causes and consequences are as dreams. In the heart, there are no three realms of desire, form and formlessness from which one has to free oneself, no enlightenment for one to seek. In the heart, no distinction exists between what is human and what is non-human, either in their nature or in their manifestation. The Way is infinitely protean and mysterious, endless and free from the encumbrance of thought and definition. If you have the Way, there is nothing lacking, and you are no different from Buddha himself. There is no other way. Follow your heart. Do not trouble yourself with self-scrutiny, or with attempts to clear your heart. Do not harbour thoughts of greed or wrath; and do

白话翻译

心就是佛，佛就是心

　　四祖道信(对法融)说："千百种佛法门径，同归于方寸之心，无数美妙的德行，也都来源于此心。一切戒律、禅定、智慧法门以及种种神通变化，都已在你心中具备。一切烦恼业障本不存在。一切前因后果都如梦幻。没有什么生死轮回的三种境界可以脱离，没有什么菩提觉悟可以追求。人与非人，本性和本相都是平等的。大道虚渺空旷，绝无思虑。这些通法，你如今已经获得，并不缺少，与佛没有两样。再没有另外的道法了，你只要随心自在，无须观察作为，无须清澄自心，别生贪婪嗔怒之念，别怀忧愁疑虑之情，坦坦荡荡，无所障碍，任随己意，不受拘束，不用作各种善事，不用作各种恶事，行、住、坐、卧之间，触目所见机缘，都是佛法的微妙作用。快乐无忧，所以称为佛。"法融问："此心既然已经具备充足，请问什么是佛？什么是心？"四祖答道："不是心就不会问佛，所问之佛就是此心。"

注释

　　① 戒门、定门、慧门：佛教称戒(戒律)、定(禅定)、慧(智慧)为三学。戒门、定门、慧门为这三学的法门路径。

　　② 三界：处在生死轮回过程中的俗世三种境界。即欲界、色界(物质)、无色界。

　　③ 性相：本性与本相。相，指事物的体貌、样状。

Excerpts from Zen Buddhist Texts

not let sorrow and doubt trouble you. Be at peace. Act as you like — spontaneously, without bounds or restrictions. You do not have to do good deeds; you do not have to do any evil. In all that you see and encounter in your daily life, at home or abroad, waking or resting, there are opportunities wherein the mysteries of enlightenment are manifested. This happiness, this absence of anxieties, is Buddha." Farong asked, "If all that is already in the heart, what then is Buddha? What is the heart?" The Fourth Patriarch replied, "It is the heart that seeks Buddha; and the Buddha that is sought after is the heart."

— Recorded Dialogues of the Fourth Patriarch Daoxin, from *A Collection from the Halls of the Patriarchs*, vol. 2

大厦之材，本出幽谷

又问:"学问何故不向城邑聚落,要在山居?"答曰:"大厦之材,本出幽谷,不向人间有也。以远离人故,不被刀斧损斫,一一长成大物,后乃堪为栋梁之用。故知栖神幽谷,远避嚣尘,养性山中,长辞俗事,目前无物,心自安宁。从此道树花开,禅林果出也。"其忍大师,萧然净坐,不出文记,口说玄理,默授与人。

——五祖弘忍语录,引自《楞伽师资记》卷一

白话翻译

建造大厦的木材,出自深山幽谷

有人又问:"学习佛法为什么不在城市,不在人群集聚之处,却要在这山里居住?"弘忍大师回答道:"建造大厦的木材,本来就出自深山幽谷,不会在人群聚集之处长成。因为远离人群,不被刀斧砍伤,能够一一长大成材,日后才能用作栋梁。所以学习佛法,应在幽谷里栖息精神;远远地避开尘世,在深山修养情性;长期辞别俗世杂事,眼前没有俗物,心中自然安宁。这样学禅,如同种树,便能开花结果。"当时弘忍大师安然端坐,不用文字记写,只是口说禅理,默默地教给别人。

Excerpts from
Zen Buddhist Texts

Timbers for buildings come from secluded valleys

Someone asked, "Why is it that when people want to learn the Way of Buddha, they do not do so in the cities, or go to places where people gather, but live here in the mountains?" Zen Master Hongren replied, "Timbers for building big manors come from secluded valleys. Big trees do not grow where crowds gather. When the trees are far from the crowds, they are not cut or bruised by the axe and the knife, and so grow to their full strength to be used for pillars and beams for a house. So when one learns the Way of the Buddha, one should nurture one's spirit in secluded valleys, away from the vanities of the crowd, and let one's true nature emerge in the mountains. Away from the trivialities of the world, untroubled by the mundane things in one's sight, one will naturally have peace in one's heart. To learn Zen in this environment is like growing a tree there. The effort will blossom and bear fruit." Zen Master Hongren sat at ease and with decorum as he taught the Way of Zen by word of mouth, without relying on the written word.

— Recorded Dialogues of the Fifth Patriarch Hongren, from *A Chronicle of the Lankavatara Masters*, vol. 1

佛性无南北

弘忍和尚问惠能①："汝何方人？来此山礼拜吾，汝今向吾边复求何物？"惠能答曰："弟子是岭南人，新州百姓，今故远来礼拜和尚。不求余物，唯求作佛。"大师遂责惠能曰："汝是岭南人，又是獦獠②，若为堪作佛！"惠能答曰："人即有南北，佛性即无南北；獦獠身与和尚不同，佛性有何差别！"

——六祖慧能语录，引自《坛经》

白话翻译

佛性无南北之分别

弘忍和尚问惠能："你是哪里人？你来此山礼拜我，向我寻求什么？"惠能答："弟子是岭南人，新州的百姓。今特远来礼拜和尚，不求别的，只求作佛。"大师斥责惠能说："你是岭南人，又是蛮人，怎么能够作佛！"惠能答："人虽有南北之分，佛性却没有南北之分；蛮人与和尚的身份不同，但蛮人的佛性与和尚的佛性有什么差别！"

Excerpts from
Zen Buddhist Texts

No regional differences

The monk Hongren asked Huineng before Huineng was ordained a monk, "Where are you from? What do you want of me in coming to this mountain to pay your respects to me?" Huineng replied, "I am a native of Xinzhou in south China, south of the mountains. I have travelled long distances to pay my respects to you. I asked for nothing other than to learn to become a buddha." The Master rebuked him and said, "You are a southerner, a barbarian. How can you expect to become a buddha?" Huineng replied, "There may be differences between southerners and northerners, but the nature and potentials for enlightenment know no regional differences. There may be differences between a barbarian and a monk, but what difference is there in the Buddha-nature in them?"

— Recorded Dialogues of the Sixth Patriarch Huineng,
from *Platform Sutra*

注释

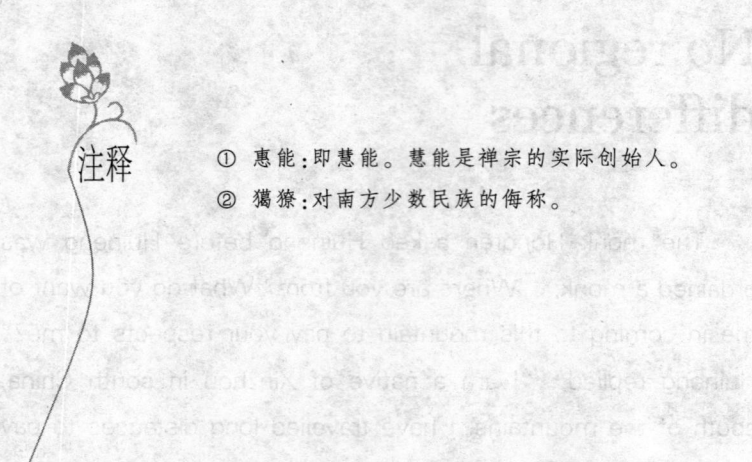

① 惠能：即慧能。慧能是禅宗的实际创始人。
② 獦獠：对南方少数民族的侮称。

阅读提示

慧能"佛性无南北"的思想正是禅宗"人人皆有佛性"这一主张的反映。

Excerpts from Zen Buddhist Texts

Observation

☆ Huineng's idea that Buddha-nature knows no regional differences clearly reflects the Zen Buddhist tenet that everyone has Buddha-nature.

仁者自心动

印宗是讲经论僧也。有一日正讲经,风雨猛动。见其幡动,法师问众:"风动也?幡动?"一个云:"风动。"一个云:"幡动。"各自相争,就讲主证明。讲主断不得,却请行者①断。行者云:"不是风动,不是幡动。"讲主云:"是什么物动?"行者云:"仁者②自心动。"

——六祖慧能语录,引自《坛经》

Excerpts from
Zen Buddhist Texts

Your minds are wavering

Yinzong was a Master monk who lectured on the scriptures. One day, as he was lecturing, there was a storm. Seeing the banners in the monastery fluttering in the wind, Yinzong asked the assembly, "Is it the wind that moves? Or is it the banners?" Some replied that it was the wind, and others replied that it was the banners that moved. An argument developed and both sides insisted that they were right. They asked Yinzong to judge, but he could not give a judgement either. So he asked the abbot's attendant Huineng to judge. Huineng said, "It is neither the wind nor the banners." The Master asked, "What is it then that is moving?" Huineng replied, "It is your minds that are wavering."

— Recorded Dialogues of the Sixth Patriarch Huineng,
from *Platform Sutra*

白话翻译

你们各自的心在动

印宗是讲说经论的僧师。有一天正在讲经时,风雨大作。看到寺院里的旗幡在风中飘摇,法师就问众人:"是风在动,还是旗在动?"有人回答:"是风动。"另有人回答:"是旗子动。"各自争执不下,要求主讲法师判定。法师也判定不了,就请行者慧能来断定。慧能说:"既不是风动,也不是旗子动。"法师问:"那么是什么东西在动?"行者说:"是你们各自的心在动。"

注释

① 行者:指入寺尚未正式剃发出家的修行者,一般在寺中承担劳役,服侍僧众。此处指慧能。

② 仁者:对对方的尊称。古时多以仁、贤等尊称对方。

经典名句 Highlights

yī dēng néng chú qiān nián àn, yī zhī huì néng miè wàn nián yú
一灯能除千年暗，一知惠能灭万年愚。

A bright lamp can clear away the darkness of ages, a single thought of wisdom can dispel the ignorance and obsession of ages.

诸佛妙理，非关文字

尼无尽藏者，常读《涅槃经》。师暂听之，即为之解说其义。尼遂执卷问字，祖曰："字即不识，义即请问。"尼曰："字尚不识，曷能会义？"祖曰："诸佛妙理，非关文字。"尼惊异之，告乡里耆艾曰："能是有道之人，宜请供养。"于是居人竞来瞻礼。

——六祖慧能语录，引自《五灯会元》卷一

白话翻译

佛法玄妙的义理跟文字无关

有位叫无尽藏的尼姑常常读《涅槃经》。慧能禅师刚听了一会儿，就为她解说其中的意义。尼姑便拿着经卷来请教不懂的字，六祖说："字我是不识的，意义请你询问。"尼姑说："连字都不认识，怎么能领会意义？"六祖说："诸佛玄妙的义理跟文字没有关系。"尼姑十分惊奇，对乡里老人们说："慧能是深通佛道的人，请大家供养他。"于是，居民们都争着来拜见慧能。

Excerpts from Zen Buddhist Texts

The wonderful mysteries of Buddhist enlightenment have nothing to do with the written word

A nun called Wujincang often recited the *Maha Parinirvana Sutra*. Soon after Huineng, the Sixth Patriarch, had listened to her recitation, he explained to her the meaning of the *Sutra*. So the nun came to consult Huineng on the characters that she didn't know in the text of the *Sutras*. The Sixth Patriarch said, "I cannot read, but you can ask me about the meaning of the text." The nun asked, "If you can't even read, how can you understand the meaning of the text?" The Sixth Patriarch replied, "The wonderful mysteries of Buddhist enlightenment have nothing to do with the written word." The nun was amazed, and she told the elders in the village, "Huineng knows the profundity of the Way of Buddha. Let us serve him well." So people in the village came to seek him out to pay their respects to him.

— Recorded Dialogues of the Sixth Patriarch Huineng,
from *Amalgamation of the Sources of the Five Lamps*, vol. 1

何名禅定

此法门中，何名坐禅？此法门中，一切无碍，外于一切境界上念不起为坐，见本性不乱为禅。何名为禅定①？外离相曰禅，内不乱曰定。外若著相，内心即乱；外若离相，内性不乱。本性自净自定，只缘触境，触即乱，离相不乱即定。外离相即禅，内不乱即定。外禅内定，故名禅定。《维摩经》云："即时豁然，还得本心。"《菩萨戒经》云："本元自性清净。"善知识②，见自性自净，自修自作自性法身，自行佛行，自作自成佛道。

——六祖慧能语录，引自《坛经》

Excerpts from Zen Buddhist Texts

Zen meditation

What is Zen meditation? In the sect to which we belong, to meditate means that we are free from all things and do not have any vain thoughts about anything in the outside world. When we see our nature untroubled, we call that state Zen. What is the tranquillity of Zen? As I said, not to be affected by things in the outside world is Zen, and when the inner peace is untroubled, that is the tranquillity of Zen. If we cling to what is in the world outside us, our inner peace will be disturbed. If we detach ourselves from things in the outside world, our inner peace will not be troubled. In truth, we are by nature pure, tranquil, at one. Only upon contact with things in the outside world do we become disturbed. When we detach ourselves from things of the outside world, our inner peace will not be disturbed, and we have tranquillity. Zen and tranquillity, that is Zen meditation. The *Vimalakirti Sutra* describes it as "a sudden realisation, a repossession of the mind in its untroubled, unperturbed state." The *Bodhisattva Sila Sutra* says, "The nature of the self is pure and tranquil." Students of the Way, discover the nature of your self, which is at peace, through your own efforts and perseverance. For in the nature of your

白话翻译

什么叫禅定

在我们这个法门中,什么叫坐禅?在此法门中,一切都没有障碍,对于外界一切事物都不起妄念称为坐,见到自身本性不乱称为禅。什么叫禅定?离开外界物相是禅,内心不散乱是定。如果执着外界物相,内心就散乱。如果离开外界物相,内性就不散乱。其实本性原是清净、专一、安定的,只是因为接触了外物,接触了便会散乱,离开外界物相,内心就不散乱,就专一安定了。外禅内定,因而称为禅定。《维摩经》上说:"顿时领悟,恢复本心。"《菩萨戒经》上说:"自性本来清净。"各位高僧,发现自性本来清净,自我努力修习,自性便是佛法,自己努力实践佛行,自然能得佛道。

注释

① 禅定:佛家指思想集中、专注一境的精神状态。
② 善知识:对有较高道德学问的僧人的称呼。这里是对听众的敬称。

Excerpts from Zen Buddhist Texts

self lies the Way of Buddha. Do what Buddha did, and you will succeed in the Way of Buddha.

— Recorded Dialogues of the Sixth Patriarch Huineng,
from *Platform Sutra*

清净法身

善知识！世人性自净，万法在自性。思量一切恶事，即行于恶；思量一切善事，便修于善行。如是一切法尽在自性。自性常清净，日月常明。只为云覆盖，上明下暗，不能了见日月星辰。忽遇惠风吹散卷尽云雾，万象森罗，一时皆现。世人清净，犹如青天，惠如日，智如月，知惠常明。于外著境，妄念浮云盖覆，自性不能明。故遇善知识开真法，吹却迷妄，内外明彻，于自性中，万法皆见。一切法自在性，名为清净法身。

——六祖慧能语录，引自《坛经》

Excerpts from Zen Buddhist Texts

The nature of man is pure

Students of the Way, the nature of man is basically pure, and all things arise from that nature. If you think of all manners of evil, then you will be evil; but if you think of all manners of good, then you will do good deeds. Thus all arise out of that nature. That nature is always pure, just as the sun and the moon are always bright. But when dark clouds obscure the sun and the moon, then the brightness is hidden behind the clouds and there is darkness below, and we do not see the sun, the moon and the stars. If the breeze of wisdom blows away the clouds and the mist, then all is revealed again in clarity. The nature of man is pure, like the clear sky, and the wisdom of man shines bright as the sun and the moon. But if you persist in taking things of the outside world as all important, then vain thoughts will rise like dark clouds to obscure your nature and it will not appear pure. That is why when you meet enlightened monks and listen to their teachings, the vain thoughts will be blown away, and all is clarity, all things are revealed to be in the nature of man. This is the meaning of "the nature of man is pure".

— Recorded Dialogues of the Sixth Patriarch Huineng, from *Platform Sutra*

白话翻译

清净法身

　　各位，世上人性本来清净，万事万物都在自性中产生。如果思量一切恶事，就会作恶；如果思量一切善事，就会行善。所以一切事物都在于自性。自性永远清净，如日月永远明亮一样。只因乌云覆盖，上面明亮而下面昏暗，所以就不能清楚地看到日月星辰。如果有智慧之风吹散卷尽云雾，那万事万物，纷然罗列，就全部显现出来。世上人性清净，犹如青天，智慧如同日月常明。如果执着外界事物，虚妄之念像浮云覆盖，自性便不能明净。因此遇上得道高僧宣讲真法，驱除迷妄之念，使内外通明透彻，在自性中，万物都显现出来。一切事物本在自性中，这就叫做清净法身。

经典名句 Highlights

金屑虽珍宝,在眼亦为病。
(jīn xiè suī zhēn bǎo, zài yǎn yì wéi bìng)

Gold dust may be valuable, but it can hurt the eyes if you put it there.

禅宗语录

一灯能除千年暗

不思量，性即空寂；思量即是白化。思量恶法，化为地狱；思量善法，化为天堂。毒害化为畜生，慈悲化为菩萨，知惠化为上界，愚痴化为下方。自性变化甚多，迷人自不知见。一念善，知惠即生。一灯能除千年暗，一知惠能灭万年愚。

——六祖慧能语录，引自《坛经》

白话翻译

一盏灯能驱除千年黑暗

如果不思量，自性就空寂不变；如果思量就造成自性的变化。思量恶事，化为地狱；思量善事，化为天堂。心生毒害化为畜生，心生慈悲化为菩萨，心生智慧化为上界乐土，心生愚痴化为下方苦海。自性变化很多，痴迷的人自己不了解，看不到。心中善念一起，就会产生智慧。一盏灯能驱除千年黑暗，一念智慧能消灭万年愚痴。

Excerpts from Zen Buddhist Texts

One bright lamp can clear away the darkness of ages

If one does not think, one's nature remains static and nothing happens. When one thinks, changes occur in one's nature and that in turn changes the state one is in. When one thinks of evil, the thought makes a hell for the person; when one thinks of good, the thought makes a heaven for the person. Thoughts of killing and aggression turn one into a beast; thoughts of kindness and compassion turn one into a *bodhisattva*. Thoughts of wisdom turn the world into the supreme paradise; ignorance and obsession turn the world into the depths of the sea of suffering. The nature of man undergoes many changes, but the benighted do not understand or perceive them. As soon as a kind thought turns in the mind, wisdom is born. Just as a bright lamp can clear away the darkness of ages, a single thought of wisdom can dispel the ignorance and obsession of ages.

— Recorded Dialogues of the Sixth Patriarch Huineng,
from *Platform Sutra*

无别之性

师云："《涅槃经》上云：'明与无明，凡夫见二，智者了达其性无别。'无别之性，即是实性。处凡不减，在圣不增。住烦恼而不乱，居禅定①而不寂。不断不常，不来不去，不在中间及其内外，不生不灭。性相常住，恒而不变，名之曰道。"

——六祖慧能语录，引自《祖堂集》卷二

白话翻译

没有差别的性质

慧能大师说："《涅槃经》上讲：'明和无明，凡俗之人看来是相对立的两个方面，有智慧者却了解它们的性质没有差别。'没有差别的性质，就是事物的真实本性。处在凡人的地位不减少什么，处在圣人的地位不增加什么。在尘世烦恼中而其心不乱，在专注禅定中而其心不寂。不断绝也不连续，不来也不去，不在中间也不在里外，不生也不灭。本性和相状长久存在，永恒而不变化，这就叫做道。"

注释

① 禅定：见第30页注释。

Excerpts from
Zen Buddhist Texts

No qualitative difference

Zen Master Huineng said, "It is written in the *Maha Parinirvana Sutra* that 'Light and no-light are, to the ordinary man, opposites. But the wise man knows that there is no qualitative difference between the two.' The quality that does not change is the real nature of all living things. A man who loses nothing for being an ordinary man, who gains nothing for being a wise man, whose heart is at ease in the midst of the world's turmoil, whose mind is not lonely in meditation, who seeks neither severance nor continuance, who aims not to come nor to go, not to be within nor without, not to create nor to destroy, whose nature goes through eternity without change — a man like this is the embodiment of the Way."

— Recorded Dialogues of the Sixth Patriarch Huineng, from *A Collection from the Halls of the Patriarchs*, vol. 2

识心见性

缘在人中有愚有智，愚为小人，智为大人。迷人问于智者，智者与愚人说法，令彼愚者悟解心解。迷人若悟解心开，与大智人无别。故知不悟，即是佛是众生；一念若悟，即众生是佛。故知一切万法，尽在自身中。何不从于自心顿现真如本性？《菩萨戒经》云："我本元自性清净。"识心见性，自成佛道。《维摩经》云："即时豁然，还得本心。"

——六祖慧能语录，引自《坛经》

白话翻译

认识自心，发现本性

因为在人群里有愚有智，愚迷的是小人，睿智的是大人。愚迷者向睿智者请教。睿智者向愚迷者讲说佛法，使他们醒悟理解。愚迷者如能醒悟理解，就跟大智者没有区别。因此，如果没有领悟，佛也就如同众生；而如果一念顿悟，众生就都可以成佛。由此可知，一切佛法都在自身心中。何不追随在自心中顿现真实本性呢？《菩萨戒经》说："我本来自性清净。"认识自心，发现本性，自然成功佛道。《维摩经》说："顿时领悟，恢复本心。"

Excerpts from Zen Buddhist Texts

Know your own mind, discover your own nature

There are among people the wise and the foolish. The foolish and the benighted are the lesser among men, and the wise are the greater. The foolish seek to learn from the wise, and the wise talk to them about the Way of Buddha to help them understand and be enlightened. If the foolish and benighted can understand and are enlightened, then they are no different from the man of great wisdom. That is why, without enlightenment, a buddha is just like any other man, but in a moment of enlightenment, any man can become a buddha. This means that the Way of Buddha is in one's mind. So why do we not discover our own nature in the instant of revelation in our minds? The *Bodhisattva Sila Sutra* says, "The nature of the self is pure and tranquil." Therefore know your own mind, discover your nature, and you will attain the Way of Buddha. The *Vimalakirti Sutra* describes this as a sudden realisation, a repossession of the mind in its untroubled, unperturbed state."

— Recorded Dialogues of the Sixth Patriarch Huineng, from *Platform Sutra*

顿悟见佛

今生若悟顿教门,悟即眼前见世尊。

若欲修行云觅佛,不知何处欲求真。

若能心中自有真,有真即是成佛因。

自不求真外觅佛,去觅总是大痴人。

顿教法者是西流,救度世人须自修。

今报世间学道者,不于此见大悠悠。

大师说偈已了,遂告门人曰:"汝等好住,今共汝别。吾去已后,莫作世情悲泣,而受人吊问钱帛,著孝衣,即非正法,非我弟子。如吾在日一种,一时端坐,但无动无静,无生无灭,无去无来,无是无非,无住无往,但然寂静,即是大道。吾去已后,但依修行,共吾在日一种。吾若在世,汝违吾教,吾住无益。"大师云此语

Excerpts from Zen Buddhist Texts

In the moment of enlightenment you see Buddha

In the moment of enlightenment,
You'll see Buddha with your own eyes.
If you seek Him not in enlightenment,
Where with you your nature find?

If you know there is Buddha-nature in you,
The key to Buddhahood you've found.
If you seek Him without and not within you,
You're a fool to waste your time.

The Way of enlightenment comes from heaven:
But salvation depends on efforts of your own.
This I tell all who study Buddha's Way:
If you don't know this, benighted you'll stay.

When the Master Huineng had recited these words to his disciples, he said, "You will have to manage on your own. I bid you farewell today. When I die, do not grieve as ordinary

已，夜至三更，奄然迁化。

——六祖慧能录，引自《坛经》

白话翻译

顿悟见佛

今生如能领悟顿教法门，立刻可以亲眼见到世尊。如不领悟徒然修行觅佛，不知何处可求真实本性。

如能明了自身具有佛性，这便是成佛的关键原因。不求自心却向外界觅佛，枉费气力就是愚痴之人。

顿教法门本从西天传来，救度世人还须各自修行。如今奉告世间学佛之人，不明此理实在糊涂愚钝。

慧能大师说完了三则偈语，对众位门徒说："你们好自为之，我今天和你们告别了。我去世之后，别以世俗之情悲泣，如果接受他人吊问和钱帛，穿着孝衣，就不是正宗佛法，不是我的弟子。应该跟我在世时一样，一齐端坐着，无动无静，无生无灭，无去无来，无是无非，无住无往，只是一片寂静，这就是大道。我去世后，你们依然修行，和我在世一样。我如果在世，你们违背我的教导，我活着也无益。"大师说完这番话，到夜里三更，忽然去世。

Excerpts from Zen Buddhist Texts

people do. Do not wear mourning clothes, nor accept condolences or mourning gifts, for that is not in keeping with proper Buddhist teachings. I would not consider you my disciples if you did that. You should behave as if I were alive: sit decorously together, neither rush about nor refrain from movement, think neither of life nor of annihilation, neither of coming nor going, neither of right nor wrong, neither of abiding nor departing. Just be still. That is the supreme Way. After my death, you should continue in your spiritual efforts just as if I were alive. For if you go against my teachings, then even if I were alive, my presence would have been pointless." After the Master had said all this, he passed away quite suddenly in the middle of the night.

— Recorded Dialogues of the Sixth Patriarch Huineng,
from *Platform Sutra*

法地若动，一切不安

梁武帝请讲《金刚经》，士①才升座，以尺挥按一下，便下座。帝愕然，圣师曰："陛下还会么？"帝曰："不会。"圣师曰："大士讲经竟。"又一日讲经次，帝至，大众皆起，唯士端坐不动。近臣报曰："圣驾在此，何不起？"士曰："法地若动，一切不安。"大士一日披衲②、顶冠③、跋履朝见。帝问："是僧邪？"士以手指冠。帝曰："是道邪？"士以手指跋履。帝曰："是俗邪？"士以手指衲衣。

——善慧语录，引自《五灯会元》卷二

白话翻译

法地如果起动，一切都会不安

梁武帝请善慧大士讲《金刚经》，大士才升法座，把挥尺拍了一下，就走下法座。武帝十分吃惊。供奉僧问："陛下可领会了吗？"武帝答："不懂。"供奉僧说："大士讲经完

Excerpts from Zen Buddhist Texts

If the foundations of *dharma* stir, all will be upset

Emperor Wu of the Liang Dynasty (AD 502–557) invited Zen Master Shanhui of Heze to expound the teachings in the *Diamond Sutra*. As soon as the Master ascended the *dharma* seat from where he was to deliver his lecture, he took up the ritual baton, banged it on the table, and got off his seat. Emperor Wu was amazed and bewildered. A serving monk asked, "Have you got the point, Your Majesty?" Emperor Wu replied, "No." The serving monk said, "The Master has finished expounding the meaning of the *sutra*." On another occasion, Emperor Wu entered the room when Shanhui was lecturing. Everyone stood up respectfully except the Master, who sat quite still. The Emperor's attendant said to him, "Why don't you stand up in the presence of His Majesty?" The Master replied, "If the foundations of *dharma* stir, all will be upset." One day, the Master dressed himself in the robe of a Buddhist monk, donned the hat of a Taoist priest, put on shoes worn by ordinary folk, and went to the Emperor's court. The Emperor asked, "Are you a monk?" The Master pointed at his Taoist hat. The Emperor asked, "A Taoist

毕。"又有一天,大士讲经的时候,武帝驾到,大家都站起迎接,只有大士端坐不动。武帝的侍臣对他说:"圣驾在此,为什么不起立?"大士答:"法地如果起动,一切都会不安。"大士有一天穿着僧人的百衲衣,戴着道冠,拖着鞋子上朝。武帝问:"是和尚吗?"大士指指道冠。武帝问:"是道士吗?"大士指指拖着的鞋子。武帝又问:"那么是俗人吗?"大士指指百衲衣。

注释

① 士、大士:指善慧禅师。
② 披衲:穿上衲衣。衲衣为僧人的服装。
③ 顶冠:这里指戴着道士印帽子。

阅读提示

禅法以心传心,不立文字,不落言句,是不言之言,所以善慧大士只拍一下镇尺,就下法座,表示讲经已毕。

梁武帝驾到,大士不起立,说:"法地若动,一切不安。"因为禅宗说离开外界物相是禅,内心不散乱是定。如果见了皇帝就起立,那就没有摆脱外界事物的干扰;没有做到内心清静。善慧在这里是见机说法。

善慧大士穿着僧衣,戴着道冠,拖着俗人的鞋子,打扮得非僧、非道、非俗,意在说明:佛、道、俗只是外表穿着上不同,他们在本质上是完全相同的。

Excerpts from Zen Buddhist Texts

priest?" The Master pointed at his shoes. The Emperor asked, "Are you a layman, then?" The Master pointed at his Buddhist robe.

— Recorded Dialogues of Shanhui,
from *Amalgamation of the Sources of the Five Lamps*, vol. 2

Observation

☆ The Master does not speak because he is wary of the interference which words impose on intuitive perception. Later on, the Master remarks, "If the foundations of *dharma* stir, all will be upset." This is in keeping with the teachings of the Sixth Patriarch, Huineng, that "not to be affected by things in the outside world is Zen; when the inner peace is untroubled, that is the tranquillity of Zen". If the Master Shanhui should rise to his feet upon seeing the Emperor, that means he has not freed himself from disturbances of the outside world, and has not achieved tranquillity of the mind. The Master here is employing the method of teaching as the opportunity arises. In the last part of the story, the Master dresses as he does to illustrate the point that although they may dress differently and differ in outward appearances, Buddhist monks, Taoist priests, and lay people are the same in essence.

本无所断，亦无所得

问师："夫言圣人者，当断何法，当得何法，而言圣人？"答："一法不断，一法不得，此谓圣人。"进曰："不断不得，与凡夫有何异？"师曰："有异。何以故？一切凡夫皆有所断，妄计所得。真心圣人则本无所断，亦无所得。故曰有异。"

——法融语录，引自《祖堂集》卷一

白话翻译

无所断除，无所取得

僧徒问法融禅师："所谓圣人，应当断除何种法，得到何种法，而后可称为圣人呢？"禅师回答："什么法也不必断除，什么法也不必得到，这叫做圣人。"又问："既不断除也不得到，跟凡夫有什么区别呢？"禅师答："有区别。为什么呢？一切凡夫都有所断除，并且虚妄地考虑所得到的。而明了自心是佛的圣人则本无所断除，也无所取得。所以说是有区别的。"

Excerpts from Zen Buddhist Texts

Nothing to give up, and nothing to acquire

A disciple asked Zen Master Farong, "What teachings and ideas must one give up, and what teachings and ideas must one acquire before one could become a saint?" The Zen Master replied, "A saint doesn't have to give up any teachings or ideas, and doesn't have to acquire any teachings or ideas." The disciple asked, "Well, if a saint doesn't have to give up anything, and he doesn't acquire anything, what makes him different from the ordinary man?" The Master replied, "There is a difference. What is the difference? There are many things the ordinary man wants to give up or get rid of, and there are many things that he vainly hopes to acquire. But a man who realises that his mind is buddha and enlightenment itself has nothing to give up or get rid of, and he has no need to acquire anything. That is the difference."

— Recorded Dialogues of Farong,
from *A Collection from the Halls of the Patriarchs*, vol. 1

无心恰恰用

问曰:"恰恰用心时,若为安隐好?"师曰:"恰恰用心时,恰恰无心用。曲谭名相劳,直说无繁重。无心恰恰用,常用恰恰无。今说无心处,不与有心殊。"

——法融语录,引自《五灯会元》卷二

白话翻译

无所用心,恰恰是在用心

僧徒问:"正当用心思虑的时候,如何能使此心安稳些呢?"法融禅师回答:"正当你用心的时候,恰恰是心无可用。曲折委婉的谈论使互相造成疲劳,简单直率的话语可以避免繁琐重复。无所用心恰恰是在用心,常常用心恰恰是未曾用心。现在说的无所用心,和用心思虑并没有什么两样。"

Excerpts from Zen Buddhist Texts

When you are not concentrating, you are concentrating

A disciple asked Zen Master Farong, "When I am thinking carefully, how can I hold that concentration in my mind?" The Zen Master replied, "When you are concentrating, your mind is too occupied to do anything. Complicated and circuitous discussions tire out both the speaker and the listener. Simple and direct discourse avoids minute details and repetitions. When you are not trying to concentrate, you can use your mind. If you are always trying to concentrate, you have not really used your mind. What I am saying is that not trying to concentrate is the same as thinking carefully."

— Recorded Dialogues of Farong,
from *Amalgamation of the Sources of the Five Lamps*, vol. 2

一切自看

问:"达摩未来此土时,还有佛法也无?"师曰:"未来且置,即今事作么生?"曰:"某甲不会,乞师指示。"师曰:"万古长空,一朝风月。"僧无语。师复曰:"阇梨①会么?"曰:"不会。"师曰:"自己分上作么生,干他达摩来与未来作么?他家来,大似卖卜汉,见汝不会,为汝锥破,卦文才生吉凶,尽在汝分上,一切自看②。"

——崇慧语录,引自《五灯会元》卷二

Excerpts from
Zen Buddhist Texts

You have to work things out for yourself

A monk asked Zen Master Chonghui, "Was there Buddhism in China before *Bodhidharma* came to China?" The Master replied, "We'll put this question aside for the moment. What are you going to do about the present?" The monk said, "I don't understand. Please explain." The Master said, "The sky has been there for centuries. The breeze and the moon are different every night." The monk was silent. The Master asked, "Do you get the point?" The monk replied, "No." The Master explained, "The way you work things out for yourself — what has that got to do with whether or when *Bodhidharma* came to China? His coming to China is like a visit by a fortune-teller. Seeing that you can't work things out in your life, the fortune-teller tells you your fortune. But whether your fortune is going to be good or bad actually depends on yourself. That's why you have to work things out for yourself."

— Recorded Dialogues of Chonghui,
from *Amalga mation of the Sources of the Five Lamps*, vol. 2

白话翻译

一切自己留意

僧人问道:"菩提达摩尚未来中国时,中国可有佛法吗?"崇慧禅师答道:"尚未来时的事暂且不论,如今的事怎么样?"僧人说:"我不领会,请师指点。"禅师说:"万古长空,一朝风月。"僧人无语。禅师又说:"你领会了吗?"僧人答:"不领会。"禅师说:"自己身上的事情怎么样,跟他这摩来与不来有什么关系?他来中国很像个占卦人,看到你不领会,就为你占一卦。卦文是吉是凶,其实都在你的身上,一切都应自己留意。"

注释

① 阇梨:也作"阇黎",梵语,意为僧人之师,也泛称僧人。

② 一切自看:看:注意,留心。这里意思是:领悟佛法应立足眼前,以自我为主,不要管祖师来或没来,也不关他人之事。

经典名句 Highlights

jǔ shǒu pān nán dǒu, huí shēn yǐ běi chén.
举手攀南斗,回身倚北辰。
chū tóu tiān wài kàn, shéi shì wǒ bān rén
出头天外看,谁是我般人?

My hands stretch to touch the constellations,
I lean against the Northern Star.
I crane my head and see beyond the heavens,
Who, like me, on earth, there are?

禅宗语录 中华传统文化精粹

八十老人行不得

元和中,白居易侍郎出守兹郡,因入山谒师。问曰:"禅师住处甚危险!"师曰:"太守危险尤甚!"白曰:"弟子位镇江山,何险之有?"师曰:"薪火相交,识性不停,得非险乎?"又问:"如何是佛法大意?"师曰:"诸恶莫作,众善奉行。"白曰:"三岁孩儿也解恁么道。"师曰:"三岁孩儿虽道得,八十老人行不得。"白作礼而退。

——道林语录,引自《五灯会元》卷二

Excerpts from
Zen Buddhist Texts

Not even an eighty-year-old can do it

Sometime in the Yuanhe Period (AD 806-820) in the Tang Dynasty, the famous poet Bai Juyi, while serving as Governor of Hangzhou, went to a mountain to visit Zen Master Daolin who made his abode on an ancient pine tree. Bai Juyi observed, "Master, you live in great danger!" The Zen Master said, "Governor, you live in greater danger than I do!" Bai Juyi asked, "My work is to keep order in the land. What danger is there?" The Zen Master replied, "Affairs of the world burn ceaselessly, and troubles never end. Is that not dangerous?" Bai Juyi then asked, "What is the main principle of Buddha's teachings?" The Master replied, "Do no evil, and perform what is good." Bai Juyi said, "Even a three-year-old knows that!" The Master responded, "A three-year-old may know it, but not even an eighty-year-old can do it." The poet bowed and left.

— Recorded Dialogues of Daolin,
from *Amalgamation of the Sources of the Five Lamps*. vol. 2

白话翻译

八十岁老人做不到

唐元和年中(806-820)白居易侍郎出任杭州太守,入山谒见道林禅师。白居易说:"禅师的住处很危险啊!"(按:道林住在古松枝上)禅师说:"太守更加危险!"白居易问:"弟子的职务位镇江山,有什么危险?"禅师答:"俗世如薪火相煎迫,烦恼不停息,难道不危险吗?"白居易又问:"什么是佛法的主要意旨?"禅师回答:"各种恶事都别去做,众多善事应当去做。"白居易说:"三岁小孩也会这样说。"禅师说:"三岁的小孩虽然说得出,八十岁的老人却做不到。"白居易行礼而退。

经典名句 Highlights

<pre>
zhí xū zài yì   mò kōng guò shí
直须在意，莫 空 过 时。
</pre>

Be careful. Do not waste time.

吾不如也

（志诚）少于荆南当阳山玉泉寺奉事神秀禅师，后因两宗盛化，秀之徒众往往讥南宗曰："能大师不识一字，有何所长？"秀曰："他得无师之智，深悟上乘，吾不如也。且吾师五祖亲付衣法，岂徒然哉？吾所恨不能远去亲近，虚受国恩。汝等诸人，无滞于此，可往曹溪质疑，他日回复还为吾说。"师闻此语，礼辞至韶阳。

——神秀语录，引自《景德传灯录》卷五

我比不上他

志诚年少的时候在荆南当阳山玉泉寺侍奉神秀禅师，后来南、北两宗教化盛行，神秀的门徒们往往朝讽南宗说："慧能大师不识一字，有什么本领？"神秀说："他具有无须开导的智慧，深刻领悟了大乘佛理，我不如他啊。而且我的老师五祖亲自把衣法传给他，难道是没有道理的吗？我所遗憾的是相隔遥远，不能去向他请教，虚受着国家的恩惠。你们各位不要滞留在这里，可去曹溪向他请教，日后回来再说给我听。"志诚听了这话，就告辞神秀来到韶阳。

Excerpts from Zen Buddhist Texts

I am not as good as he is

When Zhicheng was young, he served Zen Master Shenxiu in the Jade Fountain Monastery in Dangyang Mountain (situated in what is now the Jiangling county in Hubei Province). Later, as both the Southern and the Northern Schools of Zen Buddhism flourished, Shenxiu's disciples often sneered at the Southern School, "Their Zen Master Huineng is illiterate. What does he know?" But Shenxiu said to them, "He has wisdom that needs no learning to bring out, and he has a profound understanding of *Mahayana* Buddhism. I am not as good as he is. Besides, my Master the Fifth Patriarch himself appointed Huineng his successor. Would he have done that for no reason? My regret is, we are so far apart that I cannot go to learn from him, but have to see time slip by while I serve here and live on the bounties bestowed by the country. You, my disciples, should not tarry here. You should go to Caoxi in Guangdong to learn from him, and then come back to tell me about his teaching." When Zhicheng heard this, he bade Shenxiu farewell and headed south to Shaoyang.

— Recorded Dialogues of Shenxiu,
from *Jingde Record of the Transmission of the Lamp*, vol. 5

不见不闻

后归东洛，遇秀禅师，言下知微。乃卜寿州三峰山，结茅而居。常有野人，服色素朴，言谈诡异，于言笑外，化作佛形及菩萨、罗汉①、天仙等形，或放神光，或呈声响。师之学徒睹之，皆不能测。如此涉十年，后寂无形影。师告众曰："野人作多色伎俩，眩惑于人。只消老僧不见不闻，伊伎俩有穷，吾不见不闻无尽。"

——道树语录，引自《五灯会元》卷二

Excerpts from
Zen Buddhist Texts

See nothing, hear nothing

When the monk Daoshu returned to Luoyang[①], he met Zen Master Shenxiu, and came to an understanding of the meaning of Zen Buddhism in the course of their discussions. So he chose a place in the Three Peaks Mountain, built a hut and settled there. To this place came many strange visitors. They were plainly dressed, and their discourse was strange. When they talked, they often transformed themselves into buddhas, *bodhisattvas*, *arhat* and other celestial beings, and they radiated mysterious light and made strange noises. When Daoshu's disciples saw these strange phenomena, they were bewildered. This went on for ten years, and then the strange visitors all disappeared. The Zen Master later told his disciples, "Those strange people used their many tricks to deceive and confuse people. If I would see nothing and hear nothing of them, there is an end to the tricks they can play, and I can persist in seeing nothing and hearing nothing."

— Recorded Dialogues of Daoshu,
from *Amalgamation of the Sources of the Five Lamps*, vol. 2

不看不听

    道树后来回到东都洛阳,遇上神秀禅师,言谈之中,当下领悟禅旨。于是选择寿州三峰山,造茅屋而住。这里常有野人来往,衣服朴素,言语怪异,谈笑之余,变化成佛、菩萨、罗汉、天仙等形状,或放出神秘的光,或发出奇怪的声响。道树的学徒们看到这些现象都不知是怎么回事。如此经过十年,野人完全消失了。禅师告诉众人:"野人使出多种伎俩迷惑他人,只要老僧我不看不听,他的伎俩是有穷尽之日的,而我的不看不听却没有穷尽之时。"

① 罗汉:佛教称断绝了一切嗜欲,解脱了烦恼的僧人。

Excerpts from Zen Buddhist Texts

Note

① Luoyang: the ancient capital of China.

不记年岁

武后徵至辇下，待以师礼，与秀禅师同加钦重。后尝问师："甲子多少？"师曰："不记。"后曰："何不记邪？"师曰："生死之身，其若循环。环无起尽，焉用记为？况此心流注，中间无间。见沤起灭者，乃妄想耳。从初识至动相灭时，亦只如此。何年月而可记乎？"后闻稽颡，信受。

——慧安语录，引自《五灯会元》卷二

白话翻译

不记年岁

武后召慧安禅师来到京都，当作老师接待，与神秀禅师一样看重。武后曾经问慧安禅师："年纪多大了？"禅师回答："不记得。"武后说："怎么会不记得呢？"禅师答道："此身有生有死，如同圆环转动，圆环没有起点也没有尽头，哪用得着记岁数呢？何况此心如水流动，中间没有间隙。看到水泡（喻人的生死）的生灭，不过是虚妄的思想罢了。从初有意识到此身毁灭，也是如此，有什么年月可记呢？"武后听了便行礼道歉，相信、接受了禅师的说法。

Excerpts from
Zen Buddhist Texts

I remember not my age

Empress Wu summoned Zen Master Huian to the capital, and received him with the honour accorded to a Master, in the same manner as she honoured Zen Master Shenxiu. Empress Wu once asked Huian, "How old are you?" The Master replied, "I remember not my age." The Empress asked, "How could that be?" The Master replied, "One goes through lives and deaths, in cycles, as in a ring. A ring has no beginning and no end. What is the point of noting its progress in years? Besides, the mind flows, like water, and nothing marks the flow. And the birth and death of its bubbles are nothing but vain thoughts. Life, from the first moment of consciousness to the moment of death, is just the same. Why mark it in months and years?" When Empress Wu heard this, she bowed, apologised for her ignorance, understood and accepted the Master's vision.

— Recorded Dialogues of Huian,
from *Amalgamation of the Sources of the Five Lamps*, vol. 2

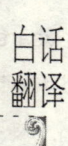

如人饮水，冷暖自知

卢曰："不思善，不思恶，正恁么时，阿那个是明上座本来面目？"师当下大悟，遍体汗流，泣礼数拜，问曰："上来密语密意外，还更别有意旨否？"卢曰："我今与汝说者，即非密也。汝若返照自己面目，密却在汝边。"师曰："某甲虽在黄梅随众，实未省自己面目。今蒙指授入处，如人饮水，冷暖自知。今行者即是某甲师也。"

——道明语录，引自《五灯会元》卷二

白话翻译

如人饮水，冷暖自知

卢行者（六祖慧能）说："既不思虑善，也不思虑恶，正当这个时候，什么是你的本来面目？"道明立刻彻底省悟了，他浑身流汗，哭泣着连连礼拜，问道："除了刚才的密语密意外，是不是还有其他意旨呢？"卢行者回答："我现在对你说的话，就不隐密了。你如果回转眼光返照自己的面目，那么隐密正在你的身边。"道明说："我虽然在黄梅（五祖弘忍）跟随大众学道，其实并没有省悟自己的面目。今天蒙您指教门路，如人饮水，冷暖自知。如今您就是我的老师了！"

Excerpts from
Zen Buddhist Texts

When you drink water, you know if it is hot or cold

The Lay Brother Lu, who later became the Sixth Patriarch Huineng, asked the monk, Daoming, "When you are not thinking of good, or evil, at that instant, what is the real you?" Daoming came to a sudden realisation. He broke out into a sweat, and in tears he bowed to the Patriarch and asked, "Apart from these profound words and their profound message, is there some other point to be observed?" Lu replied, "What I have told you is not profound or mysterious. If you turn your attention inward and observe yourself, the profound mystery is in you." Daoming said, "Although I have been studying under our Fifth Patriarch Hongren, I have not really looked at my real self. I am grateful to you for showing me the way to inward knowledge. It is like when one drinks water, one knows if it's hot or cold. From now on, you are my teacher and master."

— Recorded Dialogues of Daoming,
from *Amalgamation of the Sources of the Five Lamps*, vol. 2

善恶如浮云

僧问:"如何是修善行人?"师曰:"担枷带锁。"曰:"如何是作恶行人?"师曰:"修禅入定。"曰:"某甲浅机,请师直指。"师曰:"汝问我恶,恶不从善;汝问我善,善不从恶。"僧良久。师曰:"会么?"曰:"不会。"师曰:"恶人无善念,善人无恶心。所以道善恶如浮云,俱无起灭处。"僧于言下大悟。后破灶堕闻举,乃曰:"此子会尽诸法无生。"

——峻极语录,引自《五灯会元》卷二

Excerpts from Zen Buddhist Texts

Good and evil are like floating clouds

A monk asked Zen Master Junji, "What sort of people do good deeds?" The Master replied, "Those in hand-cuffs and chains." The monk asked, "And what sort of people do evil?" The Master replied, "Those who practise Zen meditation." The monk said, "I am not experienced at catching the meaning of these hints. Please speak plainly that I may learn." The Master said, "You asked about evil. Evil resides not in good. You asked about good. Good resides not in evil." The monk was silent for a long while. The Master asked, "Do you understand?" "No," the monk replied. The Master explained, "Good men have no evil thoughts, and evil men have no good thoughts. Good and evil are like floating clouds, they come and go." At this, the monk was enlightened. Later, when the Master Po Zao Duo heard about this, he said, "The man had a total realisation of the nature of impermanence and the absence of absolutes."

— Recorded Dialogues of Junji,
from *Amalgamation of the Sources of the Five Lamps*, vol.2

白话翻译

善与恶如同浮云

僧徒问:"怎样是修习善行的人?"峻极禅师答:"披带枷锁。"问:"怎样是为非作恶的人?"师答:"修禅入定。"僧徒说:"我初学禅机,请老师直截指示。"禅师说:"你问我恶,恶人不从善;你问我善,善人不从恶。"僧徒默然。禅师问:"领会了吗?"答:"不领会。"禅师说:"恶人无善念,善人无恶心。所以说善恶如同浮云,都无生无灭。"僧徒立即大悟。后来破灶堕禅师知道了这番话,就说:"此人把事物本性为无生无灭的道理领悟透彻了。"

Excerpts from Zen Buddhist Texts

Observation

★ Men are neither good nor bad, they are what their thoughts make them. A villain who thinks a good thought becomes a good man; a good man who thinks evil becomes a villain. Thoughts of good and evil come and go like floating clouds, thus defining us as they change.

磨砖作镜

开元中有沙门道一住传法院，常日坐禅。师知是法器，往问曰："大德坐禅图什么？"一曰："图作佛。"师乃取一砖，于彼庵前石上磨。一曰："师作什么？"师曰："磨作镜。"一曰："磨砖岂得成镜耶？"[师曰：]"坐禅岂得成佛耶？"一曰：如何即是？"师曰："如人驾车，不行，打车即是，打牛即是？"一无对。师又曰："汝学坐禅，为学坐佛？若学坐禅，禅非坐卧；若学坐佛，佛非定相。于无住法不应取舍，汝若坐佛即是杀佛，若执坐相非达其理。"一闻示诲，如饮醍醐①。

——怀让语录，引自《景德传灯录》卷五

Excerpts from
Zen Buddhist Texts

Polishing a brick to make a mirror

Sometime in the Kaiyuan Period (AD 713–741) in the Tang Dynasty, there was a monk called Daoyi who spent all his time sitting in meditation in a monastery. Zen Master Huairang of Nanyue, knowing that he had some potential for spiritual enlightenment, approached him and asked, "What do you hope to achieve by meditation?" Daoyi replied, "I hope to become a buddha." The Master took a brick and started to polish it by grinding it against a rock outside Daoyi's room. Daoyi asked him, "What are you doing, Master?" The Master replied, "Polishing it to make a mirror." Daoyi said, "How can you make a mirror out of a brick?" The Master said, "If you can't make a mirror out of a brick, how can you become a buddha by sitting in meditation?" Daoyi asked, "Then what is the right way to do it?" The Master answered, "If a man is driving a cart, and the cart stops, should he whip the cart or the ox that pulls it?" Daoyi did not know how to answer the question. The Master went on, "If you want to practise Zen meditation, you don't have to sit here all the time, because Zen is neither sitting down nor lying down. If you want to become a buddha, you should know that buddhas have no fixed form or shape either.

白话翻译

磨砖作镜子

　　开元年(713—741)间,有个叫道一的僧人住在传法院,整天坐禅。怀让禅师知道他具有佛法才器,就去问他:"和尚您坐禅谋求什么?"道一答:"谋求作佛。"禅师就拿了一块砖头,在房前的石头上磨起来。道一问:"禅师做什么?"禅师答:"磨作镜子。"道一说:"磨砖怎能成镜呢?"禅师说:"既然磨砖不能成镜,那么坐禅怎能成佛呢?"道一问:"怎么做才正确?"禅师说:"好比有个人驾车,车不前进,应该打车呢,还是打牛?"道一无法回答。禅师又说:"你学习坐禅,还是学习坐佛?如果学坐禅,禅并不是坐或卧;如果学坐佛,佛也没有固定的相状。事物变化不定,不应有所取舍,你如坐佛就是杀佛,如果执着于坐相是不能达到真理的。"道一听了这番教诲,如饮醍醐一般地清醒了。

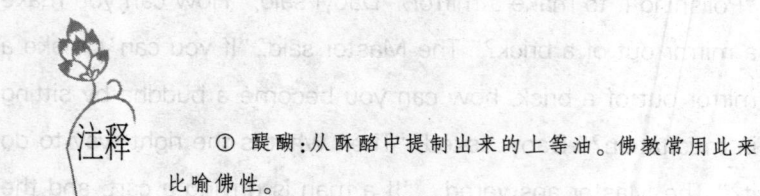

注释

① 醍醐:从酥酪中提制出来的上等油。佛教常用此来比喻佛性。

Excerpts from Zen Buddhist Texts

All things change in a flux, and one should not be fixated on any particular form. If you think of buddhas as sitting, you kill the idea of buddha. Being fixated on a sitting posture cannot help you see the truth." These words woke Daoyi to a new realisation about the nature of Buddhahood.

— Recorded Dialogues of Huairang,
from *Jingde Record of the Transmission of the Lamp*, vol. 5

小乘是大乘

齐寺主问曰："云何是大乘？"答曰："小乘是。"又问曰："今问大乘，因何言小乘是？"答："因有小故，而始立大；若其无小，大从何生？今言大者，乃是小家之大。今言大乘者，空无所有，即不可言大小。犹如虚空，虚空无限量，不可言无限量；虚空无边，不可言无边，大乘亦尔。是故经云：虚空无中边，诸佛身亦然。今问大乘者，所以小乘是也。道理极分明，何须有怪？"

——引自《神会语录》

白话翻译

小乘是大乘

姓齐的寺院主持僧问："什么是大乘？"神会禅师答："小乘就是。"又问："今问大乘，为何却说小乘就是呢？"答："只因有小，才设立大；如果没有小，大从何而来？现在你问的大，便是小者的大。所谓大乘，空寂无物，就不能说大小。好比虚空，虚空无限，但不可说无限，虚空无边，但不可说无边，大乘也是这样。所以佛经说：虚空没有中间，没有边际，诸佛法身也如此。因此你问大乘，我便答是小乘。道理极其分明，何必奇怪？"

Excerpts from
Zen Buddhist Texts

Hinayana is Mahayana

The abbot, surnamed Qi, of a monastery asked, "What is *Mahayana*, the Big Vehicle?" Zen Master Shenhui of Heze replied, "It is *Hinayana*, the Small Vehicle." Qi asked, "I am asking about *Mahayana*. Why do you say it is *Hinayana*?" Shenhui replied, "Only when you have an idea of 'small' can you set up an idea of 'big'. Without the notion of what is 'small', how can you have a notion of what is 'big'? The 'big' that you ask about is big only to those who are used to what is 'small'. The so-called Big Vehicle, *Mahayana*, is not a thing, it has no size, so you cannot say it is big or small. Rather it is like a void. A void has no limits, but you cannot say it is limitless; a void has no boundaries, but you cannot say it is boundless. So it is with *Mahayana*. That is why, in the *sutras*, it is said: a void has no centre, no boundaries. So it is with the Way of Buddha. That is why when you asked about the Big Vehicle, I answered that it is the Small Vehicle. The reason is clear. There is nothing strange in such an answer."

— From *Recorded Dialogues of Shenhui*

是法平等

……儿子①便问禅师："乞师慈悲摄受，度得一个众生。某甲切要投禅师出家。"禅师曰："是我宗门中，银轮王嫡子，金轮王②孙子，方始得继续，不坠此门风。是你三家村里男女③，牛背上将养的儿子，作么生投这个宗门？不是你分上事！"儿子曰："启禅师，是法平等，无有高下，那得有这个言辞，障于某甲善心？再乞禅师垂慈容纳。"

——南阳慧忠国师语录，引自《祖堂集》卷三

Excerpts from
Zen Buddhist Texts

All creatures are equal

A young man, Huizhong, said to a Zen Master, "Show some compassion, Master, take me as your disciple, and save a soul. I want desperately to follow you." The Zen Master said, "In the School of Zen, only the sons and grandsons of gods and mythical kings bearing wheels of gold and silver can carry on the heritage of its teachings. That is how we have kept up the tradition. You are a nobody from a tiny village, a mere child who grew up minding buffaloes! How can you be accepted into the School? It is not for the likes of you!" The young man replied, "All creatures are equal, none is superior to another. How can you use such a lame excuse to curb my yearning to learn compassion? Please, I beg of you, show some compassion, and accept me as your disciple."

— Recorded Dialogues of Imperial Buddhist Master Huizhong of Nanyang, from *A Collection from the Halls of the Patriarchs*, vol. 3

白话翻译

万物平等

……少年便对禅师说:"求禅师发慈悲心,收我为徒,救度一个众生。我迫切要求投奔禅师出家。"禅师说:"我禅宗门中,银轮王的嫡子,金轮王的孙子,才能继承法嗣,不损坏宗门风气。你是乡野小村里的俗人,牛背上长大的孩子,怎能投入这个宗门?这不是你分上的事!"少年说:"万物平等,没有高低,您怎能用这种话来阻拦我向善之心?再次求您发慈悲心,收我为徒。"

注释

① 儿子:少年。这里指慧忠,当时十多岁。
② 银轮王……金轮王:佛教传说中手持宝轮的神仙。
③ 三家村里男女:只有几户人家的偏僻村子里的人。男女,是对人轻贱的称呼。

经典名句 Highlights

měi shí bù zhōng bǎo rén chī
美食不中饱人吃.

The food may be nice, but it has no attraction for a man who is full.

佛还曾迷也无

师问璘供奉①："佛是什么义？"对曰："佛是觉义。"师曰："佛还曾迷也无②？"对曰："不曾迷。"师曰："既不曾迷，用觉作什摩③？"无对。

——慧忠语录，引自《祖堂集》卷三

白话翻译

佛可曾迷惑过

南阳慧忠禅师问璘供奉："佛是什么意思？"璘回答："佛是觉悟的意思。"禅师问："佛可曾迷惑过？"回答："不曾迷惑过。"禅师说："既然不曾迷惑过，还要觉悟干什么？"璘供奉无法回答。

Excerpts from Zen Buddhist Texts

Was Buddha ever deluded?

   Zen Master Huizhong of Nanyang asked a follower called Lin, "What does 'Buddha' mean?" "Buddha means enlightenment," Lin replied. The Master asked, "Was Buddha ever deluded?" "No," Lin replied. The Master said, "If he was never deluded, what need is there for enlightenment[①]?" Lin could not give an answer.

— Recorded Dialogues of Huizhong,
from *A Collection from the Halls of the Patriarchs*, vol. 3

注释

① 师问璘供奉：师，即慧忠禅师。璘供奉，指一个名叫璘的佛教信徒。

② 还曾……也无：疑问格式，相当于"可曾……吗？"

③ 用觉作什摩：此句慧忠禅师的意思是：佛既然是觉悟的意思，表明佛也曾迷惑过，否则还要觉悟干什么？佛是由凡入圣，再堕凡普度众生的。

Excerpts from
Zen Buddhist Texts

Note

① If he was ... enlightenment: Huizhong's point is: since Buddha means enlightenment, it implies that Buddha was once deluded, or else enlightenment would be pointless. Buddha underwent a transition from an ordinary person to Buddha through enlightenment, and returned to the world to save all living things.

Observation

★ Huizhong's last question embraces two possibilities of interpretation: (a) Buddha was once deluded, like the rest of us. This enhances the human aspect of Buddha, and raises hopes that enlightenment can effect a similar attainment for us; (b) If Buddha is, by definition, enlightenment, then Buddha could not have been deluded. What was deluded was the man that Buddha was before enlightenment made him a buddha.

何不自看自静

师天竺人也。行至太原定襄县历村，见秀大师弟子结草为庵，独坐观心。师问："作什么？"对曰："看静。"师曰："看者何人？静者何物？"僧遂起礼拜，问："此理为何？乞师指示。"师曰："何不自看，何不自静？"僧无对。师见根性迟回，乃曰："汝师是谁？"对曰："秀和尚。"师曰："汝师只教此法，为当别有意旨？"对曰："只教某甲看静。"师曰："西天下劣外道①所习之清，此土以为禅宗，也大误人！"其僧问："三藏②师是谁？"师曰："六祖。"又曰："正法难闻，汝何不往彼中？"其僧闻师提训，便去曹溪礼见六祖，具陈上事。六祖曰："诚如崛多所言，汝何不自看，何不自静？教谁静汝？"其僧言下大悟也。

——崛多三藏语录，引自《祖堂集》卷三

Excerpts from
Zen Buddhist Texts

Why not keep peace in your own mind

Zen Master Jueduo was an Indian. When he travelled to the village of Li in the county of Dingxiang in Taiyuan, he found one of Shenxiu's disciples there. This monk had built himself a thatched hut, and meditated there all by himself. The Zen Master asked him, "What are you doing here?" "I'm looking for peace," he replied. The Master asked, "Who is looking for peace? And what is peace?" Upon hearing this, the monk stood up, bowed respectfully and asked, "What do your words mean? Could you please explain to me?" The Master replied, "Why don't you look into your own mind? Why not keep peace in your mind?" The monk was silent. Seeing that he was slow to understand, the Master asked him, "Who is your teacher?" He replied, "The monk Shenxiu." The Master asked, "Did he teach you only this method? Did he teach you anything else?" "He taught me to look for peace," came the reply. The Master said, "The unorthodox ways of the West have been taken for the Way of Zen here. That's going to lead many astray!" The monk asked the Master, "Who is your teacher, Master?" The Master replied, "The Sixth Patriarch." Then he added, "It is not easy to learn the true ways of Zen. Why don't you go and

何不自心清静

崛多禅师是印度人。他游历到太原定襄县历村,看见神秀大师的弟子结草为庵,独自坐禅。禅师问:"干什么呢?"答:"探寻清静。"禅师问:"探寻者是什么人?清静又是什么东西?"那僧人便起立礼拜,问:"这话什么意思?请您指点。"禅师说:"何不探寻自心,何不自心清静?"僧无话回答。禅师见他迟钝,便问:"你的老师是谁?"答:"神秀和尚。"禅师问:"你的老师只教这种方法,还是另有他法?"答:"只教我探寻清静。"禅师说:"西方低劣的外道修行方法,这里以为是禅宗,真是太误人!"该僧问:"法师您的老师是谁?"师答:"六祖。"又说:"真正的禅法难以听到,你何不到他那里去?"该僧听了训导便去曹溪参见六祖慧能,并叙说了上面的事。六祖说:"确实像崛多所说,你何不探寻自心,何不自心清静?让谁来使你清静?"该僧一听,立即大悟。

① 外道:指佛教以外的其他宗教。
② 三藏:此处是对僧人的敬称。

Excerpts from
Zen Buddhist Texts

learn from him?" The monk took his advice and set out to Caoxi. There the monk found the Sixth Patriarch Huineng, paid his respects and recounted his meeting with Jueduo. Huineng said, "Jueduo was right. Why not look into your own mind, and keep peace in your mind? If you don't do that, who can keep peace for you?" When the monk heard this, he was enlightened.

— Recorded Dialogues of Jueduo,
from *A C llection from the Halls of the Patriarchs*, vol. 3

禅宗语录　中华传统文化精粹

但看弄傀儡，线断一时休

又白马寺惠真问："禅师说无心是道？"师曰："然。"问曰："道既无心，佛有心耶？佛之与道，是一是二？"师曰："不一不二。"问："佛度众生，为有心故；道不度人，为无心故。一度一不度，是二不是二？"师曰："此是大德妄生二见，山僧不然。何者？佛是虚名，道亦妄立。二俱不实，都是假名。一假之中立何二？"又问："佛之与道，纵是假名，当立名时，是谁为立？若有立者，何得言无？"师曰："佛之与道，因心而立。推究心本，心亦是无。二俱虚妄，犹如花翳。即悟本空，强立佛道。"……师《无修偈》曰："见道方修道，不见复何修？道性如虚空，虚空何处修？遍观修道者，拨火觅浮沤。但看弄傀儡，

94

Excerpts from
Zen Buddhist Texts

Watch the puppeteer

Huizhen, the abbot of Baima Monastery, asked Zen Master Benjing, "You said that the Way is not a matter of intention or the heart. Did you not?" Benjing replied, "I did." Huizhen asked, "If the Way is not a matter of intention or the heart, then does Buddha have any intention or heart? The Way, and Buddha, are they the same? Or are they different?" The Zen Master replied, "Not the same. And not different." Huizhen said, "Buddha wanted to save all beings, and that is an intention. The Way is not for saving others, for the Way has no intention. One is out to save and the other is not. Are they not, then, different?" The Zen Master replied, "This distinction is created by your reverence. This humble recluse does not see such a distinction. Why? Buddha is a name invented to stand for something, as is the Way. Neither has any substance, both are unreal. What distinction is there to draw between the two unrealities?" Huizhen said, "It may be true that the two are unreal and exist only in name, but then who first invented the two names? And, if someone had invented and established the names, how can you say they do not exist?" The Zen Master replied, "Those names had been set up with an intention, but even that

xiàn duàn yī shí xiū
线　断　一　时休。"

běn jìng yǔ lù   yǐn zì   zǔ táng jí   juǎn sān
——本净语录，引自《祖堂集》卷三

白话翻译

如演木偶戏，线断一齐倒

又有白马寺的惠真问："禅师您说无心是道？"本净禅师答："是的。"惠真问："道既然无心，佛有心吗？佛与道，是一回事还是两回事？"禅师答："既不是一回事，也不是两回事。"问："佛教度众生，因为佛有心，道不救度人，因为道无心。一个度一个不度，是不是两回事呢？"禅师答："这是大德您虚妄的见解，因此看作两回事。山僧我不是这样看的，为什么呢？佛只是虚妄的称呼，道也是虚立其名，二者都不是实际存在，都是虚假的称呼。同一虚假怎能区分为二？"惠真又问："佛与道就算是虚假的名称，那么当初是谁为它们设立的？如果有设立者，怎能说是无呢？"禅师答："佛与道由心设立名称。推究心的根本，其实心也不存在。佛与道都是虚妄不实的，好比花的阴影一样。领悟了本源虚空，便知佛与道是勉强设立的。"于是惠真称赞说："对事理的解说透彻完满，这是禅宗顿悟的真正门径。心就是佛，可以作为后世遵循的法则。"本净禅师作《无修偈》说："看见道才去修道，不见道从何修习？道的本性如虚空，既是虚空怎修习？遍看修道者，正如火里找水泡；又如台上演木偶，牵线如断一齐倒。"

Excerpts from Zen Buddhist Texts

intention has no existence. Buddha and the Way are both unreal, just as the shadows of flowers are unreal. When we understand that these names came from an unreal source, then we know that Buddha and the Way were invented only out of necessity." ....

The Master also wrote a verse entitled "No cultivation needed":

If you can seek the Way only when you've known it,

How do you start before you know it?

The Way, by nature, is empty, unreal,

How can you follow it?

So many followers of the Way,

Seek water bubbles in the fire,

Watch the puppeteer, his strings broken,

Retire.

— Recorded Dialogues of Benjing,
from *A Collection from the Halls of the Patriarchs*, vol. 3

一宿觉

初到振锡,绕祖三匝,卓然而立。祖曰:"夫沙门①者,具三千威仪,八万细行。大德自何方而来,生大我慢②?"师曰:"生死事大,无常迅速。"祖曰:"何不体取无生,了无速乎?"师曰:"体即无生,了本无速③。"祖曰:"如是!如是!"于时大众无不愕然。师方具威仪参礼,须臾告辞。祖曰:"返太速乎?"师曰:"本自非动,岂有速邪!"祖曰:"谁知非动?"师曰:"仁者④自生分别。"祖曰:"汝甚得无生之意。"师曰:"无生岂有意邪!"祖曰:"无意谁当分别?"师曰:"分别亦非意!"祖叹曰:"善哉!善哉!少留一宿。"时谓"一宿觉"⑤矣。

——玄觉语录,引自《五灯会元》卷二

Excerpts from Zen Buddhist Texts

The one-night enlightenment

When Zen Master Xuanjue of Yongjia first arrived at an assembly conducted by the Sixth Patriarch Huineng, he shook his ritual staff, walked three times round Huineng's seat, and stood bolt upright. The Patriarch said, "The behaviour and bearing of a monk should be in accordance with the three thousand regulations and eighty thousand examples. Where are you from that you should be so arrogant?" The Master replied, "Life and death are big changes, and they happen too fast to know." The Patriarch said, "Then why don't you learn the mystery that there is neither life nor death, and understand the principle that nothing is too fast or too slow?" The Master replied, "But learning is not subject to birth or death, and understanding in itself is neither too fast nor too slow." The Patriarch said, "That is so. Quite so." All who were gathered there were amazed at the exchange. Only then did Xuanjue pay his respects to the Patriarch in the proper manner and with the appropriate ceremony. As soon as he had done that, he took his leave of the Patriarch. The Patriarch said, "Are you leaving so soon?" The Master replied, "I haven't really moved. Soon or not doesn't come into it." The Patriarch asked, "Who would

白话翻译

留宿一晚得觉悟

玄觉禅师初到六祖慧能的法会,振动锡杖,绕六祖法座走了三圈,笔直地站着。六祖说:"作为僧人,行为动作应具备三千仪则和八万规范,您从哪里来,怎么如此傲慢?"禅师说:"生死是大事,变化很迅速。"六祖说:"那为什么不去领会无生无灭的法旨,了悟无快无慢的道理呢?"禅师说:"领会就是无生无灭,了悟本来无快无慢。"六祖说:"是这样!是这样!"当时众人没有一个不惊讶。玄觉禅师此时才按照礼仪参拜六祖,接着便要告辞。六祖说:"回去得太快了吧?"禅师说:"本来就没有动过,怎么谈得上快呢?"六祖说:"谁知道没有动过?"禅师说:"您人为地区分动过和没有动过。"六祖说:"你很懂得无生无灭的意思。"禅师说:"无生无灭难道还有意思吗?"六祖说:"无意思有意思是谁在区分?"禅师说:"区分也不是意思。"六祖赞叹说:"妙啊,妙啊,小住一宿再走吧。"当时人称此为留宿一晚得觉悟。

注释

① 沙门:梵语 śramana,称僧侣。

② 我慢:傲慢,自大。

③ 体即无生,了本无速:体,即体会,领悟;了,即了悟。这两句说:道本无生无灭,万物也本无迟无速。

④ 仁者:尊称对方。

⑤ 一宿觉:仅留宿一晚,便得觉悟;又因其名玄觉,故称为"一宿觉"。

Excerpts from Zen Buddhist Texts

know that you haven't moved?" The Master replied, "Only those who insist on arbitrary distinctions note whether one has moved." The Patriarch said, "You truly understand the meaning of not being limited by life or death." The Master said, "Is there any point in not being limited by life or death?" The Patriarch asked, "And who is now making an arbitrary distinction between there being a point or not being a point?" The Master said. "There is no point, is there, in making a distinction." "Wonderful! Truly wonderful!" said the Patriarch with approbation, and he added, "Won't you stay the night before you go?" Those who were there spoke of this encounter as the one-night enlightenment.

— Recorded Dialogues of Xuanjue,
from *Amalgamation of the Sources of the Five Lamps*, vol.2

禅宗语录 中华传统文化精粹

阅读提示 玄觉禅师与六祖慧能的问辩往来体现了禅宗"无生无灭"、"无分别"的思想。六祖为接引后学,以身作靶;玄觉领悟透彻,句句中的,使整段对话词锋锐利,禅机紧凑。

经典名句 **Highlights**

fēi xīn bú wèn fó　wèn fó bù fēi xīn
非心不问佛，问佛不非心。

The heart is Buddha, and Buddha is the heart.

常定无出入

游方时届于河溯,有隍禅师者,曾谒黄梅,自谓正受。师知隍所得未真,往问曰:"汝坐于此作么?"隍曰:"入定。"师曰:"汝言入定,有心邪?无心邪?若有心者,一切蠢动之类,皆应得定。若无心者,一切草木之流,亦合得定。"曰:"我正入定时,则不见有有无之心。"师曰:"既不见有有无之心,即是常定,何有出入?若有出入,则非大定①。"隍无语。

——玄策语录,引自《五灯会元》卷二

Excerpts from Zen Buddhist Texts

Mindless in meditation

When in his travels the monk Xuance came to the lower reaches of the Yellow River, he met a certain Zen Master by the name of Huang. Huang, since he had the honour of having visited the Fifth Patriarch, Hongren, claimed that he had learned the orthodox teachings from the Patriarch himself. Xuance knew that the Zen Master had not really understood the Way of Zen. He went and asked the Master, "What are you doing, sitting here?" Huang replied, "I'm entering into the state of Zen meditation." Xuance asked, "When you enter into a state of meditation, do you do so with a mind intent on it, or do you do it mindlessly? Because if you enter into meditation with a mind, then any creature should be able to do it; and if you do it mindlessly, then any plant or vegetable can do it too." Huang replied, "When I enter into meditation, I am not conscious of whether I have a mind to it or am mindless." Xuance said, "Well, if you are not conscious of it, then you are already in a state of meditation. Why say you have to enter into it or get out of it? If you have to enter or get out of it, then it is not true

白话翻译

心常定，无出入

玄策游历各地，来到河溯地区，有位隍禅师曾经参见过黄梅（五祖），自称是正宗传授。玄策知道隍禅师尚未得到真法，去问他："你坐在这里干什么？"隍禅师答："进入禅定。"玄策问："你说进入禅定，是有心呢，还是无心呢？如果有心的话，一切动物都应能禅定；如果无心的话，一切植物也应能禅定。"隍禅师说："当我进入禅定时，就看不到有心和无心。"玄策说："既是看不到有心和无心，就是常定不变，哪有什么进入或出离呢？如有入和出，就不是大定了。"隍禅师无言回答。

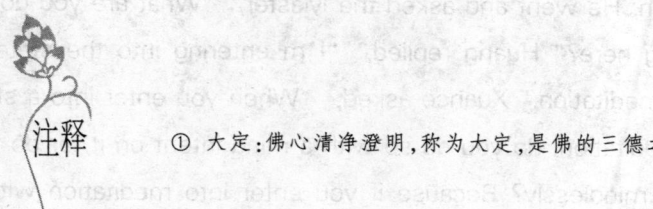

注释

① 大定：佛心清净澄明，称为大定，是佛的三德之一。

Excerpts from Zen Buddhist Texts

meditation." Zen Master Huang was left speechless.

— Recorded Dialogues of Xuance,
from *Amalgamation of the Sources of the Five Lamps,* vol. 2

石头路滑

邓隐峰①辞师，师云："什么处去？"对云："石头②去。"师云："石头路滑！"对云："竿木随身，逢场作戏③。"便去。才到石头，即绕禅床一匝，振锡一声，问："是何宗旨？"石头云："苍天！苍天④！"隐峰无语，却回，举似于师。师云："汝更去，见他道'苍天'，汝便'嘘嘘⑤'。"隐峰又去石头，一依前，问："是何宗旨？"石头乃"嘘嘘"。隐峰又无语。归来，师云："向汝道：'石头路滑！'"

——道一语录，引自《景德传灯录》卷六

Excerpts from
Zen Buddhist Texts

That stone is a slippery one

Deng Yinfeng took his leave of his teacher, Patriarch Ma[①]. Patriarch Ma asked, "Where are you heading for?" Deng replied, "I'm going to visit Zen Master Stone[②]" Patriarch Ma cautioned him, "That Stone is a slippery one!" Deng replied, "I'll take a staff with me, and perhaps we'll have fun." Then he set out. When he arrived at Zen Master Stone's place, he walked round the Master's seat, rattled his ritual staff and asked, "What is the principle?" Stone said, "The sky, the sky[③]!" Deng had no rejoinder for this, so he went back to tell Patriarch Ma about it. Patriarch Ma said to him, "Go to him again, and when he says 'the sky, the sky', you should say 'shush, shush[④]'." Deng went to see Stone again, repeated what he did, and asked, "What is the principle?" Stone replied, "Shush, shush!" Deng was again left without a rejoinder. When he went back to tell Patriarch Ma about it, the Patriarch said, "I told you, that Stone is a slippery one!"

— Recorded Dialogues of Daoyi,
from *Jingde Record of the Transmission of the Lamp*, vol. 6

石头路滑

白话翻译

邓隐峰向马祖告辞,马祖问:"到什么地方去?"答:"到石头禅师那儿去。"马祖说:"石头路滑!"答:"竿木随身,逢场作戏。"说完就出发了。到了石头禅师那儿,就绕着法座走了一圈,振动了一下锡杖,问:"宗旨是什么?"石头说:"苍天,苍天!"隐峰无话应对,回来告诉马祖。马祖说:"你再去,听他说'苍天',你就'嘘嘘'。"隐峰又去石头那儿,重复了上次的动作,同样又问:"宗旨是什么?"石头却发"嘘嘘"声。隐峰又无话答对,回来后马祖说:"我早跟你说石头路滑嘛!"

注释

① 邓隐峰:道一禅师的弟子。道一俗姓马,世称马祖。
② 石头:希迁禅师法号,也是希迁的住处。
③ 竿木随身,逢场作戏:本指江湖艺人随身携带着竿木等道具,遇到合适的场合就随时演出。这里比喻事先有准备,可随机应变。
④ 苍天:隐指空。
⑤ 嘘嘘:隐指虚。

Excerpts from Zen Buddhist Texts

Notes

① Patriarch Ma: This is the literal translation of Ma Zu, a term of respect popularly used by Buddhist followers to address Zen Master Daoyi. Patriarch Ma was the successor of Zen Master Huairang of Nanyue, who was one of the two major successors of the Sixth Patriarch Huineng, generally considered to be the founder of the Southern School of Zen Buddhism in China.

② Zen Master Stone: Shitou in transliteration. He was the successor of Zen Master Xingsi of Qingyuan, who was the other major successor of the Sixth Patriarch, Huineng.

③ the sky: In Chinese, the sky is often referred to as "the empty sky", so Stone uses it as a metaphor for emptiness.

④ shush: In Chinese the word "shush" is the same sound as the word "empty" ("xu").

莫道我解佛法

僧问:"如何是玄妙之说①?"师②曰:"莫道我解佛法。"僧曰:"争奈学人疑滞何?"师曰:"何不问老僧?"僧曰:"问了也。"师曰:"去!不是汝存泊③处。"

——道悟语录,引自《景德传灯录》卷十四

别以为我懂得佛法

有一个僧人问:"什么是玄妙的佛理?"道悟禅师说:"别以为我懂得佛法。"僧人问:"学人我有疑问怎么办呢?"禅师说:"何不问老僧我?"僧人说:"刚才已经问过了。"禅师说:"走吧,这里不是你停留的地方。"

Excerpts from Zen Buddhist Texts

Don't think that I can explain Buddha's Way

A monk asked, "What is the mystery of Buddha's Way?" Zen Master Daowu of the Tianhuang Monastery replied, "Do not think that I can explain Buddha's Way." The monk asked, "So what do I do if I have problems in learning?" The Master said, "Why don't you ask me?" The monk said, "But I just did." The Master sighed, "Oh, go away! This place is not for you."

— Recorded Dialogues of Daowu,
from *Jingde Record of the Transmission of the Lamp,* vol. 14

注释

① 玄妙之说:指禅法、佛法。
② 师:指天皇寺道悟禅师。
③ 存泊:停留、落脚。

阅读提示

道悟禅师说"别以为我懂佛法",意思是佛法是可悟而不可说的自心,自心只能靠自己去感悟,别人说什么都没有用处。但是这个僧人根本听不懂,反而问:"我有问题怎么办?"道悟说:"何不问老僧我?"这句话本是为启发僧人反观自心的,无奈僧人仍不懂,道悟只得失望地让他离开。

Excerpts from
Zen Buddhist Texts

Observation

☆ When Daowu says, "Do not think that I can explain Buddha's Way," he means that Buddha's Way cannot be explained but can only be realised through personal experience. The realisation depends on the person, and what other people say cannot effect any change. But the monk just does not understand and persists in asking "What do I do if I have problems in learning?" Daowu's answer, "Why not ask me?" is a subtle attempt to tell the monk that we each have our own way of solving problems, and the person to consult is the "me" in each of us. But since the monk has no idea what Daowu is talking about, Daowu can only sigh in resignation and send him away.

一切不为

一日师坐次，石头睹之问曰："汝在遮里①作么？"曰："一切不为。"石头曰："恁么即闲坐也。"曰："若闲坐即为也②。"

——药山惟俨禅师语录，

引自《景德传灯录》卷十四

白话翻译

什么都不做

一天，药山惟俨禅师在坐禅，石头和尚见后问他："你在这里做什么？"药山说："什么都不做。"石头说："那么就是闲坐了。"药山说："如果闲坐，就是有所做了。"

注释

① 遮里：即这里。唐宋时期"这"也写作"遮"。

② 若闲坐即为也：药山禅师主张坐禅时要"一切不为"，即不去想坐禅达到什么境界，也不要想通过坐禅成佛等，因为一有想法就会落入执着，连闲坐都不是，如果是就变成有所为了。

Excerpts from Zen Buddhist Texts

Doing nothing

One day, the Buddhist monk Stone saw Zen Master Weiyan of Yaoshan sitting in meditation, and he asked the Master, "What are you doing?" "Nothing," came the reply. Stone said, "That means you are sitting here in leisure." The Master said, "If I am sitting in leisure, I am already doing something.① "

— Recorded Dialogues of Zen Master Weiyan of Yaoshan, from *Jingde Record of the Transmission of the Lamp*, vol. 14

Note

① already doing something: The Master's view is that in meditation one should do nothing, that is, with no intention of achieving a certain state or of attaining enlightenment, because that would be an assertion of the will. Even the intention to just sit in leisure would be a choice to exclude other possibilities.

龙生龙子，凤生凤儿

师一日谒忠国师，先问侍者："国师在否？"曰："在即在，不见客。"师曰："太深远生。"曰："佛眼也觑不见。"师曰："龙生龙子，凤生凤儿。"国师睡起，侍者以告，国师乃鞭侍者二十棒遣出。后丹霞①闻之乃云："不谬为南阳国师！"至明日却往礼拜，见国师便展坐具，国师云："不用，不用。"师退步，国师云："如是，如是。"师却进前，国师云："不是，不是。"师绕国师一匝便出。国师云："去圣时遥，人多懈怠。三十年后觅此汉也还难得。"

——天然语录，引自《景德传灯录》卷十四

Excerpts from Zen Buddhist Texts

Dragons beget dragons, phoenixes beget phoenixes

One day, Zen Master Tianran of Danxia Mountain went for an audience with the Imperial Buddhist Master Huizhong of Nanyang. He asked the attendant, "Is the Imperial Master in?" The attendant replied, "He is in, but he is not seeing anybody." Tianran said, "He keeps himself too secluded!" The attendant said, "Not even Buddha can see him." The Zen Master observed, "Dragons beget dragons, phoenixes beget phoenixes." When Huizhong woke up from his sleep, and the attendant told him what happened, Huizhong punished the attendant by giving him twenty strokes of the staff, and having him expelled from the monastery. Later, when Tianran heard about this, he exclaimed, "Quite becoming of an Imperial Master!" The next day, he went to pay his respects to Huizhong. As soon as he met Huizhong, he began to spread out his meditation mat in preparation for Huizhong's teaching. Huizhong said, "Please, there is no call for this." Tianran took a couple of steps back from him, and Huizhong said, "Quite so." Then Tianran approached Huizhong again, and he said, "No, no. It won't be right." Whereupon Tianran walked once around him and left. The Imperial Master observed, "How distant we are from the days of saints and sages! How lax people have

龙生龙,凤生凤

白话翻译

有一天,丹霞禅师去谒见慧忠国师,先问侍者:"国师在吗?"侍者答:"在虽然在,只是不见客。"禅师说:"太深远啦!"侍者说:"佛眼也看不见。"禅师说:"龙生龙,凤生凤。"国师睡醒起床后,侍者把情况告诉他,国师就责打侍者二十棒,并赶出寺院。后来丹霞知道了说:"不愧是南阳国师!"第二天就去礼拜,见了国师就要打开坐具,国师说:"不用,不用!"丹霞就退后,国师说:"是这样,是这样。"丹霞又进前,国师云:"不对,不对。"丹霞绕着国师走了一圈,就出去了。国师说:"离开圣人的时代远了,人们大多懈怠。三十年后寻找(像丹霞)这样的人也难得啊!"

注释

① 丹霞:天然禅师住邓州丹霞山,故也称丹霞禅师。

阅读提示

慧忠国师的侍者回答问题不俗,所以丹霞禅师说"龙生龙子,凤生凤儿"。丹霞禅师去拜见慧忠国师要坐未坐,要进未进,绕一圈就走了。这说明他领悟到佛法以心传心,不须多言,不须从他人寻求。

120

Excerpts from Zen Buddhist Texts

grown! In thirty years, it would be difficult to find a man like him!"

— Recorded Dialogues of Tianran,
from *Jingde Record of the Transmission of the Lamp*, vol. 14

Observations

☆ Tianran thinks quite highly of the attendant for his reply, that is why he makes the remark, "Dragons beget dragons, phoenixes beget phoenixes". Tianran's behaviour towards Huizhong when he sees him indicates his understanding of a central tenet of Zen Buddhism: the teachings of Buddha do not necessarily have to be learned through the written word and preaching, but can be obtained through an individual's own perceptions and realisations. Enlightenment is to be sought not from others, but via the individual's own effort.

★ It is possible that Tianran's remark, "Dragons beget dragons, phoenixes beget phoenixes" is intended as an ironic comment on the arrogance of the attendant — learned perhaps from his master? The Imperial Master himself probably also thinks that the attendant's behaviour towards Tianran is arrogant. That is why he punishes him and expels him from the monastery.

Tianran's behaviour in front of Huizhong is a demonstration of the courteous interaction between masters. First, Tianran assumes the role of a pupil and asks for comment on his spiritual attainment by offering to meditate in front of Huizhong. Huizhong politely declines since he does not presume to comment on the attainment of a fellow Zen master. Taking the cue from Huizhong that their relationship is that of equals, Tianran then approaches as the lesser of the equals to ask for advice. Huizhong says "it won't be right" for Tianran to ask him for advice, thus putting Tianran in a superior position. So Tianran assumes the role of a superior, walks round Huizhong once to observe him and departs. What Huizhong appreciates in Tianran is his genuine humility. When Huizhong shows that he has nothing to teach this Zen master, Tianran learns from him through observation and takes his leave.

丹霞烧木佛

（丹霞天然禅师）后于惠林寺遇天大寒，取木佛烧火向①，院主诃②曰："何得烧我木佛？"师以杖子拨灰曰："吾烧取舍利③。"主曰："木佛何有舍利？"师曰："既无舍利，更取两尊烧。"主自后眉须堕落④。

——丹霞天然禅师语录，引自《五灯会元》卷五

白话翻译

丹霞禅师烧木佛

丹霞天然禅师后来在惠林寺，有一天天气十分寒冷，他就用木佛烧火取暖。院主斥责说："你怎么能把我的木佛烧掉！"丹霞用棍子拨灰说："我烧木佛是为了取佛的舍利子（骨头）。"院主说："木佛怎么会有舍利子？"丹霞说："既然没有，再拿两尊来烧火。"院主吓得后来眉毛胡子都脱落了。

Excerpts from Zen Buddhist Texts

Danxia burnt a Buddha carved in wood

Zen Master Danxia (also known as Zen Master Tianran) was in the Huilin Monastery. It was a very cold day, and Danxia made a fire to keep warm by burning a buddha carved in wood. The abbot of the monastery shouted at him, "How could you burn my wooden buddha?" Danxia poked among the ashes and replied, "I burnt it to get the holy crystallised relics buddhas leave behind." The abbot said, "How can you get relics from a wooden buddha!" Danxia said. "Well, if there are no holy relics, I might as well burn a couple more." The abbot had such a shock that his beard and his hair fell off.

— Recorded Dialogues of Zen Master Tianran of Danxia, from *Amalgamation of the Sources of the Five Lamps*, vol. 5

注释

① 向：向火，烤火取暖。

② 院主诃：院主，指惠林寺的主持僧。诃：责骂，喝斥。

③ 舍利：释迦牟尼佛遗体火化后结成的坚硬珠状物，也叫舍利子。

④ 主自后眉须堕落：主持僧因丹霞焚烧木佛而惊恐，以致后来眉毛、胡须全都脱落。

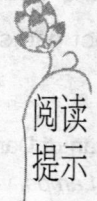

阅读提示

丹霞天然禅师认为木佛等同于木头，烧木佛就是烧木头，他看到的是本质，能不被外形所拘束；而院主看到的是形式，拘泥于对佛的崇拜与执着。

Excerpts from Zen Buddhist Texts

Observations

- ☆ Danxia treated the wooden buddha statue as wood. He sees the nature rather than the form. The abbot sees the form only and is fettered by the idea of respect for Buddha.
- ★ The abbot might have charged Danxia for firewood, or the price of the statue and saved his beard and hair!

洪炉上一点雪

潭州攸县长髭旷禅师,初往曹溪礼祖塔,回参石头。石头问:"什么处来?"曰:"岭南来。"石头曰:"岭头一尊功德①成就也未?"师曰:"成就久矣,只欠点眼②在。"石头曰:"莫要点眼么?"师曰:"便请。"石头乃翘一足,师礼拜。石头曰:"汝见什么道理便礼拜?"师曰:"据某甲所见,如洪炉上一点雪。"

——旷禅师语录,引自《景德传灯录》卷十四

白话翻译

熔炉上一点雪

潭州攸县的长髭旷禅师,当初曾到曹溪礼拜六祖的墓塔,回来时参见石头禅师。石头问:"从哪里来?"答:"从岭南来。"石头问:"岭上的一尊佛像完成了吗?"答:"早就完成了,只缺点上眼睛了。"石头问:"莫非要点上眼吗?"答:"请您点眼。"石头就翘起了一只脚。旷禅师忙礼拜。石头问:"你看到什么道理就礼拜?"旷禅师回答:"据我见到的,好似熔炉上的一点雪。"

Excerpts from
Zen Buddhist Texts

A snowflake on the stove

Zen Master Kuang, also known as Zen Master Long Beard, was from Tanzhou in the county of You. He had at one time visited Caoxi to pay his respects to the memorial pagoda of the Sixth Patriarch. After that, he went to call on Zen Master Stone (or Shitou). Stone asked him, "Where did you come from?" Kuang replied, "From the south, south of the mountain." Stone asked, "The statue of Buddha on top of the mountain, is it finished[1]?" Kuang replied, "Yes, for some time now. What is needed is the dotting of the eyes[2]." Stone asked, "Shall I dot the eyes?" Kuang said, "Please." Stone raised one foot, and Kuang quickly bowed. Stone asked, "What did you see that made you bow?" Kuang replied, "I saw a snowflake on the stove."

— Recorded Dialogues of Zen Master Kuang,
from *Jingde Record of the Transmission of the Lamp*, vol. 14

注释

① 岭头一尊功德：本指山上的佛像，此处指领悟佛法禅旨。

② 点眼：本指为佛像画上眼睛，此处指点化使省悟禅旨。眼，省悟佛法者独具的眼光。

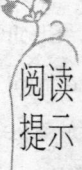

阅读提示

洪炉上一点雪：雪在洪炉上很快融化，不留痕迹。旷禅师的意思是，你翘起一足，是自性自用；我对你礼拜，是我领悟到了这一点。这表现得十分自然，如同烘炉上的一点雪，溶化后无迹可寻一样。

Excerpts from Zen Buddhist Texts

Notes

① is it finished: This is a figurative way of asking Kuang whether he has achieved enlightenment on the mountain.

② dotting of the eyes: This could mean that work on the statue of Buddha is finished and needs only to have the eyes dotted in. On a figurative level, Kuang is also saying that he has achieved enlightenment on the mountain but since Stone asks him, he would welcome further teaching from Stone as yet another opportunity for enlightenment, for seeing the Way of Zen. Hence the image of the eyes.

Observation

☆ Snowflakes on a stove melt quickly, leaving not a trace. Kuang sees in Stone's gesture of raising a foot an oblique hint to "get a move on", i.e. to put what one has learnt into practice. In appreciation of this point, he bows to Stone. The point comes naturally and needs no elaboration, it is just like a snowflake melting on a stove, leaving not a trace behind.

汝无佛性

初参马祖,祖问:"汝来何求?"曰:"求佛知见。"祖曰:"佛无知见,知见乃魔耳。汝自何来?"曰:"南岳来。"祖曰:"汝从南岳来,未识曹溪心要。汝速归彼,不宜他往。"师归石头,便问:"如何是佛?"头曰:"汝无佛性。"师曰:"蠢动含灵,又作么生?"头曰:"蠢动含灵,却有佛性。"曰:"慧朗为什么却无?"头曰:"为汝不肯承当。"师于言下信入。住后,凡学者至,皆曰:"去!去!汝无佛性。"其接机①大约如此。

——慧朗语录,引自《景德传灯录》卷五

Excerpts from Zen Buddhist Texts

You have no Buddha-nature

When Huilang first went to visit Patriarch Ma, the Patriarch asked him, "What do you seek here?" He answered, "I seek the knowledge and understanding of Buddha." Patriarch Ma said, "Buddha has no knowledge, no understanding. Knowledge and understanding are devils of confusion. Where have you come from?" Huilang replied, "From Nanyue where Zen Master Stone is." Patriarch Ma said, "You have come from Stone, but you have not understood the essence of the Way of Zen practised by the Sixth Patriarch. Go back to your Master. Don't go anywhere else." Huilang went back to Zen Master Stone and asked him, "How can I become a buddha?" Stone said, "You have no Buddha-nature." Huilang asked, "But why? Even animals have some spiritual nature." Stone said, "Yes, animals have some spiritual nature, and they have Buddha-nature." Huilang persisted, "But why do I have no Buddha-nature?" Stone replied, "Because you have refused to respond to enlightenment." Then Huilang understood. Later, when he was abbot in a monastery, to all who came to learn the Way of Zen, he would say, "Go! Go away! You have no Buddha-nature." That was how he responded to those who

白话翻译

你没有佛性

慧朗初次参见马祖,马祖问:"你来寻求什么?"答:"寻求佛的知识见解。"马祖说:"佛没有知识见解,知识见解恰恰是魔。你从哪儿来?"答:"从南岳(石头禅师处)来。"马祖说:"你从南岳来,却没有领会曹溪(六祖慧能)的禅法要领。你快返回去,不宜到其他地方。"慧朗回到石头禅师处,就问:"怎样才是佛?"石头说:"你没有佛性。"慧朗问:"连动物都含有灵性,这又怎么理解?"石头答:"动物含有灵性,倒是有佛性的。"慧朗问:"慧朗为什么却没有呢?"石头答:"因为你不肯承接禅机。"慧朗一听就领悟了。他住持寺院后,凡有学禅的人来到,他都说:"去!去!你没有佛性。"他(慧朗)启发问禅僧人的方法大体就是这样的。

注释

① 接机:应对禅法机要、机密。

Excerpts from Zen Buddhist Texts

sought the way to enlightenment.

— Recorded Dialogues of Huilang,
from *Jingde Record of the Transmission of the Lamp,* vol. 5

野鸭子什么处去也

师侍马祖行次①,见一群野鸭飞过。祖曰:"是什么?"师曰:"野鸭子。"祖曰:"什处去也?"师曰:"飞过去也。"祖遂把师鼻扭,负痛失声。祖曰:"又道飞过去也。"师于言下大悟。

——百丈怀海禅师语录,引自《五灯会元》卷三

白话翻译

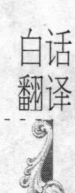

野鸭飞到什么地方去了

百丈怀海禅师随侍马祖道一禅师外出时,见一群野鸭子飞了过去。马祖问:"那是什么?"怀海说:"野鸭子。"马祖问:"它飞到什么地方去了?"怀海答:"飞过去了。"马祖就拧怀海的鼻子,痛得他叫出声来。马祖说:"还说飞过去了!"怀海此时马上大悟。

Excerpts from Zen Buddhist Texts

Where are the ducks going?

When Zen Master Huaihai of Baizhang Mountain was still a disciple of Patriarch Ma, he attended the Patriarch on a journey. They saw a flock of wild ducks fly by. Patriarch Ma asked, "What are those?" Huaihai replied, "Wild ducks." Patriarch Ma asked, "Where are they going?" Huaihai replied, "They've flown away." The Patriarch caught hold of Huaihai's nose and tweaked it until Huaihai cried out in pain. Patriarch Ma said, "And you still say away." Then Huaihai understood.

— Recorded Dialogues of Zen Master Huaihai of Baizhang, from *Amalgamation of the Sources of the Five Lamps*, vol. 3

注释

① 师侍马祖行次：师，指百丈怀海禅师，为马祖道一禅师的弟子。行次：外出走路时。

阅读提示

禅宗讲无住为本，即对事物变化的反应持事过境迁的态度，鸭子飞走了，心却不能随野鸭飞走。马祖拧怀海的鼻子，并逼责他"还说飞走了"，是以眼前的事物、场景传示弟子：心不可随物而去，不能丧失自心。

Excerpts from Zen Buddhist Texts

Observations

- ☆ A central tenet of Zen Buddhism is impermanence. The proper attitude towards the impermanence of things is to tell oneself that the incident is over and the circumstances are different rather than get obsessed with things. The wild ducks have flown away, but the mind should not fly away with the ducks. Patriarch Ma scolds Huaihai because he wants to use this incident to teach Huaihai a lesson: the mind should not get carried away by things and occurrences in the world, otherwise one will lose touch with one's own mind.
- ★ Pranks are not unknown to Zen Masters. Zen Masters are highly conscious psycholinguists as well. To say that the wild ducks have flown "away" suggests an egocentric way of assessing other creatures and their positions, i.e. relative to oneself. The psychological implication of such an assumption is that one interprets and evaluates things and events in the world only in relation to oneself.

自家宝藏

初至江西参马祖，祖问曰："从何处来？"曰："越州大云寺来。"祖曰："来此拟须何事？"曰："来求佛法。"祖曰："自家宝藏不顾，抛家散走作什么！我遮里一物也无，求什么佛法？"师遂礼拜问曰："阿那个是慧海自家宝藏？"祖曰："即今问我者，是汝宝藏，一切具足，更无欠少，使用自在，何假向外求觅？"师于言下自识本心，不由知觉。踊跃礼谢，师事六载，后以受业师年老迁归奉养。

——慧海语录，引自《景德传灯录》卷六

Excerpts from
Zen Buddhist Texts

Your own treasure

Before Huihai became a Zen Master, he went to Jiangxi Province to visit Patriarch Ma. The Patriarch asked him, "Where have you come from?" He replied, "From Daiyun Monastery in Yuezhou." "And what do you want to do here?" "To seek the Way of Buddha," he replied. Patriarch Ma said, "Why have you ignored your own treasure and run around away from home? I have nothing here. What Way of Buddha can I give you?" Huihai bowed respectfully to the Patriarch and asked, "What is my own treasure?" Patriarch Ma replied, "He who now asks this question is your own treasure. He has all that you need, and nothing lacking. Make free use of that. Why seek it from outside?" Upon hearing these words, Huihai realised the worth of his nature. He thanked Patriarch Ma joyfully, and stayed to serve him for six years. Then he left and went back to his home in Yuezhou to look after his former teacher in his old age.

— Recorded Dialogues of Huihai,
from *Jingde Record of the Transmission of the Lamp*, vol. 6

白话翻译

自己的宝藏

　　慧海初到江西参见马祖,马祖问:"从哪儿来?"答:"从越州大云寺来。"马祖问:"来这里打算干什么?"答:"来求佛法。"马祖说:"自己的宝藏不顾,离家乱跑什么!我这里什么也没有,求什么佛法?"慧海就向马祖礼拜,问:"哪个是慧海我自己的宝藏?"马祖说:"如今问我的人,就是你的宝藏,一切具备,绝不缺少,可以自在地使用,何必再向外寻找?"慧海一听,立即意识到自己的本心,不由省悟,十分欢喜,礼谢马祖,并在马祖身边侍奉了六年。后来因为他的老师年老,就回越州奉养老师去了。

经典名句 Highlights

dà shà zhī cái　běn chū yōu gǔ
大厦之材，本出幽谷。

Timbers for buildings come from secluded valleys.

饥来吃饭，困来即眠

有源律师①来问："和尚修道还用功否？"师曰："用功。"曰："如何用功？"师曰："饥来吃饭，困来即眠。"曰："一切人总如是，同师用功否？"师曰："不同。"曰："何故不同？"师曰："他吃饭时不肯吃饭，百种须索；睡时不肯睡，千般计较。所以不同也。"律师杜口。

——慧海语录，引自《景德传灯录》卷六

Excerpts from
Zen Buddhist Texts

Eat when I'm hungry, sleep when I'm sleepy

One day, a monk by the name of Yuan who was in charge of discipline in the monastery asked Zen Master Huihai, "Do you work hard at your spiritual quest?" Huihai replied, "Yes." Yuan asked, "How?" Huihai replied, "I eat when I am hungry, sleep when I am sleepy." Yuan said, "But that's what everybody does. Would you say they all work as hard as you do?" The Zen Master said, "No." "Why not? In what way are they different?" The Zen Master replied, "Some people don't eat when they should eat, don't sleep when they should sleep, but spend their time calculating and scheming. That's what makes the difference." The Master of Buddhist Discipline was lost for words.

— Recorded Dialogues of Huihai,
from *Jingde Record of the Transmission of the Lamp*, vol. 6

白话翻译

饿了吃饭,困了睡觉

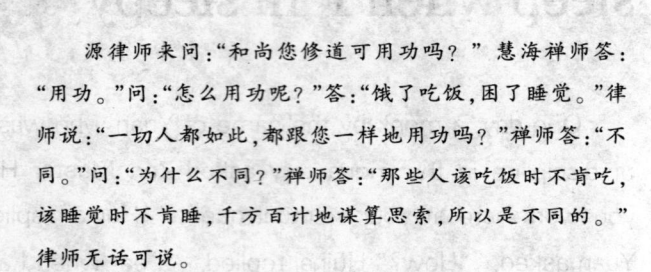

　　源律师来问:"和尚您修道可用功吗?"慧海禅师答:"用功。"问:"怎么用功呢?"答:"饿了吃饭,困了睡觉。"律师说:"一切人都如此,都跟您一样地用功吗?"禅师答:"不同。"问:"为什么不同?"禅师答:"那些人该吃饭时不肯吃,该睡觉时不肯睡,千方百计地谋算思索,所以是不同的。"律师无话可说。

注释

① 律师:佛教典籍分经、律、论三部分,专门研究佛律的称律师。

经典名句 Highlights

一念若悟，众生是佛。
yī niàn ruò wù, zhòng shēng shì fó

One sudden awareness would make a man a buddha.

师子身中虫，自食师子肉

师普请①次，曰："因果历然②，争奈何！争奈何！"时有僧出，以手托地。师曰："作什么？"曰："相救！相救！"师曰："大众，这个师僧犹较些子③。"僧佛袖便走。师曰："师子④身中虫，自食师子肉。"

——智藏禅师语录，引自《五灯会元》卷三

Excerpts from
Zen Buddhist Texts

The fleas on the lion eat of the lion's flesh

When Zen Master Zhicang was doing group chores[①] with the monks of the monastery, he said, "It is so clear that we have to pay for our sins, what shall we do? What shall we do?" A monk came forward and went down on the ground rather in the manner of someone doing a push-up. The Master asked, "What are you doing?" The monk shouted, "Help! Help!" The Master said to the monks around him, "He is doing all right." The monk got up and left. The Master observed, "The fleas on the lion[②] eat of the lion's flesh."

— Recorded Dialogues of Zhicang,
from *Amalgamation of the Sources of the Five Lamps*, vol. 3

Notes

① group chores: the collective labour that is part of the duties of the monks in the monastery. It was a practice started by Zen Master Huaihai of Baizhang.
② the lion: This is often used as a symbol of Buddha.

白话翻译

狮子身上的虫儿，吃着狮子的肉

智藏禅师跟僧徒们一起劳动时说："因果报应分明，怎么办！怎么办！"当时有一个僧人走出来，用手撑着地。禅师问："你干什么？"那僧大叫："救人！救人！"禅师说："诸位，这个师僧倒还可以。"那僧拂袖便走。禅师说："狮子身上的虫儿，吃着狮子的肉。"

注释

① 普请：指寺院里的集体劳动。这是由百丈怀海禅师创立的规定。

② 历然：分明的样子。

③ 较些子：差一点，差不多。这里是肯定的意思。

④ 师子：即狮子。佛经中多以狮子比喻佛。

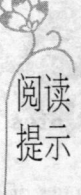

阅读提示

智藏禅师说："因果报应分明，怎么办！怎么办！"意思是：堕入尘世苦海，如何解脱！这是一句机锋话头。那位僧人以手撑地，喊人相救，说明他领会了禅师的意思，承接得机灵，所以禅师夸奖他差不多。僧人拂袖便走，是表示体悟了自性，入圣又不执着于圣。禅师最后两句话是说：作为佛的信徒，见性成佛，才是安身立命的处所。

Excerpts from
Zen Buddhist Texts

Observations

☆ When the Zen Master observes that one has to pay for one's sins, and asks what one should do, he is asking for an answer as to how one can be rid of suffering and punishment. As a reply, the monk supports himself on his arms and yet asks for help. This is to tell the Master that he has the answer, since he could easily help himself if he wanted to get up. Then, having won the approval of the Master, the monk turns round and leaves. This is a demonstration of self reliance. The monk has been inspired by the Zen Master to realise his own Buddha-nature, he will continue to seek for himself the Way of Buddha. The Zen Master's last observation means that the disciples of Buddha should realise their nature the way Buddha did.

★ It seems that the Zen Master's last remark can be interpreted in a different way. Fleas are parasitic creatures, they feed on the flesh of their host. As the lion is a conventional symbol of Buddha, the fleas obviously refer to Buddha's disciples. The remark, therefore, can well be a subtle criticism of the other monks in the monastery. The Zen Master is saying that unlike the wise monk who realises the importance of self reliance in the search for enlightenment and deliverance from suffering and punishment, the other monks in the monastery rely too heavily on Buddha and the teachings of Buddha, on their Zen Masters and the teachings of the Masters. They have not looked into their own selves to discover their nature.

有与无

师住西堂后,有一俗士问:"有天堂地狱否?"师曰:"有。"曰:"有佛、法、僧宝①否?"师曰:"有。"更有多问,尽答言有。曰:"和尚恁么道莫错否?"师曰:"汝曾见尊宿来耶?"曰:"某甲曾参径山和尚来。"师曰:"径山向汝作么生道?"曰:"他道一切总无。"师曰:"汝有妻否?"曰:"有。"师曰:"径山和尚有妻否?"曰:"无。"师曰:"径山和尚道无即得。"俗士礼谢而去。

——智藏语录,引自《景德传灯录》卷七

Excerpts from Zen Buddhist Texts

Yes and no

One day, after Zen Master Zhicang had taken charge of the West Hall, a man asked him, "Is there a heaven and a hell?" He replied, "Yes." The man asked, "Are there the 'three gems' of Buddhism — Buddha, the *dharma*, the *sangha*①?" He said, "Yes." The man asked a lot of other questions to which he also answered "Yes." Finally the man said, 'I'm afraid your answers are not correct, are they?" He replied. "Perhaps you have met some enlightened monks?" The man said, " I've met the Reverend Jingshan." "And what did the reverend monk say to you?" he asked. The man said, "Well, his answers to those questions were all 'No.' "The Zen Master asked the man, "Do you have a wife?" The man said, "Yes." The Master asked the man, "Does the Reverend Jingshan have a wife?" The man said, "No." The Zen Master said, "'No' is a very good answer from the Reverend Jingshan." The man bowed, apologized and took his leave.

— Recorded Dialogues of Zhicang,
from *Jingde Record of the Transmission of the Lamp*, vol. 7

有与无

智藏禅师住持西堂后,有一次,一位俗家人士问:"有天堂和地狱吗?"禅师答:"有。"问:"有佛、法、僧三宝吗?"答:"有。"另有许多问题,禅师都回答说"有"。那人说:"和尚这么回答恐怕不对吧?"禅师问:"莫非你曾见过得道高僧吗?"答:"我曾参见过径山和尚。"禅师问:"径山对你怎么说的?"答:"他说一切都无。"禅师问:"你有妻子吗?"答:"有。"又问:"径山和尚有妻子吗?"答:"没有。"禅师说:"径山和尚说'无'是对的。"那人行礼道歉之后离去了。

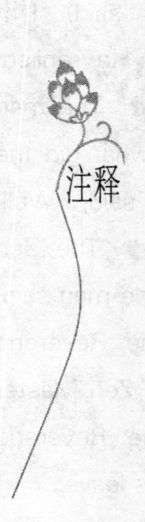

① 佛、法、僧宝:见第8页注③。

Excerpts from Zen Buddhist Texts

Note

① Buddha, the *dharma*, the *sangha*: See P.9 Note②.

禅宗语录　中华传统文化精粹

梅子熟也

大寂闻师住山,乃令一僧到问云:"和尚见马师得个什么,便此住山?"师云:"马师向我道即心是佛,我便向遮里住。"僧云:"马师近日佛法又别。"师云:"作么生别?"僧云:"近日又道非心非佛。"师云:"遮老汉惑乱人未有了日,任汝非心非佛,我只管即心即佛。"其僧回举似马祖,祖云:"大众,梅子熟也[①]!"僧问禾山:"大梅恁么道,意作么生?"禾山云:"真师子儿!"自此学者渐臻,师道弥著。

——法常语录,引自《景德传灯录》卷七

Excerpts from Zen Buddhist Texts

The plum is ripe

Patriarch Ma (also known as Daji) heard that the monk Fachang (also known as Damei, meaning "big plum") was made the abbot of a monastery. He sent a disciple to the monastery to inquire, "Reverend, what did you learn from your teacher, Patriarch Ma, to qualify you to be an abbot here?" Fachang answered, "He told me that the mind is buddha." The disciple said, "Ah, but recently the Master is teaching something different." Fachang asked, "What is it that is different?" The disciple replied, "Now he is saying: It is not true that the mind is buddha." Fachang said, "The old man is always trying to confuse people. Whether he says it's true or not true that the mind is buddha, to me the mind is buddha." The disciple returned to Patriarch Ma and recounted all this. Patriarch Ma exclaimed, "Hear this, all of you. The Plum is ripe[①]!" Later, when the incident was recounted by Zen Master Heshan, a monk asked, "Fachang's reply ..., what's the meaning of it?" Heshan said, "Fachang has come from a line of lions!" From then on, many who wanted to learn the Way of Zen gathered at Fachang's monastery, and his teachings

白话翻译

梅子熟啦

大寂(马祖)听到法常住持山寺,就派一个僧人到寺询问:"和尚参见马祖大师学到了什么,就在这里住持山寺?"法常答:"马师对我说心就是佛,我就在这里住持。"僧人说:"马师的佛法近来又不同了。"法常问:"怎么个不同?"僧人答:"近来又说不是心不是佛。"法常说:"这个老头迷惑人没完没了,任你不是心不是佛,我只管心就是佛。"那僧人回去告诉马祖,马祖说:"大众,梅子熟啦!"(后来)有僧人问禾山:"大梅(法常)那么说,意思怎么样?"禾山说:"真是狮子的后代!"从此之后,学禅的人逐渐聚集在法常处,法常的道法更加兴盛了。

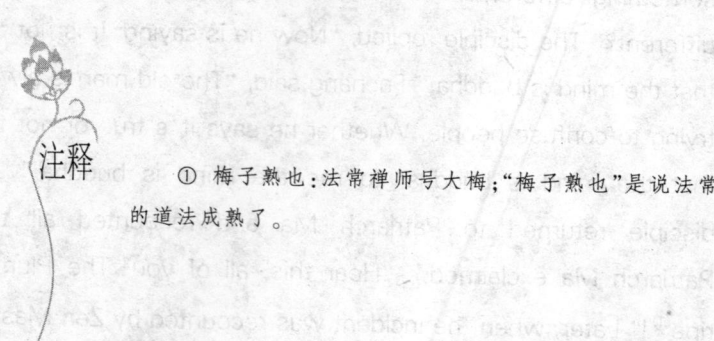

注释

① 梅子熟也:法常禅师号大梅;"梅子熟也"是说法常的道法成熟了。

Excerpts from Zen Buddhist Texts

spread far and wide.

— Recorded Dialogues of Fachang,
from *Jingde Record of the Transmission of the Lamp,* vol. 7

Note

① The Plum is ripe: meaning that Fachang has matured spiritually.

亲者不问,问者不亲

夹山与定山同行言语次,定山云:"生死中无佛即非生死。"夹山云:"生死中有佛即不迷生死。"二人上山参礼,夹山便举问师:"未审二人见处那个较亲?"师云:"一亲一疏。"夹山云:"那个亲?"师云:"且去,明日来。"夹山明日再上问师,师云:"亲者不问,问者不亲。"夹山住后自云:"当时失一只眼。"

——法常语录,引自《景德传灯录》卷七

近者不问,问者不近

夹山和定山一同行走说着话,定山说:"生死轮回中没有佛就没有生死。"夹山说:"生死轮回中有了佛就不被生死所迷惑。"两个人上山参拜法常禅师,夹山就举出上面的话问:"不知两个人的看法哪个跟禅旨比较接近?"禅师答:"一近一远。"夹山问:"哪个近?"禅师说:"暂且下去,明天再来。"第二天,夹山又上前问禅师,禅师答道:"近者不问,问者不近。"夹山住持寺院后自己说:"当时失落了一只眼。"

Excerpts from
Zen Buddhist Texts

He who is closer does not ask

Two monks, Jiashan and Dingshan, had a conversation one day as they were walking along together. Dingshan said, "In the Wheel of *Karma*, the cycle of life and death, if there is no buddha, there will be no life and death." Jiashan said, "In the Wheel of *Karma*, the cycle of life and death, because of buddha, we need not be troubled and confused by life and death." The two went up to a mountain monastery to visit Zen Master Fachang. Jiashan recounted their conversation and asked, "Which of us holds a view closer to yours?" The Zen Master replied, "One is nearer, the other farther." Jiashan asked, "Who is nearer?" The Master said, "Go home now. Come again tomorrow." The next day, Jiashan went to the Master again. The Master said, "He who is closer does not ask, he who asks is not close." When Jiashan became an abbot later, he looked back on that day and said, "That day I was blind in one eye!"

— Recorded Dialogues of Fachang,
from *Jingde Record of the Transmission of the Lamp*, vol. 7

万灵归一

师元和十三年三月二十三日沐浴焚香,端坐告众云:"法身圆寂①,示有去来。千圣同源,万灵归一。吾今沤散,胡假兴哀?无自劳神,须存正念。若遵此命,真报吾恩;倘固违言,非吾之子。"时有僧问:"和尚向什么处去?"师曰:"无处去。"曰:"某甲何不见?"师曰:"非眼所睹。"洞山云:"作家②!"言毕,奄然顺化③。寿七十有二,腊四十一。

——灵默语录,引自《景德传灯录》卷七

Excerpts from Zen Buddhist Texts

All return to the One

On the 23rd day of the third month of the lunar calendar, in the thirteenth year of the Yuanhe Period (AD 818) in the Tang Dynasty, Zen Master Lingmo cleansed himself, lit some incense, seated himself ceremoniously and instructed his disciples thus, "When the body, the vehicle for knowing the truth, vanishes, it signifies that all things come and go. All things in the world come from the same source, and they return to the One. Today, I shall disappear as do bubbles in water, but there is no cause for grief. Do not be upset, but keep a proper understanding of the event. If you can do this, it would be proper recompense for my time with you. If you do otherwise, you are no disciple of mine." One of the monks asked, "Where will you be going?" The Master answered, "To nowhere." The monk asked, "Why don't I see this place?" The Master replied, "It is not what the eyes can see." Zen Master Liangjia of Dongshan said, "You are truly a Master of the Way." Soon after this, Zen Master Lingmo passed away. He was seventy-two, and had lived as an ordained monk for forty-one

白话翻译

万物终归于一

元和十三年(818)三月二十三日,灵默禅师沐浴烧香,端然而坐,告诫众人:"法身消逝,显示有去有来。世间万物来源相同,终归于一。我今天如同浮泡散灭,何必悲伤?大家不用劳神,须存正念。如果遵从此命,是真正地报答我;如果定要违背我的话,那就不是我的弟子。"当时有个僧人问:"和尚要到什么地方去?"师答:"无处去。"又问:"我为什么看不见?"禅师答:"不是眼睛所能看到的。"洞山说:"行家!"禅师说完话后,忽然去世,享年七十二岁,受戒四十一年。

注释

① 圆寂:指僧尼逝世。

② 作家:内行人,行家,指得道彻悟的僧人。这里洞山称赞灵默彻底领悟了禅宗万灵归一,一切皆空的大道。

③ 顺化:同注①。

Excerpts from
Zen Buddhist Texts

years.

— Recorded Dialogues of Lingmo,
from *Jingde Record of the Transmission of the Lamp,* vol. 7

捉虚空

师问西堂："汝还解捉得虚空么？"堂曰："捉得。"师曰："作么生捉？"堂以手撮虚空。师曰："汝不解捉。"堂却问："师兄作么生捉？"师把西堂鼻孔拽，堂作忍痛声，曰："太煞拽人鼻孔，直欲脱去。"师曰："直须恁么捉虚空始得。"

——慧藏语录，引自《五灯会元》卷三

白话翻译

抓虚空

慧藏禅师问西堂："你会抓虚空吗？"西堂答："能抓到。"慧藏问："怎么样抓？"西堂用手在空中抓握。慧藏说："你不会抓。"西堂反问："师兄怎么抓？"慧藏抓住西堂的鼻子就拽，西堂痛得叫起来，说："拽得太狠啦，鼻子都要被拽掉啦！"慧藏说："必须这样抓虚空才行。"

Excerpts from
Zen Buddhist Texts

Grasping the intangible

One day, Zen Master Huicang asked Xitang, a monk junior to himself, "Can you grasp the intangible?" Xitang said, "Yes." Huicang asked, "How?" Xitang waved his hand and grasped at the air. Huicang said, "You don't know how." Xitang asked, "How would you do it then?" Huicang grasped Xitang's nose and pulled it. Xitang cried in pain and shouted, "Lay off, will you? You're pulling my nose off!" Huicang said, "That's how you grasp the intangible."

— Recorded Dialogues of Huicang,
from *Amalgamation of the Sources of the Five Lamps*, vol. 3

不可思议

问:"狗子还有佛性否?"师曰:"有。"曰:"和尚还有否?"师曰:"我无。"曰:"一切众生皆有佛性,和尚因何独无?"师曰:"我非一切众生。"曰:"既非众生,莫是佛否?"师曰:"不是佛。"曰:"究竟是何物?"师曰:"亦不是物。"曰:"可见可思否?"师曰:"思之不及,议之不得,故曰不可思议。"

——惟宽语录,引自《五灯会元》卷三

Excerpts from Zen Buddhist Texts

Beyond comprehension

Someone asked Zen Master Weikuan, "Do dogs have Buddha-nature?" Weikuan replied, "Yes." The man then asked, "Do you have it, Master?" The Master replied, "I don't." The man said, "All living creatures have Buddha-nature, why is it that you don't?" The Master replied, "I'm not part of all living creatures." The man asked, "If you are not part of all living creatures, are you Buddha himself?" "No, I'm not Buddha himself." The man persisted, "Then what thing are you?" "I'm not a thing," came the reply. The man said, "Whatever you are — can it be seen? Is it something one can comprehend?" The Master replied, "It can neither be attained through an effort of the mind, nor can it be encompassed through discourse. It is beyond comprehension."

— Recorded Dialogues of Weikuan,
from *Amalgamation of the Sources of the Five Lamps*, vol. 3

不可思议

有人问:"狗可有佛性吗?"惟宽禅师答:"有。"问:"和尚您有吗?"禅师答:"我没有。"问:"一切众生都有佛性,和尚为什么独独没有?"禅师答:"我不是一切众生。"问:"既然不是众生,莫非是佛吗?"禅师答:"不是佛。"问:"那究竟是什么东西呢?"禅师答:"也不是东西。"问:"可以看到、可以思虑吗?"禅师答:"思之不能到达,议之不可认识,所以是不可思议。"

Excerpts from Zen Buddhist Texts

Observation

★ One perceives here the possibility of a mind-game in which the questioner is trying to force the Master into an admission (a) that he makes no distinction between a man and a dog, or (b) that he has much in common with a dog, or indeed with any living creature, or (c) that if he refuses to be identified with a dog, then he may be guilty of a hubristic claim to be identified with Buddha himself, or (d) that he is nothing. The Master's answers indicate a dissociation from the suggested identifications so that an independent description of an individual's Buddhahood can be posited. Here one sees a Zen Master's manoeuvre at divergent thinking as a counter for a game of logic.

金屑虽珍宝，在眼亦为病

元和四年，宪宗诏至阙下，侍郎白居易尝问曰："既曰禅师，何以说法？[①]"师曰："无上菩提者，被于身为律，说于口为法，行于心为禅。应用者三，其致一也。譬如江湖淮汉，在处立名，名虽不一，水性无二。律即是法，法不离禅，云何于中妄起分别？"曰："既无分别，何以修心？"师曰："心本无损伤，云何要修理？无论垢与净，一切勿念起。"曰："垢即不可念，净无念可乎？"师曰："如人眼睛上，一物不可住。金屑虽珍宝，在眼亦为病。"

——惟宽语录，引自《五灯会元》卷三

Excerpts from Zen Buddhist Texts

Gold dust may be valuable, but it can hurt the eyes

In the fourth year of the Yuanhe Period (AD 809) in the Tang Dynasty, the Emperor summoned Zen Master Weikuan to preach to him in the capital. The famous poet Bai Juyi, who was also an attendant gentleman at court, asked Weikuan, "You are a Zen master, why do you bother to teach?" The Master replied, "The highest wisdom of Buddha, when manifested in the way one lives, is known as discipline; when manifested through what one says, it is known as teaching; and when practised in the mind, it is Zen. The manifestations are different, but they come from the same source. In the same way, although rivers, lakes and streams all have their different names, they have in common the water in them. Discipline is teaching, and teaching cannot really be separated from Zen. Why draw arbitrary distinctions?" Bai then asked, "If there is no distinction, what does one do to put the mind in order?" The Master replied, "The mind itself is neither in disorder nor damaged, why does one have to put it in order or mend it? If one thinks neither pure nor impure thoughts, there

禅宗语录　中华传统文化精粹

白话翻译

金屑虽是宝，在眼也有害

　　元和四年(809)唐宪宗诏请惟宽禅师到京城，侍郎白居易曾问道："既然称作禅师，为什么还说法？"禅师答："佛的最高智慧，显示于身为律，讲说于口为法，作用于心为禅。应用虽三种，其来源却是一致的，好比江、湖、淮(河)、汉(水)，在各地都有名称，名称虽不同，水的性质并无差别。律就是法，法也离不开禅，为什么妄加分别呢？"白居易问："既然没有分别，用什么来修心？"禅师答："此心本没有损伤，为什么要修？无论是污垢还是清净，一切念头都不要产生。"白居易问："污垢自然不可思念，清净也不思念，行吗？"禅师答："比如人的眼睛里，一样东西也不能存留。金屑虽是宝，留在眼里也有害。"

注释

① 既曰禅师，何以说法："禅"，梵语 dhyāna，原意是"静虑"，所以白居易质问为什么还说法。

Excerpts from Zen Buddhist Texts

would be nothing to put in order." Bai said, "Naturally one should not think impure thoughts, but should one not think pure thoughts?" The Master replied, "Take for example a man's eyes. Nothing should stay there. Gold dust may be valuable, but it can hurt the eyes if you put it there."

— Recorded Dialogues of Weikuan,
from *Amalgamation of the Sources of the Five Lamps,* vol. 3

禅宗语录

事怕有心人

师一日上堂，开示大众云："……劝尔兄弟家，趁色力康健时，讨取个分晓处，不被人瞒底一段大事。遮些关捩子甚是容易，自是尔不肯去下死志做工夫，只管道难了又难。好教尔知，那得树上自生底木杓？尔也须自去做个转变始得。若是个丈夫汉，看个公案①：'僧问赵州，狗子还有佛性也无？州云无。'但去二六时中②看个无字，昼参夜参，行住坐卧，著衣吃饭处，阿屎放尿处，心心相顾，猛著精彩，守个无字。日久月深，打成一片。忽然心花顿放，悟佛祖之机，便不被天下老和尚舌头瞒，便会大开口：达摩西来无风起浪，世尊拈花一场败缺。到这里说什么阎罗老子，千圣尚不奈尔何！不信道，直有遮般奇特！为什如此？事怕有心人。颂曰：尘劳迥脱事非

Excerpts from Zen Buddhist Texts

With will and perseverance

One day, Zen Master Xiyun of Huangbo preached a sermon, "... I urge you, brothers, while you are still in good health, to make the most of your life, to sort out this the most important issue, and not be deceived. It's actually very easy, only you are not willing to make the effort, and complain constantly about how difficult it is. Let me tell you this. How can you expect wooden ladles to grow on trees? You have to do something to bring about a change. If you are man enough, you should bear in mind this story: a monk once asked Zen Master Congshen of Zhaozhou whether a dog has Buddha-nature, and the Master said no. Now you should ponder on this 'no' — day and night, whether you are sitting, walking, or lying down, while changing your clothes or during a meal, or when you are in the privy. You should make it the focal point of your attention, let it stir your thoughts and spirit. In time, it becomes a part of you. Then, suddenly, like blossoms bursting forth, you would realise the point Buddha was trying to make, and you would no longer be deceived by the words of those old monks. Then you can say bravely, that *Bodhidharma*'s journey from the West was much ado about nothing, or that Buddha's wordless

常，紧把绳头做一场，不是一翻寒彻骨，争得梅花扑鼻香？"

——希运语录，引自《黄檗宛陵录》

白话翻译

事怕有心人

有一天，希运禅师上堂对大众说法："……奉劝诸位兄弟，趁着身体健康时，把那件大事探讨得分明，别被人欺瞒。这些机关很是容易，只是你们不肯下决心花工夫，一味地说难啊真难。告诉你们，树上怎会长出现成的木杓来？你们也得自己去动手加工才行。如果是男子汉，看到这一则公案：'僧人问赵州和尚，狗有没有佛性？赵州说无。'就时时刻刻留心这个无字，白天参究，晚上参究，行住坐卧、穿衣吃饭、屙屎拉尿，专心致志，振奋精神，守着这个无字。日久月深，打成一片。忽然心花顿发，省悟佛祖之机，就不会被天下老和尚的嘴巴欺瞒，就可以说大话：达摩西来本属无风起浪，世尊拈花只是一场挫败。到了这种程度，别说什么阎罗王，千位圣人也拿你没办法了！不相信吗？就是这样奇特！为什么能这样？事怕有心人。请听颂诗：远离尘缘劳碌大事非同寻常，紧握着绳头下气力做他一场，不经过一番彻骨的寒冷，哪有梅花扑鼻的芳香？"

注释

① 公案：指禅师引导学人开悟的途径，其中有禅师与学人的机锋接引与应对，有时用言语，有时用动作。

② 二六时中：古人把一昼夜分为十二个时辰，二六时中指日日夜夜，每时每刻。

Excerpts from Zen Buddhist Texts

sermon[①] was a total failure. When you reach that state, no Yama-god of the dead and not even a thousand saints and sages together can do anything to you! You don't believe me? Strangely that is how it is! How do you arrive at such a state? With will and perseverance. Attend to these lines:

It's not easy to shake off the world's dusty strife.
Take firm hold of the reins to guide your life.
Nought but the bone-piercing winter chill
Brings plum blossom fragrance your senses to thrill."

— Recorded Dialogues of Xiyun,
from *Wanling Records of Zen Master Huangbo*

Note

[①] wordless sermon: It was said that during one of his sermons, Buddha held up a flower and said nothing. One of his disciples realised the point of the wordless sermon and was enlightened.

义学沙门

师因有六人新到，五个作礼，中一个提起坐具，作一圆相。师曰："我闻有一只猎犬甚恶①。"僧曰："寻羚羊声来。"师曰："羚羊无声到汝寻。"曰："寻羚羊迹来。"师曰："羚羊无迹到汝寻。"曰："寻羚羊踪来。"师曰："羚羊无踪到汝寻。"曰："与么，则死羚羊也。"师便休去。明日升堂曰："昨日寻羚羊僧出来。"僧便出。师曰："昨日公案②未了，老僧休去，你作么生？"僧无语。师曰："将谓是本色衲僧，元来只是义学沙门！"便打趁出。

——希运语录，引自《五灯会元》卷四

Excerpts from Zen Buddhist Texts

A stickler for dogma

Six monks came to join Zen Master Xiyun of Huangbo. Five of them paid their respects to the Master, while the last one took up his prayer mat and drew a circle① on the ground. The Master observed, "I hear that there is a very fierce hound-dog." The monk said, "It's here in search of the gazelle's call." The Master said, "The gazelle has no call for you to search." The monk said, "It's here in search of the gazelle's footprints." The Master replied, "The gazelle has no footprints for you to trace." The monk persisted, "It's here in search of the gazelle's tracks." The Master said, "The gazelle has no tracks for you to follow." The monk then observed, "Well, then it's a dead gazelle." The Master let that pass. The next day, the Master was about to give a sermon when he said, "Will the monk in search of the gazelle yesterday step up please?" The monk came forward. The Master said to him, "Our exchange yesterday has not reached a conclusion. I'll let it pass. What about you?" The monk said nothing. The Master said, "What I took to be a practising Zen monk turns out to be a mere ascetic, a stickler for dogma!" So he reprimanded the monk and drove him out.

— Recorded Dialogues of Xiyun,
from *Amalgamation of the Sources of the Five Lamps*, vol. 4

死守义理之学的沙门

有六个新来的僧人,五人向希运禅师行了礼,另外一人提起坐具,画了一个圆圈。禅师说:"我听说有一只猎狗很恶。"那个僧人说:"来寻找羚羊的叫声。"禅师说:"羚羊没有叫声让你寻。"僧人说:"来寻找羚羊的足迹。"禅师说:"羚羊没有足迹让你寻。"僧人说:"来寻找羚羊的行踪。"禅师说:"羚羊没有行踪让你寻。"僧人说:"这样的话是死羚羊啦。"禅师就作罢了。第二天,禅师上堂说:"昨天要寻找羚羊的僧人出来。"僧人就站出来。禅师说:"昨天的公案还没有了结,我作罢了,你怎么样?"僧人无话应对。禅师说:"本以为是在行的禅僧,原来只是个死守义理之学的沙门!"就责打他,赶了出去。

① 猎犬甚恶:指画圆圈的僧人看来悟性甚高。
② 公案:参看第176页注①。

Excerpts from
Zen Buddhist Texts

Note

① drew a circle: In Zen Buddhism, a circle is a symbol of the universal, complete and absolute nature of the truth proclaimed by Buddha (*dharma*). Drawing a circle on the ground or in the air is a symbolic gesture alluding to the *dharma*. That is why when he sees one of the monks making this gesture, Zen Master Xiyun thinks that he is a practising Zen monk and engages him in Zen discourse. This same image is used for the explication of the *dharma* in P.69.

Observation

★ The monk has cast himself in the role of a student and has come to the Zen Master with determination to learn certain things from him. This aggressive attitude towards learning makes him a relentless hunter looking for what he seeks to find rather than someone who exposes himself to experience to draw new and unexpected perceptions of life. The Master dismisses him because his attitude would make him incapable of learning freely and creatively.

自了汉

（黄檗希运禅师）后游天台逢一僧，与之言笑，如旧相识。熟视之，目光射人，乃偕行。属①涧水暴涨，捐笠植杖而止。其僧率师同渡，僧曰："兄要渡自渡。"彼即褰②衣蹑波，若履平地，回顾曰："渡来！渡来！"师曰："咄！这自了汉③！吾早知当斫汝胫。"其僧叹曰："真大乘法器④，我所不及。"言讫不见。

——黄檗希运禅师语录，引自《五灯会元》卷四

Excerpts from
Zen Buddhist Texts

A man who only looks after himself

    Zen Master Xiyun of Huangbo was touring Tiantai when he met a monk. They got on very well and conversed as if they were old friends. Xiyun observed that this monk had sharp intelligent eyes, and they decided to travel together. They came to a turbulent stream. They stopped, took off their straw sunhats and leaned on their staves to assess the situation. The monk led the way to cross the stream. He said, "You, sir, will have to make the crossing yourself." He then girded up his robes and waded across as if he was on level ground. And he turned round to urge Xiyun, "Come on, come over here!" Xiyun cried, "Hah! You only look after yourself! Had I known that I would have broken your shin first." The monk sighed, "You are truly a dedicated follower of *Mahayana* Buddhism[①], a man far superior to myself." Having made this remark, the monk vanished.

        — Recorded Dialogues of Zen Master Xiyun of Huangbo,
        from *Amalgamation of the Sources of the Five Lamps*. vol. 4

183

白话翻译

只顾自己的家伙

　　黄檗希运禅师后来游天台山，遇到一个僧人跟他谈笑，好像是旧相识一样。仔细打量，这个僧人目光锐利有神，就跟他一同前行。当时正遇涧水暴涨，希运就丢弃笠帽拄杖而立。那个僧人领着希运一同渡水，对希运说："你要渡水就自己渡吧！"便撩起衣裳踏着水浪如同在平地行走一样，并且回头对希运说："走啊！走啊！"希运说："这个自顾自的家伙，我早知道这样就该打断你的腿！"那个僧人赞叹说："真是大乘法器啊！我比不上。"说完就不见了。

注释

① 属：正值，碰上。

② 褰：qiān，音牵。撩起（衣裳）。

③ 自了汉：自己顾自己的人。这里比喻自己得道解脱的人，在佛教宗派里属于小乘教。

④ 大乘法器：指自己得道解脱又能普度众生的真正得道之人。大乘佛教认为"自了汉"只是小我的超越，并未彻底觉悟；因为真正觉悟的人知道自己与众生为一体，不能看着众生沉溺于苦海而不顾，必定要自度度人。

Excerpts from Zen Buddhist Texts

Note

① *Mahayana* Buddhism: Followers of *Mahayana* Buddhism, or the Big Vehicle, think that a person who only looks after himself (i.e. a person who only seeks self-salvation) has not attained true enlightenment, because one who is truly enlightened realises that there is no distinction between self and others, and cannot watch with indifference others struggling in the sea of suffering. The truly enlightened one, in seeking self-deliverance, also seeks deliverance for all.

Observation

★ Interesting philsophical tension in this exchange. Zen Buddhism often stresses the individual's effort in attaining enlightenment. When that is found in the monk's attitude, Xiyun reminds him of the need to help others. But then these repartees could also have operated on the lower level of humorous exchanges between Buddhist monks.

拽出死尸著

僧问："如何是西来意？"师曰："如人在千尺井中，不假寸绳出得此人，即答汝西来意。"僧曰："近日湖南畅和尚出世，亦为人东语西语①。"师唤沙弥②："拽出死尸③著！"沙弥即仰山也。沙弥后举问耽源："如何出得井中人？"耽源曰："咄！痴汉！谁在井中？"后问沩山："如何出得井中人？"沩山乃呼："慧寂④！"寂应诺。沩山曰："出也。"

——性空语录，引自《景德传灯录》卷九

Excerpts from
Zen Buddhist Texts

Take this corpse out of here

A monk asked, "What was the purpose of *Bodhidharma*'s coming from the West?" Zen Master Xingkong replied, "If a man is at the bottom of a well a thousand feet deep, and you can get this man out of the well without a rope, then I'll answer your question about the purpose of *Bodhidharma*'s coming from the West." The monk observed, "Recently, since Reverend Chang from Hunan made his appearance, he has also been giving such irrelevant answers to people's questions." Whereupon Zen Master Xingkong summoned a novice monk and told him, "Take this corpse out of here." This novice was Huiji, who later became Zen Master Yangshan. Later, Huiji recounted the incident to the monk Danyuan and asked him, "How do you get the man out of the well?" Danyuan replied, "Oh, you fool. Who is in the well?" And then, Huiji took the question to his teacher, Zen Master Lingyou of Weishan, "How do you get the man out of the well?" The Zen Master called out, "Huiji!" Huiji shouted a reply. The Zen Master said. "There you are. He's out."

— Reccored Dialogues of Xingkong,
from *Jingde Record of the Transmission of the Lamp*, vol. 9

白话翻译

把这死尸拉出去

　　僧人问:"什么是祖师西来的意旨?"性空禅师回答:"好比有人在千尺深的井中,如果不用绳子能使此人出井,就回答你西来意旨。"僧人说:"近来湖南畅和尚出世,也是这样答非所问。"禅师唤来沙弥,说:"把这死尸拉出去!"此沙弥就是仰山。沙弥后来把此事告诉耽源,并问:"怎样让井中人出来?"耽源说:"咄!痴汉!谁在井中?"沙弥后来又问沩山:"怎样让井中人出来?"沩山就叫唤:"慧寂(仰山)!"慧寂应答。沩山说:"出来啦!"

注释

① 东语西语:指答非所问。
② 沙弥:梵语śrāmanera,指初出家的年轻和尚。
③ 死尸:比喻执迷不悟的人。
④ 慧寂:仰山禅师的名。

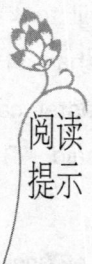

阅读提示

　　禅宗以"不立文字,直指人心"为宗旨,提倡直截了当认识自心的"顿悟",反对问佛问祖、在概念义理上纠缠不休。因此当僧徒问起这类问题时,禅师一般都不正面回答,所以僧徒称这种回答为"东语西语"。文中后一段隐喻要靠认识自性才能脱离困境。

Excerpts from Zen Buddhist Texts

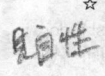

Observations

☆ Zen Buddhism stresses the attainment of enlightenment through knowing one's own mind and discovering one's own nature, and claims a special tradition handed down "from heart to heart" from Buddha himself. Zen masters therefore generally refuse to get entangled in metaphysical and conceptual speculations. To all such questions, they will respond in an oblique manner, and give "irrelevant" answers. The last part of the story illuminates the importance of knowing one's own nature as a way of deliverance from an impasse.

★ Here are three different perceptions of salvation:
1. *Bodhidharma* made his way from the West to save the benighted.
2. If one is not a lost in illusions, there is no need for salvation.
3. Salvation is a matter of heeding a call, or getting a direction and acting on it, or simply, knowing one's own nature.

※ If one does not perceive the answer when it is there but insists on an answer that meets one's expectations, one's intellect is as lively as a corpse.

见无左右

师问僧："什么处来？"曰："庄上来。"师曰："汝还见牛么①？"曰："见。"师曰："见左角，见右角？"僧无语。师代曰："见无左右②。"

——五峰常观禅师语录，引自《五灯会元》卷四

白话翻译

悟性没有左右的分别

五峰常观禅师问一僧人："你从什么地方来？"答："从村庄上来。"师问："你见到牛了吗？"答："见到了。"师问："你看见了牛的左角还是右角？"僧人不说话。禅师代他回答说："悟性没有左右之别。"

注释

① 汝还见牛么：禅宗常用牛比喻佛。这句是问僧人是否认识自性。禅宗主张自性是佛。

② 见无左右：上句僧人回答说"见"，表明自己已见本性。禅师为印证僧人开悟的程度，就问他见左角还是见右角。僧人无语，表明他并没有真正悟解，禅师代他回答说"见无左右"，意思是禅宗只讲"见"，不执着于"见"，因而没有左右的分别。

Excerpts from Zen Buddhist Texts

The left horn or the right?

Zen Master Changguan of Wufeng asked a monk, "Where have you come from?" "From the farm," the monk replied. The Master asked, "Did you see a buffalo[①]?" "Yes," the monk replied. "Did you see the left horn or the right?" The monk had no answer. The Master answered for him, "When you see, you don't make a difference between the left and the right."

— Recorded Dialogues of Zen Master Changguan of Wufeng, from *Amalgamation of the Sources of the Five Lamps*, vol. 4

Note

① buffalo: Zen masters often use the buffalo as a metaphor for buddha. When the Master asks the monk whether he has seen a buffalo, he is in fact asking the monk whether he has seen his true nature. The monk answers in the affirmative. The Master wants to test the extent of his enlightenment, and so asks about the particularities of the monk's perception. The monk is unable to answer. The Master helps him out by suggesting that particularities are not important.

发言异常

本州大中寺受业，后行脚遇百丈开悟，欲回本寺。受业师①问曰："汝离吾在外得何事业？"曰："并无事业②。"遂遣执役。一日因澡身，命师去垢，师乃拊背，曰："好所佛殿，而佛不圣。"其师回首视之，师曰："佛虽不圣，且能放光。"其师又一日在窗下看经，蜂子投窗纸求出。师睹之曰："世界如许广阔不肯出，钻他故纸，驴年③去得！"其师置经问曰："汝行脚遇何人？吾前后见汝发言异常。"师曰："某甲蒙百丈和尚指个歇处，今欲报慈德耳。"其师于是告众致斋，请师说法。

——神赞语录，引自《景德传灯录》卷九

Excerpts from
Zen Buddhist Texts

Unusual way of talking

The monk Shenzan first studied Buddhist teachings in the Dazhong Monastery in Fuzhou. On his travels, he met Zen Master Huaihai of Baizhang Mountain and was enlightened. He then returned to Dazhong Monastery. Upon his return, his tutor asked him, "What have you achieved while you were away?" Shenzan replied, "I have achieved nothing." His tutor assigned him menial duties in the monastery. One day, the tutor was bathing and asked Shenzan to scrub his back for him. Shenzan patted the tutor's back and said, "A good temple hall, only the buddha is not wise." The tutor turned round to look at him, and Shenzan added, "Not wise, but radiant." Another day, the tutor was reading a *sutra* by a window, and there was a bee bumping against the paper panes of the window trying to get out. Shenzan observed, "The world is wide open, yet you won't go out to it. If you keep banging your head against those old bits of paper, you probably won't make a breakthrough until the year of the ass[①]!" His tutor put down his book and asked, "Whom did you meet on your travels? I notice again and again your rather unusual way of talking." Shenzan replied, "Zen Master Huaihai of Baizhang Mountain taught me the basics of

193

白话翻译

说话不同寻常

　　神赞起初在本州(福州)大中寺学习佛法,后来行脚途中遇见百丈禅师而省悟,又回到原寺。业师问他:"你离开我在外面做成了什么事业?"神赞回答:"没什么事业。"业师就让他参加劳役。有一次洗澡时,业师要神赞帮他洗擦,神赞拍着业师的背,说:"好一座佛殿,只是佛不圣明。"业师回头看他,他又说:"佛虽不圣明,却能够放光。"又有一次,业师在窗下看经,一只蜜蜂扑撞着窗纸要飞出去。神赞看了说:"世界这样广阔,却不肯出去,偏要老钻着纸窗,哪年出得去!"业师放下经书问道:"你行脚时遇上过什么人?我几次听你讲话异乎寻常。"神赞答:"我曾蒙百丈和尚指明领悟门径,如今(回来)想报答您的恩德啊。"于是业师告诉大众准备斋席,请神赞说法。

注释

① 受业师:也简称业师,指教自己的老师、师僧。
② 并无事业:此句反映了神赞"无心是道"的思想。
③ 驴年:以十二生肖记年(如鼠、牛、虎、兔等),其中没有驴,故用"驴年"表示没有期限,不可能。

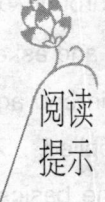

阅读提示

　　神赞已彻悟,而他的老师尚未彻悟,他反过来启发业师,用"自度度人"的方式报答业师之恩。

Excerpts from Zen Buddhist Texts

understanding, and I have come back to repay you my debt of gratitude." The tutor then ordered a meal to be prepared and invited Shenzan to preach a sermon.

— Recorded Dialogues of Shenzan,
from *Jingde Record of the Transmission of the Lamp,* vol. 9

Note

① the year of the ass: There are twelve zodiac signs in the Chinese almanac for the years of the rat, the ox, the tiger, the hare, the dragon, the serpent, the horse, the ram, the monkey, the rooster, the dog and the pig. There is no year of the ass. The expression "the year of the ass" means "never".

道在粪中

师与文远论义①曰："斗劣不斗胜②。胜者输果子。"远曰："请和尚立义。"师曰："我是一头驴。"远曰："我是驴胃。"师曰："我是驴粪。"远曰："我是粪中虫。"师曰："你在彼中作什么？"远曰："我在彼中过夏。"师曰："把将果子来！"

——赵州从谂禅师语录，引自《五灯会元》卷四

白话翻译

佛法在粪中

赵州从谂禅师跟弟子文远比赛讲论佛法，说："咱们比差不比好，胜者输果子。"文远说："请您先开头（立义）。"赵州说："我是一头驴。"文远说："我是驴胃。"赵州说："我是驴粪。"文远说："我是粪中虫。"赵州问："你在那里面干什么？"文远说："我在那里面过夏。"赵州说："你（胜了）拿果子来！"

Excerpts from
Zen Buddhist Texts

The Way is in the dung

One day, Zen Master Congshen of Zhaozhou invited his disciple Wenyuan to play a game of discourse on the Way of Buddha: "Let's see who is less competent, and he'll win a fruit." Wenyuan said, "Please start." The Master said, "I am an ass." Wenyuan countered with "I am the stomach of an ass." The Master said, "I am the dung in the ass." Wenyuan said, "I am a maggot in the dung." The master asked him, "What are you doing in the dung?" Wenyuan replied, "I am spending the summer there." The Master said, "Give me the fruit!"

— Recorded Dialogues of Zen Master Congshen of Zhaozhou, from *Amalgamation of the Sources of the Five Lamps*, vol. 4

注释

① 师与文远论义：师，指赵州从谂禅师，文远是他的门徒弟子。论义，指论说佛法。

② 斗劣不斗胜：比赛谁更差。即以不如者为赢方，胜方反而要输东西。

阅读提示

赵州从谂禅师与弟子嬉戏论义，弟子赢了，反而输了果子；赵州输了，反倒吃了果子。在禅家眼里，谁赢谁输并不重要，一切顺其自然。

Excerpts from Zen Buddhist Texts

Observations

☆ In this game, the disciple wins and loses the prize, while the Master loses yet wins the prize. In Zen Buddhism, it does not matter who wins and who loses, as long as everything is in harmony with nature.

★ It is in keeping with the spirit of Zen discourse that the Way of Buddha, the *dharma*, does not necessarily have to be analysed, discussed, or debated in high solemnity. As the title of this piece announces, "The Way is in the dung". The game of forfeits works refreshingly well as an exercise in paradoxical thinking that is crucial to attaining enlightenment. To be able to perceive, and appreciate, the truth that the winner is the loser and the loser is the winner is to be able to see beyond the surface of delusion to what lies behind — the irrelevance of winning or losing, the void, the immateriality of things and of the self.

But if the disciple's keen effort to win shows him up to be a somewhat naive novice in Zen discourse, there is yet a delightful touch of panache in his picturing himself summering in his imaginary environment. Obviously even the Master recognises this, and rules that his disciple wins.

我大悟也

初在归宗会下,忽一夜连叫曰:"我大悟也!"众骇之。明日上堂众集,宗曰:"昨夜大悟底僧出来。"师出曰:"某甲。"宗曰:"汝见什么道理,便言大悟?试说看。"师曰:"师姑元是女人作。"宗异之。师便辞去,宗门送,与提笠子。师接得笠子,戴头上便行,更不回顾。后居台山法华寺。临终有偈①曰:"举手攀南斗,回身倚北辰②。出头天外看,谁是我般人?"

——智通语录,引自《五灯会元》卷四

Excerpts from Zen Buddhist Texts

I'm enlightened

The monk Zhitong attended an assembly presided over by Guizhong. One night, to the amazement of all who were there, he shouted repeatedly, "I'm enlightened! I'm enlightened!" The next day, when everyone was gathered in the hall, Guizhong asked, "Would the monk who was enlightened last night please step forth?" Zhitong stepped forth. Guizhong asked, "What realisation did you come to that caused you to say you were enlightened? Would you tell us?" Zhitong replied, "That nuns are women." Guizhong was puzzled. Then Zhitong took his leave. Guizhong accompanied him to the gate, carrying Zhitong's straw hat. Zhitong took the straw hat, put it on and left without looking back. Later, when he became a Zen master, Zhitong lived in Fahua Monastery in Taishan. He left a verse before he died:

> My hands stretch to touch the constellations,
> I lean against the Northern Star.
> I crane my head and see beyond the heavens,
> Who, like me, on earth, there are?

— Recorded Dialogues of Zhitong,
from *Amalgamation of the Sources of the Five Lamps*, vol. 4

白话翻译

我大悟了

智通当初在归宗法会内，一天夜里忽然连声叫喊："我大悟了！"众僧大为惊骇。第二天上堂时，大众聚齐了，归宗说："昨夜大悟的僧人出来！"智通站出来说："就是我。"归宗问："你看出什么道理，就说大悟？说说看。"智通说："尼姑原来是女人做的。"归宗感到他很奇特。智通于是告辞离去，归宗送到门外，为他提着笠子。智通接过笠子，戴在头上就走，头也不回一下。后来居住在五台山法华寺。临终时作了一首偈诗："举手攀摸南斗，回身倚傍北辰。伸出头来看天外，谁跟我是一样的人？"

注释

① 偈：梵语 gatha，佛经中的唱词，为韵语。
② 南斗、北辰：泛指天上的星辰。

阅读提示

智通用"师姑元是女人作"来说明自己的大悟，似乎好笑，其实显示禅本来就是这样平常、普通。佛法没有什么神秘玄奥。

Excerpts from
Zen Buddhist Texts

Observation

☆ The realisation which Zhitong says brought him enlightenment — that nuns are women — sounds absurd and ridiculous. But that is what Zen is about — understanding the simplest and most ordinary truths of life.

禅门本无南北

唐宣宗问:"禅宗何有南北之名?"对曰:"禅门本无南北。昔如来以正法眼①付大迦叶②,展转相传,至二十八祖菩提达摩,来游此方为初祖。暨第五祖弘忍大师在蕲州东山开法,时有二弟子,一名慧能,受衣法,居岭南为六祖;一名神秀,在北扬化。其后神秀门人普寂者,立秀为六祖,而自称七祖。其所得法虽一,而开导发悟有顿渐之异,故曰南顿北渐,非禅宗本有南北之号也。"

——弘辩语录,引自《五灯会元》卷四

Excerpts from
Zen Buddhist Texts

There is no division into North and South in Zen itself

Emperor Xuan of the Tang Dynasty asked Zen Master Hongbian, "Why is the Zen sect divided into the Southern and the Northern Schools?" The Zen Master replied, "Zen at first was not divided into the Southern and the Northern Schools. In the beginning, Buddha transmitted to his disciple *Mahakashyapa* the essence of Zen. Zen teaching was passed on down the generations until the Twenty-eighth Patriarch *Bodhidharma*, who travelled here and became the First Patriarch in China. When the Fifth Patriarch Hongren taught the essence of Zen in Dongshan in Qizhou, he had two disciples. One was Huineng, who inherited the mantle of the Master, lived in south China and became the Sixth Patriarch. The other was Shenxiu, who stayed in north China to teach the doctrine of Zen. Later, Shenxiu's disciple, Puji set his master up as the Sixth Patriarch, and he himself claimed to be the Seventh Patriarch. Both Schools shared the same doctrine, but there is a difference in the way they arrive at enlightenment. The Northern School tends to progress gradually, whereas the

白话翻译

禅门本无南北之分

　　唐宣宗问："禅宗为什么有南宗、北宗的名称呢？"弘辩禅师回答："禅门本来并没有南北的区分。当初如来佛把正法眼传授给大迦叶，代代相传，到第二十八祖菩提达摩来到此地成为东土初祖。又到第五祖弘忍大师在蕲州东山宣讲禅法，当时有两个弟子：一位叫慧能，接受了衣法，居岭南成为第六祖；另一位叫神秀，在北方弘扬教化。以后神秀的门人普寂立神秀为第六祖，而自称为第七祖。他们所获得的法虽然一致，但在开导启发僧徒的省悟方面有顿悟和渐悟的不同，所以叫做南顿北渐，并不是禅宗本来就有南北的名称。

注释

① 正法眼：指禅宗的微妙旨意。

② 大迦叶：全名摩诃迦叶，又省称迦叶，释迦牟尼佛的弟子，为印度禅宗的第一祖。

206

Excerpts from Zen Buddhist Texts

Southern School tends to rely on sudden revelations and realisations. There is no division into North and South in Zen itself."

— Recorded Dialogues of Hongbian,
from *Amalgamation of the Sources of the Five Lamps,* vol. 4

指示心要

澧州龙潭崇信禅师，本渚宫卖饼家子也，未详姓氏，少而英异。初悟和尚为灵鉴潜请居天皇寺，人莫之测。师家居于寺巷，常日以十饼馈之，悟受之。每食毕，常留一饼曰："吾惠汝以荫子孙。"师一日自念："饼是我持去，何以返遗我耶？其别有旨乎？"遂造而问焉。悟曰："是汝持来，复汝何咎？"师闻之颇晓玄旨，因请出家。悟曰："汝昔崇福善，今信吾言，可名崇信。"由是服勤左右。一日问曰："某自到来不蒙指示心要。"悟曰："自汝到来，吾未尝不指示心要。"师曰："何处指示？"悟曰："汝擎茶来，吾为汝接；汝行食来，吾为汝受；汝和南[①]时，吾便低首。何处不指示心要？"师低头良久。悟曰："见则直下便见，拟思即差。"师当下开解，乃复问："如何保任？"悟

Excerpts from Zen Buddhist Texts

Show me the way of the mind

Zen Master Chongxin of the Longtan Monastery in Lizhou was the son of a baker in Zhugong, his surname unknown. He was a very bright young man. At that time, the monk Daowu had been invited by the monk Lingjian to be the abbot of the Tianhuang Monastery. Lingjian, however, did not tell anyone about the invitation as nobody knew Daowu or appreciated him. Chongxin lived with his baker father in a lane next to the Tianhuang Monastery, and he gave Daowu ten loaves of bread every day. Daowu would accept the loaves and eat them, but would always save one for the young man. And Daowu would say to him, "I give you this to bring blessings to your children." One day, the young man wondered, "I gave him the loaves, why did he give them back to me? Is there some meaning behind his gesture?" So, he came to the monastery to ask Daowu. Daowu replied; "That's right. You brought them. Is there anything wrong with giving them back to you?" When the young man heard this, he realised there was something unusual about the answer and he asked to be ordained as a monk. Daowu said, "You have always shown respect (*chong*) and kindness, and you have faith (*xin*) in what I say. I shall call

曰:"任性逍遥,随缘放旷,但尽凡心,无别胜解。"

——崇信语录,引自《景德传灯录》卷十四

指示心法的要点

澧州龙潭禅院的崇信禅师,本是渚宫卖饼人家的儿子,不知姓什么,少年时聪明异常。当初道悟和尚被灵鉴暗中邀请住持天皇寺,还没有人了解道悟。崇信家住在寺侧巷子里,一直是每天送十个饼给道悟,道悟收下吃了,常常留一个饼给崇信,说:"我送给你,会保佑子孙的。"有一天,崇信想:"饼是我拿去的,为什么反过来送给我呢?其中另有意旨吗?"就来到寺中问道悟。道悟回答:"是你拿来的,还给你有什么错?"崇信听了,知道其中大有玄妙意旨,于是请求出家。道悟说:"你从前崇敬福善,今天相信我的话,可名叫崇信。"从此在道悟身边服务。有一天崇信问:"从我来到之后,您还没有指示心法的要点。"道悟回答:"从你来之后,我时时在指示心法的要点。"崇信问:"在哪儿指示的?"道悟答:"你捧茶来,我为你接住;你拿饭来,我为你收下;你敬礼时,我就低头。哪儿不指示心法要点?"崇信低头不语。道悟说:"能领会的话,当下就领会,一思虑就错了。"崇信当下理解了。又问:"怎样保持?"道悟回答:"任性逍遥,应根据缘分做事,放达无拘,只须尽此平常之心,并没有其他特殊的见解。"

① 和南:僧人合掌行礼。

Excerpts from Zen Buddhist Texts

you Chongxin from now on." Chongxin stayed and served Daowu as a disciple. One day Chongxin asked his Master, "Since I came here, you have not shown me the crucial points in the way of the mind." Daowu replied, "Since you came here, I have been Showing you the crucial points in the way of the mind." Chongxin asked, "How?" Daowu said, "When you bring in the tea, I accept it. When you bring in the rice, I accept it. And when you bow to me, I nod. Is that not showing you the crucial points in the way of the mind?" Chongxin bowed his head and was silent. Daowu said, "If you understand this, you understand it at once. Pondering on it would take you on the wrong track." Chongxin saw the point at once. Then he asked, "And how do I persist in the way?" Daowu replied, "Freely, as your nature takes you. Do whatever is appropriate. Be not troubled or constrained. Take things naturally. Be ordinary. There is nothing more to it than that."

— Recorded Dialogues of Chongxin,
from *Jingde Record of the Transmission of the Lamp*, vol. 14

棹拨清波，金鳞罕遇

一日，泊船岸边闲坐，有官人①问："如何是和尚日用事？"师竖桡子②曰："会么？"官人曰："不会。"师曰："棹拨清波，金鳞③罕遇。"

——德诚语录，引自《五灯会元》卷五

白话翻译

桨儿拨清波，难遇金鳞鱼

有一天，船子和尚（德诚）把船停泊在岸边闲坐，有位官人问他："什么是和尚的日常事务？"和尚竖起船桨，问："明白了吗？"官人答："不明白。"和尚说："桨儿拨清波，难遇金鳞鱼。"

Excerpts from
Zen Buddhist Texts

When the oar stirs the waves

One day, Zen Master Decheng, also known as the Boat Monk, moored his boat and sat resting by the riverbank. A gentleman asked him, "What do monks do every day?" The monk raised an oar and said, "You understand?" The gentleman said, "No, I don't." The Master said, "When the oar stirs the waves, you don't see many golden scales."

— Recorded Dialogues of Decheng,
from *Amalgamation of the Sources of the Five Lamps*, vol. 5

注释

① 官人：本是对官吏的称呼，也用作对一般人的敬称。
② 桡子：船桨。
③ 金鳞：指鳞闪耀的鱼。

阅读提示

　　禅师们的日常修行完全依顺自然，无所用心。吃饭、睡觉、行走、劳作等就是和尚们的日常事务。对于别人的发问，德诚禅师竖桨回答，表示不须言说，不须用心。划桨惊走了鱼群，自然难遇金鳞鱼，禅僧的日常事务如果说出来，就是用心、执迷，就难见自性，难于彻悟。

Excerpts from Zen Buddhist Texts

Observation

☆ Zen masters, in their daily spiritual practice, do much the same things as other people — eat, sleep, get about and work. The point is that they just do what is natural for them to do. Decheng's first response to the question is to raise an oar, which means there is no need for explanation — he just does what a boatman naturally does. When the oar disturbs the water, the fish will of course swim away. When a monk goes around telling people about his everyday life, he will not be able to see his own nature, for he will no longer be doing things naturally. If he is too self-conscious, this may become an obsession, a stumbling block to realisation of the truth.

我国晏然

高沙弥初参药山，药山问师："什么处来？"师曰："南岳来。"山云："何处去？"师曰："江陵受戒去。"药云："受戒图什么？"师曰："图免生死。"药云："有一人不受戒亦免生死，汝还知否？"师曰："恁么即佛戒何用？"药云："犹挂唇齿在。"便召维那①云："遮跛脚沙弥不任僧务，安排向后庵着。"药山又谓云岩、道吾曰："适来一个沙弥却有来由。"道吾云："未可全信，更勘始得。"药乃再问师曰：'见说长安甚闹。"师曰："我国晏然。"药云："汝从看经得，请益得？"师曰："不从看经得，亦不从请益得。"山云："大有人不看经，不请益，为什么不得？"师曰："不道他无，只是他不肯承当。"

——高沙弥语录，引自《景德传灯录》卷十四

Excerpts from
Zen Buddhist Texts

My country is at peace

When Zen Master Gao was still a novice, he went to pay his respects to Zen Master Weiyan of Yaoshan. Weiyan asked him, "Where are you from?" The novice replied, "From Nanyue." Weiyan asked, "And where are you going to?" The novice replied, "To Jiangling to take my vows and be ordained." Weiyan then asked, "Why do you want to take the vows?" The novice replied, "So as to be delivered from life and death." Weiyan said, "One can be delivered from life and death without taking the vows. Did you know that?" The novice replied, "Then what is the point of taking the vows?" Weiyan observed, "Still bogged down by arguments, I see." Then Weiyan sent for the monk in charge of allocating duties in the monastery and said, "This limping novice can't handle heavy chores, get him a room in the dormitory at the back." To his disciples, Yunyan and Daowu, he added, "That novice comes with a good understanding." Daowu Said, "Well, maybe. He should be put to the test." Then Weiyan asked Gao again, "I hear that there are upheavals in Chang'an." Gao replied, "My country is at peace." Weiyan asked, "Did you learn this from reading the *sutras*? Or from talking to the masters?" Gao replied, "From

禅宗语录　中华传统文化精粹

白话翻译

我国安静

高沙弥初次参见药山禅师，药山问他："从哪儿来？"答："从南岳来。"药山问："到哪儿去？"答："到江陵受戒去。"药山问："受戒为了什么？"答："为了免生死。"药山问："有一个人不受戒也能免生死，你知道吗？"高沙弥说："如果这样，那么佛戒还有什么用？"药山说："还拘泥于言辞哩。"就召来维那说："这个跛脚沙弥不能胜任劳务，安排到后庵房去。"药山又对云岩、道吾说："刚才来的一个沙弥倒是有根底的。"道吾说："不可全信，须要再验证一下才行。"于是药山就再问高沙弥："听说长安很喧闹。"高沙弥答："我国是安静的。"药山问："你是看经学到的，还是请教别人学到的？"答："既不从看经学到，也不从请教学到。"药山又问："许多人不看经、不请教，为什么学不到？"高弥答："不是他们学不到，只是不肯承当。"

注释

① 维那：梵语 karma-dāna，音译"羯磨陀那"，意译"授事"。是佛寺中管理僧众事物的职事僧。

Excerpts from Zen Buddhist Texts

neither." Weiyan asked, "There are people who do not read the *sutras* nor talk to the masters, how come they learn nothing?" Gao replied, "It's not that they learn nothing, it's just that they do not practise what they learn."

— Recorded Dialogues of the Religious Novice Gao,
from *Jingde Record of the Transmission of the Lamp*, vol. 14

禅宗语录

切不得错用心

（义忠禅师）示众曰："今时出来尽学驰求走作，将当自己眼目，有什么相当？阿尔欲学么？不要诸余，汝等各有本分事，何不体取？作么心愤愤、口悱悱，有什么利益？分明说，若要修行路及诸圣建立化门，自有大藏教文在。若是宗门中事，汝切不得错用心！"时有僧出问："还有学路也无？"师曰："有一路滑如苔。"僧曰："学人蹑得否？"师曰："不拟心，汝自看。"

——义忠语录，引自《景德传灯录》卷十四

Excerpts from
Zen Buddhist Texts

Do not attend to the wrong things

Zen Master Yizhong said to his disciples, "Nowadays, monks all tend to wander around the country in their search, and take what they see for their eyes. Is that the Way of Zen? Do you really want to learn? Then forget all that. Why not look within yourselves for the much there is in you? What good is it to fill your hearts with excitement and anxieties and your mouths with stutterings? To put it plainly, if you want to follow the teachings of the buddhas there are the *sutras* to help you. If you want to learn the Way of Zen, do not attend to the wrong things." A monk came forward and asked, "Is there a way to learn Zen?" The Master replied, "There is a way, slippery as a mossy path." The monk asked, "Is it suitable for a beginner?" The Master replied, "Don't think about it. Try it."

— Recorded Dialogues of Yizhong,
from *Jingde Record of the Transmission of the Lamp*, vol. 14

白话翻译

不要用错了心思

义忠禅师告诫僧众说:"现在的僧人在外面都学着奔走寻求、妄自做作那一套,把它作为自己的宗旨,这和禅法有什么相同之处?你们想学吗?其余的都不要,你们各自有的本分事为什么不去领悟呢?这样心头愤懑,口头郁结,有什么好处?说得明白一点,如想了解修行途径和诸佛所建立的教化门径,自有佛教经典在。如果想了解禅宗旨意,那你们就绝不能用错了心思!"这时有个僧人站出来问:"有没有学禅的路呢?"禅师答:"有一条路,像苔藓一样滑。"僧人又问:"学人能够走吗?"禅师答:"不须思考,你们自己看。"

经典名句 Highlights

rèn xìng xiāo yáo, suí yuán fàng kuàng,
任性逍遥,随缘放旷,

dàn jìn fán xīn, wú bié shèng jiě
但尽凡心,无别胜解。

Freely, as your nature takes you. Do whatever is appropriate. Be not troubled or constrained. Take things naturally. Be ordinary. There is nothing more to it than that.

半肯半不肯

云岩讳日,师营斋。僧问:"和尚于云岩处得何指示?"师曰:"虽在彼中,不蒙指示。"云:"既不蒙指示,又用设斋作什么?"师曰:"争①敢违背他?"云:"和尚发迹南泉,为什么却与云岩设斋?"师曰:"我不重先师道德佛法,只重他不为我说破。"僧云:"和尚为先师设斋,还肯②先师也无?"师曰:"半肯半不肯。"云:"为什么不全肯?"师曰:"若全肯即孤负先师也。"

——良价语录,引自《洞山语录》

Excerpts from Zen Buddhist Texts

I half affirm him, and half do not

On the anniversary of the death of Zen Master Tansheng of Yunyan, Zen Master Liangjia of Dongshan prepared a meal of vegetables as offerings. A monk asked him, "What instructions did you get from your teacher Tansheng?" The Master replied, "Although I stayed with him, he did not give me any instructions." The monk said, "If he didn't give you any instructions, why do you make offerings to him?" The Master replied, "I wouldn't want to disobey him." The monk said, "You made your name while teaching in Nanquan. Why do you make offerings to Tansheng?" The Master replied, "I do not place a great deal of emphasis on my late master's virtues and knowledge of Buddhism. I value him because he did not make things too plain for me." The monk then asked, "Are these offerings you make to your late master an affirmation of him?" The Master replied, "I half affirm him, and half do not." The monk asked, "Why not affirm him completely?" The Master replied, "If I did that, I would have let him down."

— Recorded Dialogues of Liangjia,
from *Recorded Dialogues of Dongshan*

白话翻译

一半肯定，一半不肯定

云岩逝世纪念日，良价禅师备办斋供。僧人问："和尚在云岩那儿得到什么指示？"禅师答："虽然在他那儿，但没有得到指示。"问："既然没得到指示，那么还用设斋干什么？"禅师答："怎敢违背他呢？"问："和尚在南泉那儿发迹，为什么却为云岩设斋？"禅师答："我并不推重先师的道德和佛法，只推重他不为我说破。"问："和尚为先师设斋，是否肯定先师呢？"禅师答："一半肯定，一半不肯定。"问："为什么不全肯定？"禅师答："如全部肯定就辜负了先师啦！"

注释

① 争：即"怎"。
② 肯：赞同。

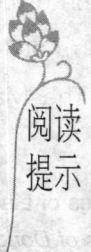

阅读提示

禅宗讲"无住为本"，"无住"即不把心定住在某一点上，肯定或否定某一事物。如六祖慧能《坛经》说："若有人问义，问有将无对，问无将有对，问凡以圣对，问圣以凡对，二法相因生中道义。"良价禅师对其老师云岩"半肯半不肯"正是这种观念的体现。

Excerpts from Zen Buddhist Texts

Observation

☆ In Zen thinking, a basic principle is "not to dwell" on things, i.e. not to get "fixated" on a thing or a point whether it be to affirm (or assert) it, or to negate (or repudiate) it. In the *Platform Sutra* it is recorded that the Sixth Patriarch said, "If someone asks about the meaning or point in something, and he thinks that there is a point, tell him there isn't, and if he thinks that there is no point, tell him there is. If he asks about the profane, talk to him about the sacred; and if he asks about the sacred, talk to him about the profane. In thinking and mediating between the two opposites, meaning would emerge." That is why Liangjia takes a half affirmative attitude towards his teacher.

柱杖子

芭蕉和尚示众云:"你有柱杖子[①],我与你柱杖子;你无柱杖子,我夺你柱杖子。"

——芭蕉禅师语录,引自《无门关》

白话翻译

拄杖

芭蕉和尚对众僧人说:"如果你有拄杖,我就给你拄杖;如果你没有拄杖,我就夺了你的拄杖。"

注释

① 柱杖子:即拄杖,俗称拐棍,是僧人外出行脚时所用。在禅宗语录中常用它比喻自性。

阅读提示

禅师接应僧徒须等对方慧根成熟,"你有拄杖子,我与你拄杖子"是说你如果能体悟自性,我就加以接应;"你无拄杖子,我夺你拄杖子"是说如果对方不能自省,反而向别处求觉悟,我就打破你向外求索的念头。

Excerpts from Zen Buddhist Texts

If you have a staff

The monk Huiqing of Bajiao said to an assembly of monks, "If you have a staff, I will give you a staff; if you have no staff, I will take away your staff."

— Recorded Dialogues of Zen Master Bajiao, from *The Gate of Gatelessness*

Observation

☆ The itinerant monks often carry a staff for support and self-defence on their travels. Zen masters often refer to it as a symbol of one's nature. The staff, therefore, has the double meaning of support and self-knowledge. The saying is a play on the two senses of the word. "If you have self-knowledge, I will give you support. But if you have no self-knowledge and hope to rely on outside support in seeking it, I will rob you of that illusion."

出门便是草

师后避世，混俗于长沙浏阳陶家坊，朝游夕处，人莫能识。后因僧自洞山来，师问："和尚有何言句示徒？"曰："解夏[①]上堂云：'秋初夏末，兄弟或东去西去，直须向万里无寸草[②]处去。'良久曰：'只如万里无寸草处作么生去？'"师曰："有人下语否？"曰："无。"师曰："何不道出门便是草？"僧回举似洞山，山曰："此是一千五百人善知识语。"因兹囊锥始露，果熟香飘，众命住持。

——庆诸语录，引自《五灯会元》

Excerpts from
Zen Buddhist Texts

There is grass when you step outside

At one time Zen Master Qingzhu of Shishuang went into retreat and lived among lay people in Taojiafang in the county of Liuyang in Changsha. He went out all day and returned at night, and mingled unrecognised among the people. Then a monk from the monastery of Zen Master Liangjia of Dongshan visited him. Qingzhu asked the monk, "What did your Master say to teach his disciples?" The monk replied, "At the end of the summer session of teaching, he said, 'Now that summer is at an end and autumn is coming, you are all going away in all directions, you must make it a point to go where no grass grows for a stretch of ten thousand miles①,' And, after a long pause, he added, 'Does anyone know how to go where grass does not grow?'" Qingzhu asked, "Did anybody give an answer?" The monk said, "No." Qingzhu said, "Why not say: when you step outside, there is grass?" The monk went back to Zen Master Liangjia and reported this exchange to him. The Zen Master remarked, "Such comments would draw a following of a thousand and five hundred." And so Qingzhu's wisdom became recognised, and his reputation spread like the fragrance of ripe fruit, and he was made an abbot by popular

白话翻译

出门就是草

　　庆诸禅师后来避世混迹于长沙浏阳陶家坊，早出晚归，没有人能够了解他。一次，有个洞山禅师会中的僧人来到这里，庆诸问他："洞山和尚有什么话语告示学徒？"僧人答道："解夏之后，和尚上堂说：'秋初夏末，兄弟们有的去东，有的去西，必须往万里无寸草的地方去。'过了会儿又说：'请问万里无寸草的地方该怎么样去呢？'"庆诸问："有人应对了吗？"僧人答"没有。"庆诸说："为什么不回答：出门就是草？"僧人回去后告诉了洞山，洞山说："这是能聚集一千五百名僧徒的高僧的话语。"因为这件事，庆诸禅师的道法被人发觉了，好像果熟香飘一样，众人请求他住持寺院。

注释

① 解夏：指僧尼夏坐安居期满（阴历七月十五日）而散去。
② 草：喻指人世的烦恼。

Excerpts from Zen Buddhist Texts

acclaim.

— Recorded Dialogues of Qingzhu,
from *Amalgamation of the Sources of the Five Lamps*

Note

① no grass ... , thousand miles: Here "grass" is used as a metaphor for the troubles of the world.

呵佛骂祖

上堂："我先祖见处即不然，这里无祖无佛。达摩是老臊胡，释迦老子是干屎橛，文殊、普贤是担屎汉，等觉、妙觉①是破执凡夫，菩提、涅槃是系驴橛，十二分教是鬼神簿、拭疮疣纸，四果、三贤、初心、十地②是守古冢鬼，自救不了。"

——宣鉴语录，引自《五灯会元》卷七

白话翻译

辱骂佛祖

宣鉴禅师上堂说："我对先祖的看法就不是这样，这里没有祖师，没有佛圣。达摩是老臊胡，释迦老头是干屎橛，文殊、普贤是挑粪汉，等觉、妙觉只是破除执见的凡夫，菩提智慧、涅槃境界是系驴绳的木桩，十二类佛经是鬼神簿，是擦拭疮疣的废纸，四类果位、三类贤者、初学佛者以及十地圣者则是守古坟的一群鬼，自身难保。"

Excerpts from Zen Buddhist Texts

Abusing the buddhas and the patriarchs

Zen Master Xuanjian of Deshan said in a lecture, "I hold a different view of the Patriarchs. There are no Patriarchs here, no buddhas and no saints. *Bodhidharma* was a red beard; old *Sakyamuni* a dry stick of dung; *Manjusri* and *Samantabhadra* carted nightsoil. The buddhas in their supreme forms of enlightenment are mere iconoclasts. *Bodhi* wisdom and *nirvana* are only stakes for tying up asses, the twelve *sutras* nothing but chronicles of spirits and ghosts, recorded on paper fit only for wiping boils and sores. The four grades of saints, the *bodhisattvas* in their three virtuous states, the beginners in the faith, the saints in their ten ranks are all phantoms guarding an old tomb, unable even to save themselves."

— Recorded Dialogues of Xuanjian,
from *Amalgamation of the Sources of the Five Lamps*, vol. 7

注释

① 等觉、妙觉：都是佛的名称。

② 四果、三贤、十地：四果是出家者获得圣果的四等阶位。三贤是三种贤者的阶位。十地是修行中的十种阶位。

阅读提示

这是一篇向佛向祖的宣战书，它痛快淋漓地打破了世人对佛祖的迷信和崇拜。宣鉴禅师示意人们：没有什么救世的佛祖，只有自己救自己，表现了他对自我及现实人生的充足信心。

经典名句 Highlights

chén láo jiǒng tuō shì fēi cháng, jǐn bǎ shéng tóu zuò yī chǎng
尘劳迥脱事非常,紧把绳头做一场

bù shì yī fān hán chè gǔ, zhēng dé méi huā pū bí xiāng
不是一翻寒彻骨,争得梅花扑鼻香?

It's not easy to shake off the world's dusty strife.
Take firm hold of the reins to guide your life.
Nought but the bone-piercing winter chill
Brings plum blossom fragrance your senses to thrill.

定取生死

师上堂告示众曰："夫有祖以来，时人错会，相承至今，以佛祖句为人师范，如此却成狂人无智人去。他只指示汝：无法本是道，道无一法。无佛可成，无道可得，无法可舍。故云目前无法，意在目前，他不是目前法。若向佛祖边学，此人未有眼目，皆属所依之法，不得自在。本只为生死茫茫，识性无自由分，千里万里求善知识。须有正眼，永脱虚谬之见。定取目前生死，为复实有，为复实无？若有人定得，许汝出头。上根之人言下明道，中下根器波波浪走。何不向生死中定当取？何处更疑佛疑祖替汝生死？有智人笑汝！"

——善会语录，引自《景德传灯录》卷十五

Excerpts from Zen Buddhist Texts

Know life and death

At a lecture, Zen Master Shanhui said to the gathering, "Since the time of Buddha and the Patriarchs, people have come under a misconception, which persists even today. They have modelled their lives on the sayings of Buddha and the Patriarchs, and this has turned them into fanatics and dullards. What Buddha and the Patriarchs did was to show you that there is no single doctrine to the way of spiritual enlightenment, that the Way is not limited to one doctrine. There is no buddha for you to model your life on, no Way for you to acquire, no doctrine for you to discard. Hence the saying: there is no doctrine before us, before us there is truth, but truth is not the doctrines before us. If we seek to learn from Buddha and the Patriarchs, we do not see with our own eyes, we rely on ways which they have used, and we are not free, nor are we at home with ourselves. After all, it is because we are bewildered by life and death, because we know we are not free, that we journey thousands of miles in search of wisdom. Therefore we must see clearly, and free ourselves from misconceptions. Know life and death for the reality and the illusion that they are. If you can see clearly, then you have

辨清生死的问题

善会禅师上堂示大众说:"从有祖师以来,当时人都领会错了,相承至今,都把佛和祖师的语句作为众人学习的典范,这样却成了狂人和没有智慧的人。其实佛和祖师只指示过你们:没有法门本身就是道,道是没有任何一种法门的。没有可以修成的佛,没有可以获取的道,也没有可以舍弃的法。所以说眼前没有法,意旨虽在眼前,但它不是眼前的法。如果向佛和祖师身上学习,这个人是没长眼睛,都属于有所依靠的方法,而不能自由自在。本来就因为生死茫茫,自身认识不能自由,才千里万里地寻求高僧。应该有正法之眼,永远脱离虚妄、谬误的见解。辨清眼前的生死,确实有呢,还是确实没有?如果有人能够辨清,就承认你已经出头。上等根器的人当下就会领悟,中等下等根器的人不停地徒然奔走。为什么不去辨清生死的问题呢?难道还指望佛或祖师代替你的生死?有智慧的人在笑你呢!"

Excerpts from Zen Buddhist Texts

broken through. Those with superior potentials will understand, and those with lesser potentials will forever run around and search in vain. Why not grasp this crucial knowledge about life and death? Why live and die vicariously the lives and deaths of Buddha and the Patriarchs, and be the laughing stock of the wise?"

— Recorded Dialogues of Shanhui,
from *Jingde Record of the Transmission of the Lamp,* vol. 15

禅宗语录

黄檗佛法无多子

师初在黄檗会下，……三度发问，三度被打。师来白首座①云："幸蒙慈悲，令某甲问讯和尚，三度发问三度被打，自恨障缘，不领深旨。今且辞去。"首座云："汝若去时，须辞和尚去。"师礼拜退。首座先到和尚处云："问话底后生，甚是如法。若来辞时，方便接他。向后穿凿成一株大树，与天下人作阴凉去在。"师去辞黄檗，檗云："不得往别处去，汝向高安滩头大愚处去，必为汝说。"师到大愚，大愚问："什么处来？"师云："黄檗处来。"大愚云："黄檗有何言句？"师云："某甲三度问佛法的大意，三度被打。不知某甲有过无过？"大愚云："黄檗与么老婆，为汝得彻困，更来这里问有过无过！"师于言下大悟云："元来黄檗

Excerpts from Zen Buddhist Texts

Huangbo's teaching is as simple as can be

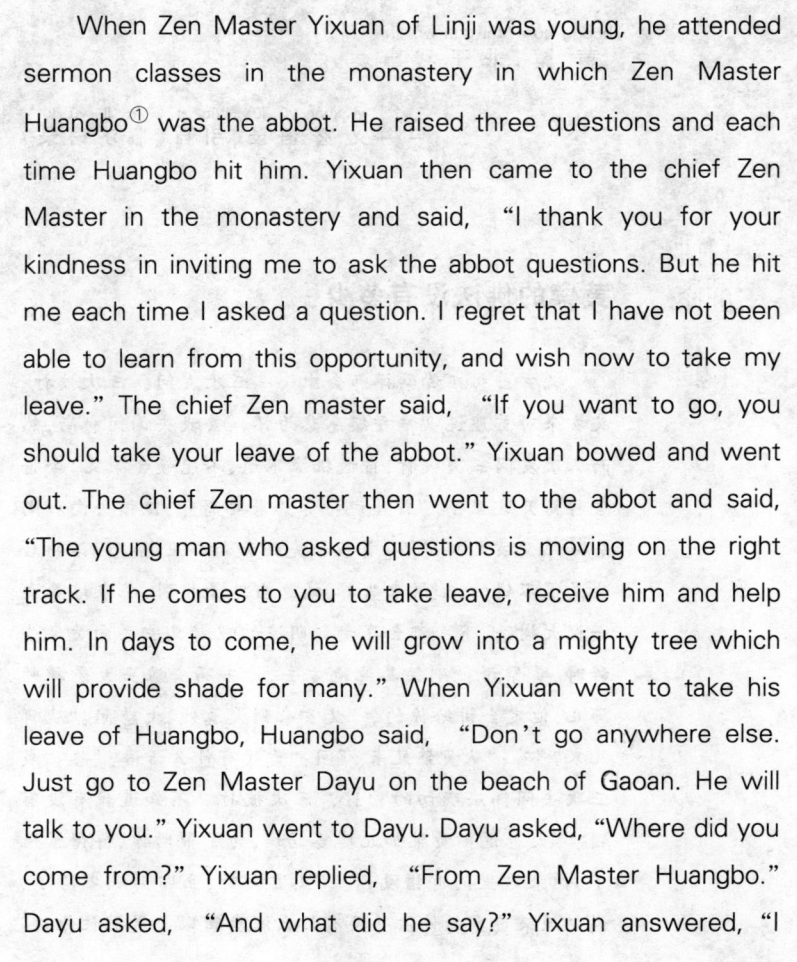

When Zen Master Yixuan of Linji was young, he attended sermon classes in the monastery in which Zen Master Huangbo① was the abbot. He raised three questions and each time Huangbo hit him. Yixuan then came to the chief Zen Master in the monastery and said, "I thank you for your kindness in inviting me to ask the abbot questions. But he hit me each time I asked a question. I regret that I have not been able to learn from this opportunity, and wish now to take my leave." The chief Zen master said, "If you want to go, you should take your leave of the abbot." Yixuan bowed and went out. The chief Zen master then went to the abbot and said, "The young man who asked questions is moving on the right track. If he comes to you to take leave, receive him and help him. In days to come, he will grow into a mighty tree which will provide shade for many." When Yixuan went to take his leave of Huangbo, Huangbo said, "Don't go anywhere else. Just go to Zen Master Dayu on the beach of Gaoan. He will talk to you." Yixuan went to Dayu. Dayu asked, "Where did you come from?" Yixuan replied, "From Zen Master Huangbo." Dayu asked, "And what did he say?" Yixuan answered, "I

禅宗语录 中华传统文化精粹

佛法无多子！"大愚挡住云："这尿床鬼子，适来道有过无过，如今却道黄檗佛法无多子！尔见个什么道理？速道！速道！"师于大愚肋下筑三拳。大愚托开云："汝师黄檗，非干我事。"

——义玄语录，引自《临济语录》

白话翻译

黄檗的佛法没有多少

义玄当初在黄檗禅师会中……三次发问，三次被打。义玄来对首座说："幸亏您慈悲为怀，要我去询问和尚，然而三次发问三次被打，自恨机缘不通，不能领会深义。今将告辞离开这里了。"首座说："你如果要离开，应该去向和尚告辞。"义玄礼拜退下。首座预先到和尚那儿说："问话的后生是很不错的，如果来告辞，请适当给予指引，将来培养成一棵大树，天下人都会享受到阴凉的哩。"义玄去向黄檗告辞时，黄檗说："别往其他地方去，你去高安滩头大愚禅师那儿，他定会讲给你的。"义玄来到大愚处，大愚问："从哪儿来？"答："从黄檗处来。"问："黄檗有什么话语？"答："我三次去问佛法确切的意旨，三次被打。不知道我有没有错。"大愚说："黄檗如此婆婆妈妈，为了帮助你，弄得累死了，你来这里问有错没错！"义玄一听，立即彻底省悟了，说："原来黄檗的佛法并没有什么深奥啊！"大愚抓住他说：

244

Excerpts from Zen Buddhist Texts

asked him three questions about Buddhist doctrines, and he hit me three times. I don't know if I was wrong about the doctrines." Dayu said, "What a fuss Huangbo made just to help you find out whether you are wrong! " Yixuan heard this and came to a realisation, and he cried out, "I see. Huangbo's teaching is as simple as can be! " Dayu grasped hold of Yixuan and demanded, "You young piss-a-bed! Just now you were still wondering whether you were wrong, and now you say Huangbo's teaching is as simple as can be! What have you seen? Tell me, quick." Yixuan punched Dayu three times in the ribs. Dayu pushed him away and cried, "Hey, Huangbo is your master, not I! "

— Recorded Dialogues of Yixuan,
from *Recorded Dialogues of Linji*

"这个尿床鬼,刚才还问有错没错,现在又说黄檗佛法没什么深奥!你看出了什么道理?快说!快说!"义玄对着大愚肋下击了三拳。大愚推开他说:"你的老师是黄檗,不关我的事。"

注释

① 首座:禅寺中属于首位的参禅者。

阅读提示

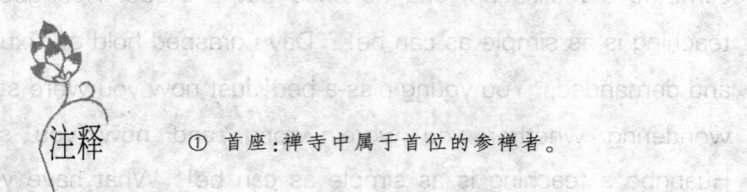

禅旨贵在以心传心,不靠语言文字来阐述,所以义玄三次询问佛法的要旨都被黄檗禅师棒打。后来义玄悟出黄檗的佛法没什么深奥的道理,并用在大愚肋下击三拳的方式表明佛法不可言传。

Excerpts from Zen Buddhist Texts

Note

① Zen Master Huangbo: also known as Zen Master Xiyun of Huangbo on PP.167—177, PP.251—253.

Observations

☆ Zen Buddhism seeks to pass on the doctrine of Zen "from heart to heart" rather than relying on the written word or verbal explication. That is why Huangbo answers Yixuan's question by hitting him. When, later on, Yixuan realises that the doctrine of Zen taught by Huangbo is based on this simple truth, he shows his understanding by doing to Dayu what Huangbo has done to him.

★ Huangbo answers Yixuan's questions by hitting him. This is a nonverbal form of acknowledging that Yixuan's questions touch on crucial points, i.e. the questions "hit" the crucial points.

佛今何在

三乘十二分教①，皆是拭不净故纸，佛是幻化身，祖是老比丘。尔还是娘生已否？尔若求佛，即被佛魔摄；尔若求祖，即被祖魔摄。尔若有求皆苦，不如无事。有一般秃比丘向学人道：佛是究竟，于三大阿僧祇劫②，修行果满方始成道。道流！尔若道佛是究竟，缘什么八十年后向拘尸罗城双林树间侧卧而死去？佛今何在？明知与我生死不别。

——义玄语录，引自《临济语录》

Excerpts from Zen Buddhist Texts

Where is Buddha now?

Zen Master Yixuan of Linji said, "All the twelve divisions of the canon of *Triyana* are paper for wiping away dirt. Buddha is an illusion; the Patriarchs are no more than old monks. Were you not born of woman too? If you appeal to Buddha for help, you are caught in a Buddha obsession; if you appeal to the Patriarchs for help, you are seized by a Patriarch obsession. All such appeals lead to suffering, it is best to let be. A monk, a mere bald-head, said to seekers after the Way, 'Buddha is the ultimate truth. He worked at his spiritual salvation through endless aeons until he reached perfection and was enlightenment itself.' But, if Buddha is the ultimate truth, why did he, at the age of eighty, lie down among the trees in the forest of Kusinagara City and die? And where is he now? He lived and died just like one of us."

— Recorded Dialogues of Yixuan,
from *Recorded Dialogues of Linji*

白话翻译

佛如今在哪儿

三乘教法的十二部类经典，都是擦拭污浊的旧纸，佛是虚幻之身，祖师是老僧侣。你是不是娘生的？你如想求佛，就被佛魔抓住；你如想求祖，就被祖魔抓住。你如果有所求，都是苦事，不如无事。有一种秃头僧侣向学道者说："佛是至极真理，经过无数劫的修行，功果圆满方才成道。各位学道者！你如说佛是至极真理，为什么他八十岁时在拘尸罗城双林树间侧卧着死去了呢？佛如今在哪儿？显然跟我们一样有生有死。

注释

① 三乘十二分教：三乘是佛教度脱众生的三种方法。十二分教是十二类体例不同的佛教经典。

② 三大阿僧祇劫：劫为佛家的计时单位，从天地的形成到毁灭为一劫。"阿僧祇劫"为无数劫，"三大阿僧祇劫"是菩萨成佛的时间。

Excerpts from
Zen Buddhist Texts

Observation

★ See also P.241, "Why do you hide your light here?", for an interesting treatment of this "where is" question.

真佛无形

道流①！真佛无形，真法无相。尔只么幻化上头作模作样，设求得者，皆是野狐精魅，并不是真佛，是外道见解。夫如真学道人，并不取佛，不取菩萨罗汉，不取三界殊胜。迥无独脱，不与物拘。乾坤倒覆，我更不疑。十方诸佛现前，无一念心喜；三途地狱顿现，无一念心怖。缘何如此？我见诸法空相，变即有，不变即无。三界②唯心，万法唯识。所以梦幻空花，何劳把捉？

——义玄语录，引自《临济语录》

Excerpts from
Zen Buddhist Texts

The real buddha has no shape or body

Seekers after the Way, the real buddha has no shape or body; the real doctrine has no form. You seek for all these in the world of delusions and illusions, imagining them to be of this shape or that form. Even if you get what you are seeking, they will merely be spirits of vixens and the like, not the real buddha, and you have but the notions of a heathen. The true seekers of the Way do not seek to reach Buddha, nor *bodhisattvas*, nor *arhats*, nor anything in the realm of sensuous desire, of form, and the formless world of pure spirit. They seek nothing except freedom, freedom from all things. Even if the world should turn upside down, they would not be perturbed. Even if all the buddhas should stand before them, they would not rejoice. Even if all hell should appear before them, they would not be afraid. Why? Because the true seekers of the Way realise that all forms are illusions; they come with change, and with change, they cease to be. The three realms of sensuous desire, of form, and the formless world of pure spirit are invented through the mind; and myriad things arise through the making of distinctions. Since these are all illusions in a dream, shadows of blossoms in the air, why

白话翻译

真实的佛没有形貌

各位学道者！真实的佛没有形貌，真实的事物没有相状。你们如此在虚幻的事物上做这做那，即使求到了，也都是野狐狸精，并不是真佛，而是其他道法的见解。至于真正的学道者，并不求取佛，不求取菩萨、罗汉，不求取三界美好之物。什么也没有，独自超脱，不与外物相拘系。哪怕乾坤倒覆，我也绝不疑惑。即使十方诸佛就在眼前，也没有一念欢喜；即使三途地狱顿时出现，也没有一念恐怖。为什么这样？因为我认识到万物都是空幻之相，变化就有，不变就无。所谓三界，都从心念而起；万千事物，全由识别而生。所以梦里幻境、空中花影，何必去辛苦地求取呢？

注释

① 道流：这是临济义玄禅师对各位学道（佛法）的僧人的称呼。

② 三界：见第14页。

Excerpts from Zen Buddhist Texts

seek to catch them?①

— Recorded Dialogues of Yixuan,
from *Recorded Dialogues of Linji*

Note

① This is an address of Zen Master Yixuan of Linji to his disciples.

佛法无用功处

道流！佛法无用功处，只是平常无心。屙屎送尿，着衣吃饭，困来即卧。愚人笑我，智乃知焉。古人云："向外作功夫[①]，总是痴顽汉。"

——引自《临济语录》

白话翻译

佛法无须用功

各位学道者，佛法无须下功夫学，平常心是道，无心是道。每天屙屎撒尿，穿衣吃饭，困了就睡。愚蠢的人讥笑我，智慧者才能理解。古人说："向别处下功夫的，都是痴迷不化的人。"

注释

① 向外作功夫：禅家认为自性是佛，体悟自心就找到了佛法，不须向他人求，也不须拜佛读经，一切顺其自然。

Excerpts from Zen Buddhist Texts

No special effort is needed

Seekers after the Way, No special effort is needed to understand the Way of Buddha. Just be natural and do what you should do. Go to the toilet, put on your clothes, eat when you are hungry, sleep when you are tired. Fools laugh at me for saying this, of course, but the wise know this is the truth. As the ancients say, "They are fools who seek enlightenment from without rather than from within."

— From *Recorded Dialogues of Linji*

Observation

★ See also P.143 "Eat when I'm hungry, sleep when I'm sleepy" for a further elaboration of this theme.

257

何汩没于此

守新安日,属运禅师初于黄檗山舍众人大安精舍,混迹劳侣,扫洒殿堂。公入寺烧香,主事祗接。因观壁画,乃问:"是何图相?"主事对曰:"高僧真仪。"公曰:"真仪可观,高僧何在?"僧皆无对。公曰:"此间有禅人否?"曰:"近有一僧,投寺执役,颇似禅者。"公曰:"可请来询问得否?"于是遽寻运师,公睹之欣然,曰:"休适有一问,诸德吝辞,今请上人①代酬一语。"曰:"请相公垂问。"公即举前问,师朗声曰:"裴休!"公应诺。师曰:"在什么处?"公当下知旨,如获髻珠②,曰:"吾师真善知识也!示人克的若是,何汩没于此乎?"时众愕然。

——裴休语录,引自《景德传灯录》卷十二

Excerpts from Zen Buddhist Texts

Why do you hide your light here?

When Peixiu was serving as a government official in Xin'an, Zen Master Xiyun of Huangbo had just left the monks at Huangbo Mountain to join the Da'an Monastery. There, he mixed with the serving monks and did menial chores like keeping the temple halls clean. When Peixiu came to the monastery to worship, the monk in charge received him respectfully. They toured the monastery and walked past some murals which they admired. Peixiu asked, "Who are these people in the portraits?" The monk in charge replied, "These are portraits of eminent monks." Peixiu asked, "One admires the portraits, but where are the eminent monks?" The monks in the entourage had no reply. Peixiu asked, "Do you have anybody who practises Zen here?" A monk answered, "We have a monk who joined us recently to do menial chores. He seems like a Zen person." Peixiu said, "Could you ask him to come here?" So they sent for Xiyun. When Peixiu saw Xiyun, he was very pleased, and he said, "I have a question. These Reverends here have no answer. Would you, Reverend, give me an answer?" The Zen Master said, "What is your question?" Peixiu repeated the question for him. Whereupon

白话翻译

为什么埋没在这里

裴休在新安任节度使的时候,恰好希运禅师离开黄檗山众僧而来到大安寺院,和干活的僧人混在一起,洒扫殿堂。裴公进寺烧香,主事恭敬地接待。观赏壁画的时候,裴公问:"是什么图相?"主事答:"这是高僧的肖像。"裴公问:"肖像可以观赏,高僧却在哪里?"僧人们无言以对。裴公问:"这里有禅人吗?"僧人回答:"最近有个僧人,投奔到本寺作劳役,很像禅者。"裴公说:"请来询问好吗?"于是立刻把希运禅师找来,裴公见了很高兴,说:"我刚才有一个问题,诸位大德没有回答,现在请您代答一语。"禅师说:"请相公问。"裴公就说了前面的问题,禅师高声叫唤:"裴休!"裴公应答。禅师问:"在什么地方?"裴公当下就知道了意旨,如获髻珠一般,说:"老师您真是高僧啊!启示人如此准确,为什么埋没在这里呢?"当时众僧愕然。

注释

① 上人:对僧人的敬称。
② 髻珠:转轮圣王髻上的明珠,常比喻佛教要旨妙义。

Excerpts from Zen Buddhist Texts

the Zen Master called aloud, "Peixiu!" And Peixiu answered. Then the Zen Master asked, "Where are you?" All at once, the point dawned on Peixiu. He was thrilled by the revelation, and as happy as if he had been given the jewel that adorned the hair of one of the gods of the universe, Cakravarti. To the amazement of all the monks present, he said to Xiyun, "Master, you are indeed a monk of deserved eminence! You can teach so effectively and economically. Why do you hide your light here?"

— Recorded Dialogues of Peixiu,
from *Jingde Record of the Transmission of the Lamp*, vol.12

阅读提示　裴休询问"高僧何在",希运禅师用大呼其名的方式启发他:无须去找寻什么高僧,每个人都有佛性,体认自性就能得道。

Excerpts from
Zen Buddhist Texts

Observations

☆ Zen Master Xiyun's way of answering Peixiu's question — "Where are the eminent monks?" — brings Peixiu to the realisation that there is Buddha-nature in everyone, and knowing one's own nature is the secret to knowing the way of spiritual enlightenment.

★ Three other points are worth noting about the question, "Where are the eminent monks?":

(1) A person is where he is. Of people who have passed away, we can only guess, but never know, where they are. In our daily life, we work at a level which presumes that our conjectures are knowledge, and we define others by our conjectures and take our own definitions as truth. The revelation of this basic falsehood in which we live should make a fundamental change in our perception of life.

(2) Another interpretation of this story — amusing, irreverent — is possible. One could say that Xiyun's action is that of a flatterer. Peixiu asks for eminent monks, and Xiyun calls Peixiu's name. No wonder Peixiu is pleased. We project what we are into the interpretation of our experiences.

(3) See P.187 "Take this corpse out of here" for a similar method used by Zen masters to bring people to realisation. See also P.249, "Where is Buddha now?", for a different, but equally illuminating, answer to the "Where is / are" question.

眼里耳里鼻里

师在沩山前坡牧牛次，见一僧上山，不久便下来。师乃问："上座何不且留山中？"僧云："只为因缘不契。"师云："有何因缘，试举看。"僧云："和尚问某：'名什么？'某答：'归真。'和尚云：'归真何在？'某甲无对。"师云："上座却回，向和尚道：'某甲道得也。'和尚问：'作么生道？'但云：'眼里耳里鼻里。'"僧回，一如所教。沩山云："脱空谩语汉！此是五百人善知识语。"

——引自《仰山语录》

Excerpts from
Zen Buddhist Texts

In the eyes, in the ears and in the nose

When Huiji (later to become Zen Master of Yangshan) was watching over the grazing buffalo on the slope of Weishan, he watched a monk go up the mountain. After a little while, the monk came down. Huiji asked him, "Sir, why don't you stay a while?" The monk replied, "The circumstances are not opportune." Huiji asked, "What circumstances? Can you explain?" The monk said, "The abbot asked me, 'What is your name?' I replied, 'Guizhen.' The abbot asked, 'Where is *guizhen*[①]?' I didn't know how to answer that question." Huiji said to the monk, "Go back and say to him, 'I have an answer.' If he asks, 'What is your answer?' then say to him, 'In the eyes, in the ears and in the nose.'" So the monk went back to the abbot, and said what Huiji taught him to say. The abbot said, "You crafty fellow! Those are words from an enlightened master who can teach a following of five hundred people!"

— From *Recorded Dialogues of Yangshan*

白话翻译

眼里耳里鼻里

慧寂在沩山前坡放牛时,看见一个僧人上山,不多久就下来了。慧寂问:"上座为什么不暂且留住山中?"僧人答:"只因为不契合机缘。"慧寂问:"有什么机缘?说说看。"僧人说:"和尚问我:'名叫什么?'我答:'归真。'和尚问:'归真在哪儿?'我无法应对。"慧寂说:"上座再回去,对和尚说:'我能回答啦。'和尚如问:'怎样回答?'就说:'眼里耳里鼻里。'"僧人又回到山上,按照慧寂教的说了。沩山说:"弄虚作假的家伙!这可是教化五百人的高僧的话语。"

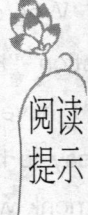

阅读提示

那个上山求教的僧人回答不出沩山禅师"归真何在"的提问,仰山告诉他"归真"(指修习佛法)在眼里耳里鼻里,就是说在日常生活中佛法无处不在。那个僧人照仰山的话返回去对沩山说了,沩山一听就知道他是从别人那里学来的,因此骂他是说谎骗人的家伙。

Excerpts from Zen Buddhist Texts

Note

① *guizhen*: This is a pun on the name. The term *guizhen* in Chinese means to return to the truth, or to return to reality.

Observation

☆ When the monk who went up the mountain could not answer where *guizhen* was, Huiji told him that *guizhen* was in the eyes, in the ears and in the nose, which means reality is everywhere in everyday life. When the monk repeated Huiji's words to Weishan, Weishan knew that he had got the answer from someone else and called him "a crafty fellow".

和尚何似驴

南塔光涌禅师,北游谒临济,复归侍师。师云:"汝来作什么?"南塔云:"礼觐和尚。"师云:"还见和尚么?"南塔云:"见。"师云:"和尚何似驴?"南塔云:"某甲见和尚亦不似佛。"师云:"若不似佛,似个什么?"南塔云:"若有所似,与驴何别?"师大惊云:"凡圣两忘,情尽体露。吾以此验人二十年,无决了者。子保任之。"师每谓人云:"此子肉身佛也。"

——引自《仰山语录》

白话翻译

和尚像不像驴

南塔光涌禅师,向北游历参见临济禅师后,又回来侍奉慧寂禅师。慧寂问:"你来干什么?"南塔回答:"参见和尚。"问:"可看见和尚了吗?"答:"看见了。"问:"和尚像不像驴?"答:"我看和尚您也不像佛。"慧寂问:"如不像佛,像个什么?"南塔回答:"如果像个什么,和驴有什么区别?"慧寂十分吃惊地说:"凡人和圣人都已忘掉,妄情除尽,实体显露。我用这个来勘验人已有二十年,没有人能辨明了悟。你要保持、巩固下去。"慧寂常对别人说:"此人是肉身佛啊!"

Excerpts from
Zen Buddhist Texts

Do I look like an ass?

Zen Master Guangyong of Nanta travelled north and visited Zen Master Yixuan of Linji, then he returned to serve his teacher, Zen Master Huiji of Yangshan. Huiji asked him, "Why have you come?" Guangyong said, "To see you." Huiji asked, "Do you see me?" Guangyong replied, "Yes." Huiji asked, "Do I look like an ass?" Guangyong replied, "To me, you don't look like a buddha either." Huiji asked, "If I don't look like a buddha, what do I look like?" Guangyong replied, "If you look like anything at all, in what way would you be different from an ass?" Huiji said in amazement, "That does away with the distinction between saints and mortals, with all distinctions, and reveals true reality. I have been using this question to test people for twenty years, and nobody has understood my point. You saw it." Huiji later often said this of Guangyong, "He is a living buddha."

— From *Recorded Dialogues of Yangshan*

智闲省悟

依沩山禅会,祐和尚知其法器,欲激发智光。一日谓之曰:"吾不问汝平生学解及经卷册上记得者,汝未出胞胎、未辨东西时,本分事试道一句来,吾要记汝。"师懵然无对,沉吟久之,进数语陈其所解,祐皆不许。师曰:"却请和尚为说。"祐曰:"吾说得是吾之见解,于汝眼目何有益乎?"师遂归堂,遍检所集诸方语句,无一言可将酬对,乃自叹曰:"画饼不可充饥。"于是尽焚之曰:"此生不学佛法也,且作个长行粥饭僧,免役心神。"遂泣辞沩山而去。抵南阳睹忠国师遗迹,遂憩止焉。一日因山中芟除草木,以瓦砾击竹作声,俄失笑间,廓然惺悟。遽归,沐浴焚香遥礼沩山,赞云:"和尚大悲,恩逾父母,当时若为我说却,何有今日事也。"

——智闲语录,引自《景德传灯录》卷十一

Excerpts from Zen Buddhist Texts

The enlightenment of Zhixian

Zhixian attended the Zen sessions of the Master Lingyou of Weishan. The Master knew that Zhixian had potentials and wanted to bring out the light of wisdom in him. One day, the Master said to Zhixian, "I would not ask you about the *sutras* and commentaries that you have read and memorised. Tell me, instead, about yourself before you were born and before you knew anything. I want to make an assessment of you." This question drew a complete blank from Zhixian. He thought for a long time, and attempted a few answers, none of which was accepted by the Master. In the end, Zhixian said, "Could you please tell me the answer?" The Master replied, "What I tell you would be my views, what good will it do to your perceptions?" Zhixian went back to his study and searched through the quotations from many learned masters, but found none that would do for an answer. He sighed, "How can I stave off hunger with the picture of a cake!" Then he burned all his books and said to himself, "I'll give up trying to learn the Way of Buddhism, for it is too taxing on the mind. I'll just eke out a living as a mendicant monk." In tears he bade farewell and left his Master Lingyou. He wandered until he reached

智闲省悟

白话翻译

智闲进入沩山禅会,灵祐和尚知道他是法器,想激发出他的智慧之光,有一天对他说:"我不问你平生的学业见解以及记得的经卷书册中的文句,你还没有出胞胎、东西不辨时的本分事,你试着说一句看,我要对你的未来进行预测。"智闲茫然不解,无言回答,想了好半天,才想出几句话陈述自己的理解,灵祐却都不认可。智闲说:"还是请和尚为我说说吧。"灵祐说:"我说了是我的见解,对你认识道法有什么好处呢?"智闲就回到僧堂,把以前收集的各地禅林的语句都翻检一遍,竟没有一句话可用来应对,就自叹自语:"画饼不可充饥。"于是将这些记录全部烧掉了,说:"今生不学佛法啦,就做个长期行脚的粥饭僧算了,免得劳心伤神。"就哭着告别沩山,来到南阳看到慧忠国师的遗迹,就栖止在那儿。一天他在山中割除草木,用瓦片碎石掷击竹子发出声音,失笑之间恍然醒悟。他立刻回来沐浴焚香,遥对沩山礼拜,赞叹说:"和尚实在慈悲,恩情超过父母!当时如果你告诉了我,哪有今天的事呢!"

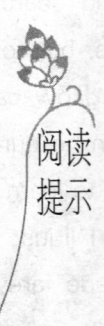

阅读提示

智闲原来只有书本知识,没有自心的体悟,所以对沩山提出的问题茫然不解。他把那些禅宗记录烧掉,表明他焚书绝路,破除文字对自心的障碍的决心。在听到瓦石击竹的响声时,他与声音融为一体,一刹那间,妄念俱灭,忽然认识到自心存在。认识自性,一悟即至佛地。

Excerpts from Zen Buddhist Texts

Nanyang where the Imperial Buddhist Master Huizhong once lived, and he settled down. One day, as Zhixian was cutting wood and clearing weeds on the mountain-side, he happened to fling some stones and broken tiles against some bamboo trees. He heard the sound that was made, and listened. Then he understood and burst out laughing. When he returned to his lodgings, he cleansed himself, burned some incense, bowed in the direction of Weishan where his Master was, and said with gratitude, "Compassionate abbot, who has given me more than my parents' gift of life! If you had told me the answer, I would not have had this experience today."

— Recorded Dialogues of Zhixian,
from *Jingde Record of the Transmission of the Lamp*, vol. 11

Observations

- ☆ Zhixian has book knowledge but no realisation of his inner self, that is why he could not understand his Master's question. His burning of the *sutras* is an indication of his resolve to break through the barrier of literature to reach the self. When he hears the sound of stones against the bamboo tree, he becomes one with the sound. In that instant, all illusions vanish, and he realises the existence of his own self. To know one's self, that realisation is Buddhahood.

- ★ Before one was born, one was in a state not dissimilar to the hollow of a bamboo tree. Nothing. No anxieties. No aspirations. At peace. External experience causes the disturbance, pleasant or unpleasant, in our lives. To be free is to be at peace again.

不较多

年十三求出家，父母许之，依乌山兴福寺行全为师。咸通乙酉落发受具。初以讲说，为众所归。弃谒雪峰，手携凫茈一包、酱一器献之。峰曰："包中是何物？"师曰："凫茈①。"峰曰："何处得来？"师曰："泥中得。"峰曰："泥深多少？"师曰："无丈数。"峰曰："还更多么？"曰："转有转深②。"又问："器中何物？"曰："酱。"峰曰："何处得来？"曰："自合得。"峰曰："还熟也未？"曰："不较多③。"峰异之，曰："子异日必为王者师。"

——澡先语录，引自《五灯会元》卷二

Excerpts from Zen Buddhist Texts

Almost ready

Zaoxian wanted to become a monk at the age of thirteen. Having got his parents' permission, he became a novice under the tutelage of a monk called Xingquan of the Xingfu Monastery in Wushan. In the sixth year of the Xiantong Period (AD 865) in the Tang Dynasty, he took the vows and was ordained a monk. He started to give sermons and commentaries on the *sutras*, and was much respected by the community. After some time, he stopped giving sermons and set off to visit Zen Master Yicun of Xuefeng. He took with him a packet of water-chestnuts and a jar of sauce and offered them to the Master. The Master asked, "What's in the packet?" Zaoxian said, "Water-chestnuts." The Master asked, "Where did you get them?" Zaoxian answered, "Out of the mud." The Master asked, "How deep was the mud?" Zaoxian answered, "Unfathomably deep." The Master asked, "Is there more?" Zaoxian answered, "The deeper it gets; the more there is." The Master then asked, "And what's in the jar?" Zaoxian answered, "Some sauce." The Master asked, "Where did you get it?" Zaoxian answered, "I made it myself." The Master asked, "Is it ready?" Zaoxian answered, "Almost ready." The Master said with some

白话翻译

差不多

澡先十三岁要求出家,父母同意了,拜乌山兴福寺行全和尚为师。咸通乙酉年(865)剃发受戒。起初因讲说经文,众僧都很信服他。后停止讲说,去参谒雪峰义存禅师,带着一包凫茈、一罐酱送给他。雪峰问:"包中是什么东西?"澡先答:"凫茈。"问:"哪里得来的?"答:"泥中挖得的。"问:"泥有多深?"答:"无数丈深。"问:"可还有吗?"答:"越深处越多。"雪峰又问:"罐中是什么东西?"澡先回答:"酱。"问:"哪儿来的?"答:"自己配制的。"问:"熟了吗?"答:"差不多。"雪峰觉得他很奇特,说:"你以后必将成为君王的老师。"

注释

① 凫茈:即荸荠。
② 转有转深:越深处越多。这里喻指对佛法的体悟。
③ 不较多:差不多。

阅读提示

在澡先与雪峰的对话中,凫茈、酱等暗指对佛法的悟性;泥有多深、酱熟没有,喻指觉悟的程度。雪峰问澡先"酱何处得来?"澡先答"自合得",即喻指自己是从自心悟得佛法的,所以雪峰对他另眼相看。

Excerpts from Zen Buddhist Texts

surprise, "You are going to be a teacher of emperors one of these days."

— Recorded Dialogues of Zaoxian,
from *Amalgamation of the Sources of the Five Lamps*, vol. 2

Observations

☆ In the dialogue, both the water-chestnuts and the sauce symbolise the ability to understand Buddhist doctrine. How deep is the mud, and whether the sauce is ready imply the degree of awareness. When Zaoxian answers that he made the sauce himself, he implies that he has arrived at his understanding independently, and that is why the Zen Master thinks so highly of him.

★ There is probably some word-play here in this dialogue which obviously operates on two levels. The words for "water-chestnut" (as written in the original text) read *fu ci* 凫茈, which sound like, though not identical to, the words *fu chi* 扶持, meaning "help and guidance". If one accepts that possibility, then the implication in the dialogue is that the deeper into the mud one penetrates, the more "help and guidance" there is. Whether that image implies profundity or ensnarement depends on one's perception. The possibility for equivocation makes this answer both a request for help and assistance to reach profound understanding, and, at the same time, a promise not to rely too heavily on the help and assistance of the Master, because such dependence is likely to hinder one's initiative. No wonder the Master sees the subtlety and sophistication of the answer as fitting for an advisor to kings. The word "sauce", pronounced "*jiang*", is the same as the word "about ready" or "will be ready", though different in tone. Zaoxian's answer implies that he has achieved much on his own initiative and with his own effort, and that he is about ready for a breakthrough in enlightenment. What tutor would not be pleased to accept such a pupil?

鳌山成道

初与岩头至澧州鳌山镇,阻雪。……师自点胸曰:"我这里未稳在①,不敢自谩。"头曰:"我将谓你他日向孤峰顶上盘结草庵,播扬大教,犹作这个话语!"师曰:"我实未稳在。"头曰:"你若实如此,据你见处一一通来。是处与你证明,不是处与你划却②。"师曰:"我初到盐官,见上堂③,举色空④义,得个人处。"头曰:"此去三十年,切忌举着。""又见洞山《过水偈》曰:'切忌从他觅,迢迢与我疏,渠今正是我,我今不是渠⑤。'"头曰:"若与么,自救也未彻在。"师又曰:"后问德山,'从上宗乘中事,学人还有分也无?'德山打一棒⑥曰:'道什么!'我当时如桶底脱相似。"头喝曰:"你不闻道,从门入者不是家珍?"师曰:

Excerpts from
Zen Buddhist Texts

Enlightenment at Aoshan

Once, Yicun of Xuefeng and Quanhuo of Yantou were travelling together. When they came to the town of Aoshan in Lizhou, there was a snow storm, and they stopped in the town. One day, Yicun pointed at his heart and said, "I don't feel sure of myself here. I don't want to deceive myself." Quanhuo said, "I thought, in time to come, you would set up a cottage on a lonely peak and preach the Way. I never thought you would say a thing like this." Yicun remarked, "I really do not feel sure." Quanhuo said, "In that case, tell me your thoughts. I will confirm what is right and clear up what is wrong." Yicun said, "When I first arrived at Yanguan, the Zen Master there gave a sermon on the false and illusory nature of all things, and that was my introduction to the Way." Quanhuo said, "Do not mention this in the next thirty years." Yicun then went on, "Then I read a verse by Zen Master Liangjia of Dongshan called 'On Crossing the Waters':

Seek not from the other,
So far removed from me.
He[①] is what I am,

"他后如何即是？"头曰："他后若欲播扬大教，一一从自己胸襟流出，将来与我盖天盖地去。"师于言下大悟，便作礼起，连声叫曰："师兄，今日始是鳌山成道！"

——义存语录，引自《五灯会元》卷七

鳌山成道

当初义存和岩头行脚来到澧州鳌山镇，碰上下雪，就暂时住下。……有一天义存手指自己的胸口说："我这里还没有安稳哩，不敢欺瞒自己。"岩头说："我以为你日后会在孤峰顶上筑起草庵，宏扬大教，没想到你说这样的话！"义存说："我确实是没有安稳哩。"岩头说："如果确实如此，就把你的见解一一说出来。对的地方给你印证，不对的给你铲除。"义存说："我当初到盐官禅师那儿，正逢他上堂举说色即是空的道理，我领会了入门的途径。"岩头说："三十年之内，切不可举说此事。"义存说："又看到洞山禅师的《过水偈》说：'切不可向别人寻求，别人的与我相隔遥远，他如今正是我，我如今不是他。'"岩头说："如果是这样，救自己还来不及哩。"义存又说："后来问德山禅师：'从前宗门中的事学人能够知道吗？'德山打我一棒说：'说什么！'我当时好像桶底脱落一样畅通明白。"岩头喝道："你没有听到吗？从门外进来的不是家藏珍宝。"义存问："今后该怎样才是？"岩头回答："今后要宏扬大教，必须一一从自己胸中流出，

Excerpts from Zen Buddhist Texts

But I am not him."

Quanhuo said, "Indeed. If you seek enlightenment from him, you can't save yourself." Then Yicun continued, "After that I asked Zen Master Xuanjian of Deshan, 'May not a pupil learn about the important events in the history of our school of teaching?' The Master whacked me with his staff and shouted, 'What are you talking about?' All at once, a glimpse of understanding shot through my mind, and I felt like a bucket with the bottom knocked out of me.[②]" Quanhuo shouted at Yicun, "Haven't you heard? Heirlooms and family treasures are not brought in from outside." Yicun asked, "What should I do from now on?" Quanhuo replied, "If you want to preach the Way, let it come out from within your heart, and let it spread over heaven and earth." On hearing this, Yicun was fully enlightened. He got up, bowed to Quanhuo and exclaimed, "My brother, today I have attained the Way at Aoshan!"

— Recorded Dialogues of Yicun,
from *Amalgamation of the Sources of the Five Lamps*, vol. 7

用此去教化普天下的人。"义存一听,顿时彻底领悟,忙起身行礼,连声叫道:"今天才是鳌山成道!"

注释

① 未稳在:指自己还没有彻悟。
② 划却:铲掉。划,通"铲"。
③ 上堂:到讲法厅堂。
④ 色空:佛教术语,指万事万物本非实有;色,有形之物。
⑤ 渠今正是我,我今不是渠:"渠",他,指佛性或真我。"渠今正是我",指的是只要能识心见性,佛就是我。"我今不是渠",是说一落于"我即是佛",就是自心的丧失,自心的执迷。
⑥ 德山打一棒:义存问以前宗门中的事,德山给了他一棒,这是告诉他不要向他人寻求佛法。这一棒使义存豁然开悟。

Excerpts from Zen Buddhist Texts

Notes

① He: "He" in the verse refers to Buddha-nature or the true self. Line 3 means if you know yourself and your true nature, Buddha is you. Line 4 means if you say "I am Buddha", then you will lose yourself or be obsessed with the self. The translators, however, think that "He" or "the other" can be anything (Buddha, a teacher, etc). Line 3 implies that any of these — Buddha or teacher — is as full of possibilities (e.g. for enlightenment) as I am. Line 4 means that everyone and everthing has his/her/its own nature and experience, and there is no point imitating or equating oneself with others.

② I felt . . . out of me: Yicun asks about the history of the Zen school of teaching, and Zen Master Xuanjian hits him with a staff. This is to tell him not to try to depend upon others in the search for Buddhist truth. This physical admonition brings Yicun his initial enlightenment.

透过祖佛

上堂示众曰:"夫参学人须透过祖佛始得。新丰和尚云:祖教佛教似生怨家,始有学分。若透祖佛不得,即被祖佛谩去。"时有僧问:"祖佛还有谩人之心也无?"师曰:"汝道江湖还有碍人之心也无?"又曰:"江湖虽无碍人之心,为时人过不得,江湖成碍人去。不得道江湖不碍人。祖佛虽无谩人之心,为时人透不得,祖佛成谩人去。不得道祖佛不谩人。若透得祖佛过,此人过却祖佛也,始是体得祖佛意,方与向上古人同。如未透得,但学佛学祖,则万劫无有得期。"

——居遁语录,引自《景德传灯录》卷十七

Excerpts from Zen Buddhist Texts

To see through the buddhas and the patriarchs

Zen Master Judun said at a sermon, "Students of the Way and those who practise Zen must see through the buddhas and the patriarchs. As Zen Master Xinfeng has said, 'You should deal with the teachings of the buddhas and the patriarchs as you would your worst enemies before you are fit to study them. If you do not see through them, you might be deceived by them.' " One of the monks asked, "Would the buddhas and the patriarchs deceive people?" The Master replied, "Would you say that rivers and lakes want to obstruct people?" Then he added, "Rivers and lakes have no intention to obstruct people, but if people cannot cross over, then the rivers and the lakes become obstructions to people. It should not be said then that rivers and lakes do not obstruct people. The buddhas and the patriarchs have no intention to deceive people, but if we cannot see through them, then we are deceived. And we cannot say that the buddhas and the patriarchs do not deceive people. But if one sees through them, one can go beyond them, and be better able to understand them, and so be as good as the best of the ancients. If one cannot see through

把祖佛看透

居遁禅师上堂对大众说："参禅学道的人必须看穿祖师和佛才行。新丰和尚说过："看待祖教、佛教好比冤家,才有学习的资格。如果不能看穿祖佛,就会被祖佛蒙骗。"当时有僧人问："祖佛有没有骗人之心?"禅师反问："你说江和湖有没有阻碍人的心?"又说:"江湖虽然没有阻碍人的心,但因为人们不能通过,江湖就成了人们的障碍。不能说江湖不阻碍人。祖佛虽然没有骗人之心,但因为人们不能看穿,祖佛也就在骗人。不能说祖佛不骗人。如果能把祖佛看穿,此人就超过了祖佛,才能体会祖佛的旨意,才与遥远的古人相同。如果没有看穿,只是学佛学祖,那永远也不会有成功的时候。"

Excerpts from Zen Buddhist Texts

them and simply tries to emulate them, one will never succeed."

— Recorded Dialogues of Judun,
from *Jingde Record of the Transmission of the Lamp,* vol. 17

禅师不看经

庄宗请入内斋，见大师大德总看经，唯师与徒众不看经。帝问："师为什么不看经？"师曰："道泰不传天子令，时清休唱太平歌。"帝曰："师一人即得，徒众为什么也不看经？"师曰："师子窟中无异兽，象王行处绝狐踪。"帝曰："大师大德为什么总看经？"师曰："水母元无眼，求食须赖虾。"

——休静语录，引自《五灯会元》卷十三

禅师不看经

唐庄宗皇帝请众僧进宫内办斋会，他见高僧们都在看经，只有休静禅师和他的徒众不看经。皇帝问："禅师你为什么不看经？"休静禅师回答说："世道和顺，无须传天子命令；时事安宁，不用唱太平歌曲。"皇帝说："禅师一个人可以不看经，徒众为什么也不看经？"禅师答："狮子的洞窟中没有其他兽类，大象行走的地方没有狐狸的踪迹。"皇帝又问："那些高僧为什么都看经？"禅师说："水母本来就没有眼睛，寻找食物要依赖虾哩！"

Excerpts from
Zen Buddhist Texts

Zen masters don't read *sutras*

Emperor Zhuang of the Tang Dynasty invited many monks to take part in a religious gathering in his palace. He noticed that many of the eminent monks spent their time reading the *sutras*, but Zen Master Xiujing and his disciples did not. The Emperor asked Xiujing, "Reverend Master, why do you not read the *sutras*?" Xiujing replied, "When all is well, there's no need for imperial decrees; and nobody sings about peace in times of peace." The Emperor said, "That may be so for you. But why don't your disciples read the *sutras*?" The Master replied, "The lion's den has no other beasts; where regal elephants walk no fox is seen." The Emperor said, "Then why do all the other eminent monks read the *sutras* all the time?" The Zen Master replied, "Jellyfish have no eyes, they have to be led by shrimps."

— Recorded Dialogues of Xiujing,
from *Amalgamation of the Sources of the Five Lamps*, vol. 13

神前酒台盘

京兆蚬子和尚,不知何许人也。事迹颇异,居无定所。自印心于洞山,混俗于闽川,不畜道具,不循律仪。常日沿江岸采掇虾蚬以充腹,暮即卧东山白马庙纸钱中。居民目为蚬子和尚。华严静师闻之,欲决真假,先潜入纸钱中。深夜师归,静把住问曰:"如何是祖师西来意?"师遽答曰:"神前酒台盘。"静奇之,忏谢而退。后静师化行京都,师亦至焉,竟不聚徒演法,惟佯狂而已。

——蚬子语录,引自《景德传灯录》卷十七

Excerpts from
Zen Buddhist Texts

The tray of wine offerings

The identity of the monk Xianzi from Jingzhao was a mystery. He had no fixed abode, and there were strange stories about him. After he had learned the Way of Zen from Zen Master Liangjia of Dongshan, he lived among ordinary people along the banks of the River Min, not carrying with him anything which signified his religious affiliation, and not observing any of the rules or vows of his religion. He usually wandered along the river in the day, picking clams and catching shrimps for food; and slept among paper offerings in the Baima Monastery in the area. The people there called him Monk Xianzi (Monk Clam). When Zen Master Xiujing of Huayan Monastery heard about this, he wanted to check if the monk was really enlightened or was just eccentric. He went to the monastery and hid among the paper offerings. Late at night, the monk returned, and Xiujing caught hold of him and asked him, "What was the intention of the *Bodhidharma* in coming to China?" The Monk answered, "The tray of wine offerings before the Buddha." Xiujing was surprised. He apologised and left. Later, when the Zen Master travelled and visited the capital, the monk was there too. But the monk did not hold any gathering

白话翻译

神面前放酒的台盘

　　京兆（今陕西省西安市）的蚬子和尚，不知是何处人。他的举动行为很怪异，没有固定的住处。自从在洞山禅师处领悟禅旨后，在闽江一带的俗世混日子。没有佛教器物，不守戒律礼仪。经常是白天沿着江岸捡蚬捉虾充饥，晚上就睡在东山白马庙中的纸钱堆里。居民叫他蚬子和尚。华严寺的休静禅师知道了，想验证他是真悟道还是假悟道，就预先藏在白马庙纸钱堆里。深夜时分蚬子和尚回庙，休静抓住他，问："什么是祖师从西方来中国的意旨？"蚬子和尚立即回答说："神面前放酒的台盘。"休静知他的确奇特，向他致歉后走了。后来休静禅师到长安说法，蚬子和尚也到了那儿，但一直不聚集僧徒演讲道法，只是伴装成疯疯癫癫的样子。

阅读提示

　　蚬子和尚答非所问的方式是禅问答的一个显著特点，是对提问者的隐晦示意，即无须问佛问祖，要悟道只要认识自心。

Excerpts from
Zen Buddhist Texts

for sermons. He merely feigned madness.

— Recorded Dialogues of Xianzi,
from *Jingde Record of the Transmission of the Lamp,* vol. 17

Observations

☆ The monk's answer is irrelevant to the question. This sort of irrelevant answers are a part of the tradition in Zen dialogue. It is an oblique hint to the questioner that it is not necessary to look for answers from Buddha and the Patriarchs. Enlightenment is a matter of knowing oneself.

★ The apparent lack of logic in the seemingly irrelevant or oblique answer either challenges the normal expectations, concepts and values to enable a new perception, or is used in defiance of normal expectations. If there is any logic in this particular answer, it could be that *Bodhidharma* might have come to China with the intention of bringing something to the people, regardless of whether the people wanted, needed or indeed could benefit from it at all. Is that not the attitude with which offerings are presented? See also P.187, "Take this corpse out of here", for the use of a similar technique in the answer given by the Zen Master to the same question about the intention of *Bodhidharma* in coming to China.

文偃契旨

师到雪峰庄,见一僧,师问:"上座今日上山去那?"僧云:"是。"师云:"寄一则因缘问堂头和尚,只是不得道是别人语。"僧云:"得。"师云:"上座到山中,见和尚上堂,众才集,便出握腕立地云:'这老汉项上铁枷①何不脱却?'"其僧一依师教。雪峰见这僧与么道,便下座拦胸把住其僧云:"速道!速道!"僧无对,雪峰托开云:"不是汝语!"僧云:"是某甲语。"雪峰云:"侍者!将绳棒来。"僧云:"不是某语,是庄上一浙中上座教某甲来道。"雪峰云:"大众!去庄上迎取五百人善知识来。"师次日上山,雪峰才见便云:"因什么得到与么地?"师乃低头,从兹契合。

——文偃语录,引自《云门广录》卷上

Excerpts from
Zen Buddhist Texts

Wenyan in harmony with Zen

When Zen Master Wenyan of Yunmen came to a village at the foot of the Xuefeng Mountain, he met a monk, and he asked, "Reverend, are you going up the mountain today?" The monk answered, "Yes." Wenyan said, "Could you take a question to the abbot, Tangtou, there? But don't tell him that the question came from someone else." The monk answered, "All right." Wenyan said, "Go up the mountain, and when you see the abbot come into the hall where the monks have assembled, take a step forward, grasp your wrist, stand firm and say, 'Why does this old man not take off the iron shackles[①] round his neck?'" The monk did what he was asked. When the abbot — Zen Master Yicun of Xuefeng — saw this, he came down from his ceremonial seat, seized the monk by the front of his collar and demanded, "Go on! Go on!" The monk had nothing more to say. Yicun pushed him away and said, "Those were not your own words!" The monk insisted, "They were." Yicun then ordered his attendants, "Get me a rope and a cudgel!" The monk hurriedly admitted, "Those were not my own words. A reverend monk from Zhejiang who is now in the village told me to do this." Yicun said, "Hey, all of you! Go to

白话翻译

文偃契合禅旨

文偃到了雪峰山下的村庄里,看见一个僧人,问道:"上座今天上山去吗?"僧人答:"是的。"文偃说:"你带一个问题去问堂头和尚,只是不能说是别人的话。"僧人说:"行。"文偃说:"你到了山中,看到和尚上堂,大众刚刚集合,你就走出来,握着手腕站着说:'这老汉颈项上的铁枷①为什么不脱掉?'"那僧人就按他说的那么做了。雪峰禅师看到僧人这样说,就走下禅座,劈胸揪住那僧人说:"快说!快说!"僧人无言应对。雪峰推开他说:"不是你的话!"僧人说:"是我的话。"雪峰吩咐说:"侍者,拿绳子和木棍来!"僧人说:"不是我的话,是村里一位浙江地区来的僧人教我来说的。"雪峰说:"大众!到庄上去迎接那位将有五百名僧徒的僧人。"文偃第二天上山,雪峰一见就问:"你为什么能达到这种程度?"文偃低下头,从此契合了禅旨。

注释

① 铁枷:文偃以此比喻对习禅人的种种形式上的束缚。脱掉铁枷,顺其自然,在日常平凡的生活中体悟自心,才是禅宗僧人修道的方式。

Excerpts from Zen Buddhist Texts

the village and welcome the sage who shall be the master of five hundred disciples." The next day, Wenyan went up the mountain. On first sight of him, Yicun asked, "How did you arrive at this level of perspicacity?" Wenyan bowed his head. Since then, Wenyan lived in accord with the Way of Zen.

— Recorded Dialogues of Wenyan,
from *Essential Sayings of Zen Masters of the School of Yunmen*, vol. 1

Note

① iron shackles: Wenyan uses this as a metaphor for the various formal disciplines imposed on those who practise Zen Buddhism.

莫趁口乱问

师云："莫道今日瞒诸人好，抑不得已，向诸人前作一场狼藉。忽被明眼人见，成一场笑具，如今避不得也。且问汝诸人，从来有什么事①？欠少什么？向汝道无事，已是相埋没也。须到者个田地始得。亦莫趁口乱问②，自己心里黑漫漫地，明朝后日大有事在！尔若根思迟回，且向古人建化门庭东觑西觑，看是什么道理。尔欲得会么？都缘是汝自家无量劫③来妄想浓厚，一期闻人说着，便生疑心，问佛问法，问向上问向下，求觅解会，转没交涉。拟心即差，况复有言。莫是不拟心是么？更有什么事？珍重！"

——文偃语录，引自《云门广录》卷上

Excerpts from Zen Buddhist Texts

Don't ask without thinking

Zen Master Wenyan of Yunmen said, "Please do not think that I undervalue your worth in saying what I have to say today. But circumstances oblige me to make a fool of myself, and a laughing stock to any perceptive onlookers. But I cannot shirk the task. First, let me ask you all: What have you achieved? What do you still lack? To say that you have achieved nothing would be to do you an injustice. After all, you have come this far. But don't be too eager to come forth with questions when there isn't a spark of understanding in your minds. If you do that, you'll have a lot to sort out tomorrow and the day after!
If you feel that understanding comes tardily, read the records of the ancients to learn from the actual examples of how they conducted their teaching, and work out the meaning for yourself. You are eager for understanding, are you not? That is because you have, for ages, been caught up in illusions. As soon as somebody says something, you are filled with doubt, and so you refer to Buddha and to the scriptures, to people of superior understanding and people of inferior understanding, in search of explanations and confirmations. This takes you away from intuitive understanding, and you are caught in a mesh of

不要抢着乱问

> 文偃禅师说:"别说我今天在蒙骗各位吧,只是不得已,才对各位做一回糊涂事。如果被明眼人看见了,就是一场笑话,如今也避免不了啦。先问你们各位,到如今做了什么?缺少什么?说你们没有事,已是埋没了你们。自然,须确实达到这个程度才行。也不要争抢着乱问,自己心里却是黑乎乎的,如果这样,明天后天事情可就多啦!你如悟性迟钝,说多看看古人的教化实例,看是个什么道理。你想领会吗?其实都因为你自己世代以来妄想浓厚,一旦听到别人说了,就产生疑心,于是问佛问法,问上问下。寻求知识见解,反而与禅旨不沾边。稍有思虑就已错了,何况用言语讲述。但是,难道不思虑就对吗?还有什么事?再会!"

① 事:即僧人修行得道的本分事。
② 莫趁口乱问:意思是要僧人反观自思,自己去体会。
③ 无量劫:见第250页注②。

Excerpts from Zen Buddhist Texts

words. Isn't that denying the intuition? But then, is intuition the way to enlightenment? Are there other ways? Farewell! Take care of yourselves."

— Recorded Dialogues of Wenyan,
from *Essential Sayings of Zen Masters of the School of Yunmen,* vol. 1

禅宗语录

各在当人分上

诸兄弟！若是得底人，他家依众遣日。若未得，切莫掠虚，不得容易过时，大须仔细。古人大有葛藤①相为处，只如雪峰和尚道：尽大地是尔。夹山和尚道："百草头上荐②取老僧，闹市里识取天子。"洛浦和尚云："一尘才起，大地全收；一毛头师子全身。"总是尔把取翻复思量看，日久岁深，自然有个入路。此个事无尔替代处，莫非各在当人分上。老和尚出世，只为尔作个证明。尔若有个入路，少许来由，亦昧汝不得。若实未得方便，拨尔即不可。

——文偃语录，引自《云门广录》卷上

Excerpts from
Zen Buddhist Texts

Do your own work

Brothers, enlightened men often live ordinary lives. Those not yet enlightened must guard against posturing and deception, and should not pass their time in idleness. They should be attentive. The ancients have left us hints and guidance to help us. For instance, Master Yicun of Xuefeng once said, "The whole world is yours." Reverend Jiashan said, "Learn the ways of old monks from how the grass grows. To learn the ways of kings to the busy market go." And Reverend Luopu said, "A speck of dust in the wind encompasses the earth; in a lion's hair is a whole lion merged." You could take ideas like these and think them over. In time, you would get some idea and attain some understanding. Nobody can do this for you. You have to do your own work. The dedicated lives and work of these old monks can only serve to illustrate what you may achieve. If you can attain some understanding, and have some potential, then nothing will escape you. If there really is no understanding at all, nobody can drag you along.

— Recorded Dialogues of Wenyan,
from *Essential Sayings of Zen Masters of the School of Yunmen*, vol. 1

都是各人本分事

白话翻译

诸位兄弟！如果是得道的人，他依随众人过日子。如果没有得道，千万不要弄虚作假，不能稀里糊涂地过日子，必须十分仔细。古人有许多启发僧徒的啰嗦话，比如雪峰和尚曾说：整个大地是你。夹山和尚说：百草顶上认识老僧，闹市里认识天子。洛浦和尚说：一粒微尘才扬起，就收摄了全部大地；一根毛的尖端上，容纳了狮子全身。你们把这些话反复思量，时间长了，自然可以有所领悟。这件事没人能代替你们，都是各人本分上的事。老和尚出世教化，也只能为你作个证明。你如果有所领悟，有些根基，也不能瞒过你。如果确实没有领悟的话，也拨不动你。

注释

① 葛藤：比喻话语纠缠、啰嗦。
② 荐：认识。

经典名句 Highlights

见道方修道，不见复何修？道性如虚空，虚空何处修？遍观修道者，拨火觅浮沤。但看弄傀儡，线断一时休。

If you can seek the Way only when you've known it,
How do you start before you know it?
The Way, by nature, is empty, unreal,
How can you follow it?
So many followers of the Way,
Seek water bubbles in the fire,
Watch the puppeteer, his strings broken,
Retire.

莫空过时

直须在意，莫空过时。游州猎县，横担拄杖，一千里二千里走。这边经冬，那边过夏。好山好水，堪取性，多斋供，易得衣钵。苦屈！苦屈！图他一斗米，失却半年粮。如此行脚有什么利益？信心檀越一把菜一粒米，作么生消得？直须自看，无人替代。时不待人，一日眼光落地，前头将何抵拟？莫一似落汤螃蟹手脚忙乱，无尔掠虚说大话处。莫将等闲，空过时光。一失人身①，万劫不复。不是小事，莫据目前。俗子尚犹道"朝闻夕死可矣"，况我沙门，各履践何事？大须努力！②

——文偃语录，引自《云门广录》卷上

Excerpts from Zen Buddhist Texts

Do not waste your time

Be careful. Do not waste time. It may be nice to wander around the country, wielding your staff and travelling great distances, spending winter in one place, summer in another. The scenery is beautiful, and you can do as you please. Offerings are plentiful and one is not short of provisions. But it is lamentable! Lamentable! Going after a mere bowl of rice may lose you half a year's provisions. What good does it do you to wander like that? In what way have you deserved the rice and vegetable that the faithful offer you? Only you yourself can do something about your spiritual life, nobody can do it for you. And time waits for no man. When death comes, how will you deal with it? Will you scurry frantically about like a crab in a boiling pot? Vain words, lies, excuses will be useless. Do not dilly dally. Do not waste your time. Once you lose the opportunity of this lifetime in human form, you will never have such an opportunity again. It is important not to trouble yourself with just the things before you. Even ordinary people say that if one learns of the Way in the morning, then even if death comes in the evening, one would have lived a worthwhile life.

白话翻译

不要虚度时光

必须留意,别虚度时光。游览州县,横挑拄杖,一千里两千里地行走。这边过冬,那边过夏。好山好水,能随心所欲,又能多受斋供,容易得到衣食之资助。苦恼啊!委屈啊!为了获得人家一斗米,失去了半年的食粮。这样行脚有什么好处?诚心施主的一把菜一粒米,怎么能够享用呢?悟道的事,必须自己留心,无人可以替代。时光不待人,一旦死期来临,今后自己用什么对付?别像放进锅里的螃蟹手脚忙乱,没有你虚妄地说大话的地方。不要漫不经心,虚度时光。一旦失去人身,万劫不能恢复。不是小事情,别只顾眼前。世俗之人尚且说"早晨得真理,即使晚间死去也值得",何况我们僧人,应该做什么事呢?必须加倍努力!

注释

① 人身:佛教以为人死后(失掉人身)会变驴变马。
② 这篇是文偃禅师教导门人的话语。

Excerpts from Zen Buddhist Texts

How much more should we monks strive? We must double our efforts.

Recorded Dialogues of Wenyan,
from *Essential Sayings of Zen Masters of the School of Yunmen,* vol. 1

自幻自怕

师云：“是诸人见有险恶，见有大虫刀剑诸事逼汝身命，便生无限怕怖。如似什么？恰如世间画师一般，自画作地狱变相①，作大虫刀剑了，好好地看了，却自生怕怖。汝今诸人亦复如是，百般见有，是汝自幻出自生怕怖，亦不是别人与汝为过。汝今欲觉此幻惑么？但识取汝金刚眼睛②。若识得，不曾教汝有纤尘可得露现，何处更有虎狼刀剑解胁吓得汝？直至释迦如此伎俩，亦觅出头处不得。所以我向汝道，沙门眼③把定世界，涵盖乾坤④，不漏丝发。何处更有一物为汝知见？知么？如是出脱，如是奇特，何不究取？"

——师备语录，引自《景德传灯录》卷十八

Excerpts from
Zen Buddhist Texts

Scaring yourself with your own delusions

Zen Master Shibei of Xuansha said, "When people are faced with danger, when they catch sight of tigers or weapons which threaten their lives, they are overcome with fear and horror. Their reaction is just like that of an artist who, having painted a picture of hell, or a picture of a tiger or a scene of violence, looks at the picture and gets frightened by it. And now, we too are like this. We take our delusions for real, and we get frightened by our own delusions. But no one, nothing, is threatening us. Do you want to be rid of these delusions and confusions? All you need is to recognise the Diamond Eye of Discernment in yourself. When you have found that, you would know that nothing in this world is real. Then what tigers, what wolves, what weapons can be a threat to you? Without discernment, even *Sakyamuni* himself would be just like you, and would not have achieved Enlightenment. That is why I say to you, the Eye of Discernment sees everything in the world, nothing escapes it. There is nothing else which can help you see so well. Do you understand? Such rare virtue, such strange

自生幻觉，自生恐惧

师备禅师说："各位看见有险恶，看见老虎，刀剑等威胁自己性命，就产生无限的恐惧。这好像什么呢？恰如世上画师一样，自己画出地狱图像，画出老虎和刀剑，仔细看后，却又自生恐惧。如今你们各位也是这样，把什么都看成真实存在，其实是你自己产生幻觉而又因此产生恐惧，并不是别人给你造成过错。现在你想澄清这种幻觉和迷惑吗？只须认识你自己的法眼。如果认识到了，就知道世间万物都不是真实的存在，哪里有什么虎狼刀剑能威胁你呢！纵然是释迦牟尼，如果像你们那样，他也不能觉悟。所以我告诉你们，佛眼、法眼能掌握世界，包容乾坤，一丝一发也漏不掉，哪里还有什么东西让你觉知和看见呢？懂了吗？如此超脱，如此奇特，为什么不去探索呢？"

① 变相：描绘佛经中神怪变异故事的佛教图画。
② 金刚眼睛：即佛眼、法眼。
③ 沙门眼：同注②。
④ 乾坤：指天地宇宙。

Excerpts from
Zen Buddhist Texts

power! Why don't you go and seek it?"

— Recorded Dialogues of Shibei,
from *Jingde Record of the Transmission of the Lamp,* vol. 18

禅宗语录　中华传统文化精粹

休从他觅

师上堂谓众曰："老僧顷年游历江外、岭南、荆湖，但有知识丛林，无不参问来。盖为今日与诸人聚会，各要知个去处。然诸方终无异说，只教当人歇却狂心，休从他觅。但随方任真，亦无真可任；随时受用，亦无时可用。设垂慈苦口，且不可呼昼作夜；更饶善巧，终不能指东为西。脱或能尔，自是神通作怪，非干我事。若是学语之辈，不自省己知非，直欲向空里采华，波中取月，还着得心力么？汝今各且退思，忽然肯去，始知瑞龙①老汉事不获已，迂回太甚。还肯么？"

——幼璋语录，引自《景德传灯录》卷二十

Excerpts from Zen Buddhist Texts

Do not seek it outside yourself

Zen Master Youzhang said in a sermon, "In recent years I have travelled in the regions north of the Yangtze River, to Guangdong and Guangxi Provinces, and to Jingzhou and Hubei Province. Wherever there are Zen monasteries, I have been to visit and learn about Zen discourse and the Buddhist Way. Perhaps all that was in preparation for our discussion today, that we should have a sense of direction. But all the Zen masters I have met only teach people to keep peace in their troubled hearts and minds, and not to seek peace outside themselves. They tell us to take things as they come and follow our nature, but then say that there isn't much in our nature to follow. They also tell us to take account of the times and make what use we can of them, and then say that there isn't much in the times for us to make use of. Even with the best intention, we cannot call the day the night; and even with the most subtle manoeuvring, we cannot call the east the west. And even if that could be done, it would be the mischief of some mysterious powers. It has nothing to do with our business. If we merely mouth the words, and know not how to reflect on or to recognise our errors, then seeking

白话翻译

不要从他人身上寻求

　　幼璋禅师上堂对大众说："老僧近年来游历江外、岭南、荆州、湖北，只要有禅宗寺院，无不去参谒问道。也是为了现在与诸位聚会，各人都要知道个去处。然而各地禅师始终没有特别的说法，只教各人自己平息狂乱之心，别向他人身上去寻求。只要依随环境，听任天性，也没什么天性可以听任；依随时势，受取使用，也没什么时势可以使用。即使以慈悲为怀，苦口婆心，也不可把白天称作黑夜；纵然是巧妙接引，总不能指东为西。或许能够这样，那是神通作怪。和我并不相干。如果是模仿话语之辈，不能反省自己，认识过错，简直就像到空中采花，水中捞月。你们能下功夫吗？现在你们各自先下去考虑，如果同意我的说法，就会知道我瑞龙老汉是迫不得已，过分啰嗦。你们同意吗？"

注释

① 瑞龙：幼璋禅师住持寺院的名称，也是他的法号。

Excerpts from Zen Buddhist Texts

enlightenment would be like plucking flowers from the air, and fishing for the moon in the water. Would you make the effort? Go and think about it. If you suddenly see my point, you would realise why this old man from Ruilong Monastery has been so circuitous against his inclinations. Would you go and think about it?"

— Recorded Dialogues of Youzhang,
from *Jingde Record of the Transmission of the Lamp*, vol. 20

竹密岂妨流水过

唐天复中,南谒乐普元安禅师,师器之,容其入室,仍典园务,力营众事。有僧辞乐普,乐普曰:"四面是山,阇黎向什么处去?"僧无对。乐普曰:"限汝十日内下语,得中即从汝发去。"其僧冥搜,久之无语。因经行偶入园中,师怪问曰:"上座岂不是辞去,今何在此?"僧具陈所以,坚请代语。师不得已,代曰:"竹密岂妨流水过,山高那阻野云飞?"其僧喜踊。师嘱之曰:"只对和尚,不须言是善静语也。"僧遂白乐普。乐普曰:"谁下此语?"曰:"某甲。"乐普曰:"非汝之语。"其僧具言园头所教。乐普至晚上堂谓众曰:"莫轻园头,他日住一城隍,五百人常随也。"

——善静语录,引自《景德传灯录》卷二十

Excerpts from Zen Buddhist Texts

A thick bamboo grove does not block the water-flow

During the last years of the Tianfu Period (AD 901–903) in the Tang Dynasty, Shanjing went south to pay his respects to Zen Master Yuan'an of Lepu. The Master thought highly of him, accepted him for a pupil, and assigned him to work in the vegetable garden. Shanjing served the community diligently. At that time, there was a monk who wanted to take his leave of Yuan'an. Yuan'an asked the monk, "There are mountains all around. Where will you go?" The monk had no answer. Yuan'an said, "I give you ten days to come up with an answer. If it shows any Zen perception, you can go." The monk thought long and hard but still could not come up with an answer. One day, as he was taking a walk, he wandered into the vegetable garden. Shanjing was surprised to see him, "Haven't you taken your leave of the abbot to go away, Reverend?" The monk told him what Yuan'an said, and insisted on Shanjing helping him with an answer. Reluctantly, Shanjing composed a verse for him, "However thick the bamboo grove, it blocks not the water-flow; however high the mountains, they stop not the

319

竹子虽密岂会妨碍流水通过

唐天复年中(901—903),善静到南方参谒乐普元安禅师,乐普很器重他,收为入室弟子,并让他从事菜园劳务,善静努力地为大家做事。有个僧人打算辞别乐普,乐普问:"四面是山,你往哪里去?"僧人无法回答。乐普说:"限你十天之内做出答语,如契中旨意就任你离去。"那僧人苦思冥想,一直找不到答语。有一天他在散步,无意中走进菜园,善静惊奇地问:"上座不是告辞离去了吗?怎么现在还在这里?"僧人就把事因告诉了他,并一定要他代拟答语。善静不得已,只得代僧人拟道:"竹子虽密岂会妨碍流水通过?山峰虽高怎能阻止野云飞越?"僧人高兴得跳了起来。善静叮嘱他说:"应对和尚时,不要说是我的话。"僧人就去答复乐普。乐普说:"谁拟的答语?"僧人说:"我。"乐普说:"不是你的话。"那僧人只好把管菜园子的僧人代拟的事一一说了出来。乐普晚间上堂时对众僧人说:"别小看管菜园子的,将来住持城中寺院,会有五百僧徒经常追随他哩!"

Excerpts from Zen Buddhist Texts

clouds that float." The monk jumped for joy at his help. Shanjing reminded him, "When you talked to the abbot, don't say these are my words." So the monk went to see Yuan'an. Yuan'an said, "Whose words are these?" The monk answered, "Mine." Yuanan said, "Not your words." So the monk told him all about the help he had from the monk in the vegetable garden. That night, when the Zen Master held a class, he told the assembled monks, "Don't underestimate the man who minds the vegetable garden. Some day, when he is the abbot of a monastery in the city, he will have a following of five hundred monks!"

— Recorded Dialogues of Shanjing,
from *Jingde Record of the Transmission of the Lamp*, vol. 20

一时抛与诸人

上堂次,大众拥法座而立。师曰:"这里无物,诸人苦怎么相促相拶作么?拟心早没交涉,更上门上户,千里万里。今既上来,各着精彩,招庆一时抛与诸人,好么?"乃曰:"还接得也无?"众无对。师曰:"劳而无功。"便升座,复曰:"汝诸人得怎么钝?看他古人一两个得怎么快,才见便负将去,也较些子。若有此个人,非但四事①供养,便以琉璃为地,白银为壁,亦未为贵;帝释②引前,梵王③随后,搅长河为酥酪,变大地为黄金,亦未为足。直是如是,犹更有一级在,还委得么?珍重!"

——道匡语录,引自《五灯会元》卷八

Excerpts from
Zen Buddhist Texts

I will toss it all to you

When Zen Master Daokuang of Zhaoqing gave a class, the people stood crowding round his ceremonial seat. The Master said, "There is nothing here to be had. Why do you crowd round and push to be near me? Any exertion of the mind or will estranges one from the Way of Zen. Going to other people's door for it further alienates one from it by a thousand miles. But since you are here, please pay attention, I will toss it all to you, all right?" Then he asked, "Did you catch it?" The crowd had no answer. The Master said, "Effort wasted." And he ascended his ceremonial seat and continued," Why are you so slow? How swiftly the ancients responded. What they saw they took away in an instant. That was more like it. If there was such a one here, one would offer him clothing, victuals, bedding, and medicine, one would offer him a floor made of crystal, walls of silver, and it would not be excessive. What's more, even if Sakra, the mighty lord of the heavens, was to usher him, and King Brahma of the heavens was to bring up the rear, churning the river into cream, and turning the earth into gold, it would still be fitting. And even then, there are

白话翻译

一起抛给各位

　　道匡禅师上堂时，大众簇拥法座而站立。道匡禅师说："这里没有什么东西，各位如此苦苦催促、逼迫我干吗？稍一存心，就已跟禅法不相干，何况还要上门上户求问，就更加远隔千里万里了。现在既然上堂来了，各位就多加注意，我招庆一起抛给你们，好吗？"接着问："接住了吗？"众人无言以对。禅师说："劳而无功。"就登上法座，继续说："你们各位怎么这样迟钝？看那一两个古人怎么如此敏捷？一见到就背负着走了。这样的人还差不多。如果有这样的人，不但样样供养，就是用琉璃铺成地面，白银做成墙壁，也不为奢侈；就是帝释在前引路，梵王在后随驾，把长河搅成奶酪，把大地变为黄金，也不为过。即使如此，还有更高一等的，能明白吗？再会！"

注释

① 四事：衣服、饮食、卧具、汤药。
② 帝释：忉利天之主。
③ 梵王：大梵天王，为初禅天之主。

Excerpts from Zen Buddhist Texts

others with an even greater potential for enlightenment. Do you see the point? Farewell."

— Recorded Dialogues of Daokuang,
from *Amalgamation of the Sources of the Five Lamps,* vol. 8

赚杀人

师问僧："什么处去来？"僧曰："劈柴来。"师曰："还有劈不破底也无？"僧曰："有。"师曰："作么生①是劈不破底？"僧无语。师曰："汝若道不得，问我，我与汝道。"僧曰："作么生是劈不破底？"师曰："赚杀人②！"

——招庆道匡律师语录，
引自《景德传灯录》卷二十一

白话翻译

作弄死人

招庆道匡禅师问一僧人："你到什么地方去了？"僧人回答："我劈柴去了。"禅师问："可有劈不开的木柴？"僧人答："有。"师问："什么是劈不开的？"僧人答不上来。禅师说："如果你说不出来，可以问我，我替你说。"僧人问："什么是劈不开的？"禅师答："作弄死人。"

Excerpts from
Zen Buddhist Texts

Split a joke with the dead

Zen Master Daokuang of Zhaoqing asked a monk, "Where have you been?" The monk replied, "I've been chopping firewood." The Master asked, "Was there any that you couldn't split?" The monk replied, "Yes." The Master asked, "What can't you split?" The monk did not know how to answer the question. The Master said, "If you can't answer that, ask me the question, and I'll answer it." The monk asked, "What can't you split?" "I can't split a joke with the dead," the Master replied.

— Recorded Dialogues of Zen Master Daokuang of Zhaoqing, from *Jingde Record of the Transmission of the Lamp*, vol. 21

注释

① 作么生：怎么，什么。"生"为词缀。

② 赚杀人：赚：欺哄，作弄。"赚杀人"即作弄死人，骗死人。此处暗指无明烦恼。

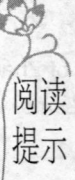

阅读提示

禅师问有无劈不开的，实际是问僧人有没有开悟。僧人不理解，照直回答说："有"。禅师认为僧人不觉悟是因为烦恼没有破除，人被烦恼所困，自性迷障，因此说作弄死人。

Excerpts from
Zen Buddhist Texts

Observations

☆ The question "Was there any that you couldn't split?" is another way of asking the monk whether there is any trouble that bars him from enlightenment. The monk does not get the point. Thinking that "any" refers to firewood, he answers "yes". The Master thinks that the monk lacks enlightenment because he has not broken through his troubles, and that troubles and illusions would torment people to death.

★ The Master's question "Was there any you couldn't split?" might well have a double meaning: arising from the context, it means any firewood that the monk could not split, but, taking off into the metaphysical plane, it could also mean "Was there any illusion you could not break through?" But since the monk stays solidly on the literal level of discourse and fails to take up the Master's cue to go into an intellectual discussion, the Master, out of exasperation — a nice human touch — laments that he cannot share an intellectual digression with the dull-witted monk.

元本契书

上堂："是汝诸人，尽是担钵囊，向外行脚。还识得性也未？若识得，试出来道看。若识不得，只是被人热谩将去。且问汝诸人，是汝参学，日久用心，扫地煎茶，游山玩水，汝且钉钉①唤什么作自性？诸人且道，始终不变不异，无高无下，无好无丑，不生不灭，究竟归于何处？诸人还知得下落所在也未？若于这里知得所在，是诸佛解脱法门，悟道见性，始终不疑不虑，一任横行，一切人不奈汝何，出言吐气，实有来处。如人买田，须是收得元本契书。若不得他元本契书，终是不稳。遮莫②经官判状，亦是不得其奈。不收得元本契书，终是被人夺却。汝等诸人，参禅学道，亦复如是。还有人收得元本契书么？试拈出看。……"

Excerpts from
Zen Buddhist Texts

The deeds of the land

Zen Master Chengyuan of Xianglin said to a class, "All of you are itinerant monks who have travelled far and wide with your alms bowls, practising the Way of Zen. Have you come to know your true nature? If you have, tell us about it. If you have not, then you have been deceived. Let me ask you this: since you have long worked hard at your spiritual search and at the Way of Zen, since you have performed your duties well at sweeping the floor and making tea, and have travelled through many places, what is it that you call your nature? Please also tell me, that which is immutable, that which is neither high nor low, neither good nor ugly, and has neither beginning nor end — where does that belong? And do you know where it is? If you know where it is, that is the key to the freedom of the buddhas, that is enlightenment and revelation of true nature, and you have obtained deliverance from doubt and uncertainty. You will be free, and nobody can do anything to you. And every word, everything you say will have their roots in reality. It is just like when you buy land, you must have the deeds. Without the deeds, nothing is secure. Without the deeds, even if the court ruled in your favour, you

——澄远语录，引自《五灯会元》卷十五

原本契据

澄远禅师上堂说："你们各位，都是挑着行李，到外面行脚的，是否已认识自性了呢？如果认识了，站出来说说看。如果没认识，就总被别人欺骗。我问你们，你们参禅学道，用心已久，扫地煮茶，游山玩水，你们究竟确实把什么称为自性？各位再说，始终没有变化，无高无低，无好无丑，不生不灭，这究竟归于何处？各位知不知道它的下落所在呢？如果知道它的下落所在，就是诸佛解脱的法门，就领悟禅道，认识自性，就始终没有疑惑，任你横行四方，一切人都拿你没有办法，你出言吐气，就确实有所依据。好比人们买田，应该保存原本契据。如果没有原本契据，终归不稳当。哪怕经过官府下了判状，仍是拿他没办法。没有保存原本契据，最后还是会被他人夺去的。你们各位参禅学道也是这样，有人已经得到原本契据了吗？拿出来看看！……"

① 钉钉：确实。
② 遮莫：尽管，纵然。

Excerpts from Zen Buddhist Texts

would still be helpless. Without the deeds, you could still be robbed of your land. It is the same for you all who study the Way of Zen. Have you got your deeds? Show us."

— Recorded Dialogues of Chengyuan,
from *Amalgamation of the Sources of the Five Lamps,* vol. 15

做个无事衲僧

初参云门,门问:"近离什处?"师曰:"查渡。"门曰:"夏在什处?"师曰:"湖南报慈。"曰:"几时离彼?"师曰:"八月二十五。"门曰:"放汝三顿棒。"师至明日却上问讯:"昨日蒙和尚放三顿棒,不知过在什么处?"门曰:"饭袋子!江西湖南便恁么去?"师于言下大悟,遂曰:"他后向无人烟处,不蓄一粒米,不种一茎菜,接待十方往来,尽与伊抽钉拔楔,拈却炙脂帽,脱却鹘臭布衫,教伊洒洒地,作个无事衲僧,岂不快哉!"门曰:"你身如椰子大,开得如许大口!"师便礼拜。

——守初语录,引自《五灯会元》卷十五

Excerpts from Zen Buddhist Texts

Be carefree monks

When the monk Shouchu first went to see Zen Master Wenyan of Yunmen, Wenyan asked, "Where have you been?" He answered, "Chadu." Wenyan asked, "Where were you in the summer?" He answered, "In Baoci, Hunan Province." Wenyan asked, "When did you leave that place?" He answered, "On the twenty-fifth day of the eighth month." Wenyan said, "I spare you three strokes of the staff." The next day, Shouchu came to ask Wenyan, "Thank you for sparing me three strokes of the staff yesterday. But in what have I offended?" Wenyan replied, "You good-for-nothing! Do you go to Jiangxi and Hunan just like that?" When Shouchu heard this, he suddenly understood, and he said, "From now on I will go to secluded places. I'll not store a grain of rice, nor grow a stick of vegetable. But I will receive seekers of the Way from everywhere, help them over their difficulties and clear up their confusion. Help them take off their greasy hats and their stinking clothes and let them be carefree monks with not a worry in the world. Won't that be wonderful?" Wenyan said, "You are the size of a coconut, but you sure talk big!" Shouchu

做个毫无牵挂的和尚

白话翻译

守初当初参见云门禅师,云门问:"从哪儿来?"答:"查渡。"云门问:"夏季在哪儿?"答:"湖南报慈。"又问:"何时离开那儿的?"守初回答:"八月二十五日。"云门说:"饶你三顿棒。"第二天守初又来问:"昨天蒙和尚饶了我三顿棒,不知我有什么过错?"云门说:"饭桶,江西、湖南就这样去?"守初一听,立刻大悟,就说:"以后到没人烟的地方,不存一粒米,不种一棵菜,接待十方往来的学道者,都给他们排除疑滞梗塞,摘去油腻的帽子,脱掉臊臭的衣衫,让他们毫无牵挂地做个无事和尚,岂不快活!"云门说:"你的身体不过像椰子一般大小,却开出如此大口!"守初就向云门礼拜。

阅读提示

守初参见云门禅师,一问一答,守初处于被动回答的状态,毫无开悟的表现,所以云门要棒打他,让他起疑团,这是禅宗接机度人的方式,即先让对方起疑,然后大疑促使大悟。果然守初第二天问自己错在何处。云门说,"江西、湖南就这样去?"守初一听大悟,悟见了那个使他自己能到处行走的自我。守初开悟之后,进一步接引学人扫除妄念,做一个无牵无挂、来去自由的僧人。

Excerpts from
Zen Buddhist Texts

bowed to Wenyan.

— Recorded Dialogues of Shouchu,
from *Amalgamation of the Sources of the Five Lamps*, vol. 15

Observation

☆ Shouchu responds to the Zen Master's questions with factual replies and shows no awareness that the Master is engaging him in a Zen dialogue. Applying the strokes of the staff is intended to arouse a person's doubts to make him come to a realisation. The Master's subsequent remark, "You good-for-nothing! Do you go to Jiangxi and Hunan just like that?" helps Shouchu discover his own nature and understand his true self so that he knows what he should do as he goes on his travels. With this realisation, Shouchu can also help others become carefree monks.

知音即不恁么问

问:"和尚百年后①,忽②有人问'和尚向什么处去',如何酬对?"师曰:"久后遇作家③,分明举似④。"曰:"谁是知音者?"师曰:"知音者即不恁么⑤问。"

——罗汉匡果禅师语录,
引自《景德传灯录》卷二十三

白话翻译

知音人不会那么发问

有僧人问:"和尚您百年之后如果有人问'和尚到什么地方去了?'我该怎么回答?"罗汉匡果禅师说:"今后如遇上高明的禅师就好好向他请教。"僧人问:"谁是行家知音?"禅师说:"知音者就不会那么问了。"

Excerpts from Zen Buddhist Texts

The enlightened would not have asked this question

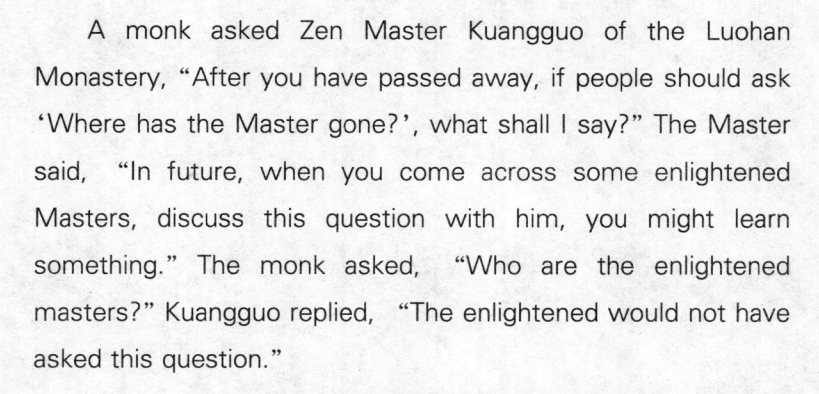

A monk asked Zen Master Kuangguo of the Luohan Monastery, "After you have passed away, if people should ask 'Where has the Master gone?', what shall I say?" The Master said, "In future, when you come across some enlightened Masters, discuss this question with him, you might learn something." The monk asked, "Who are the enlightened masters?" Kuangguo replied, "The enlightened would not have asked this question."

— Recorded Dialogues of Zen Master Kuangguo of Luohan, from *Jingde Record of the Transmission of the Lamp*, vol. 23

注释

① 百年后：指去世时。
② 忽：如果。
③ 作家：见第162页注②。
④ 举似：说给对方（听）。
⑤ 恁么：那么，如此。

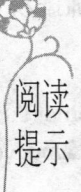

阅读提示

　　禅家认为悟道者超越生死，没有生死之别，因此百年后到什么地方去是个无须问也无法回答的问题。僧人提出这个问题，说明他还没有悟道。

Excerpts from Zen Buddhist Texts

Observations

- ☆ Zen masters think of enlightenment as transcending life and death, as well as the distinction between life and death, therefore where one goes after death is a question which need not be asked, and is impossible to answer. That the monk raises the question shows he has not yet come to such a realisation.
- ★ "The enlightened would not have asked this question". "This question" could refer not only to the question about where one goes after death but also to the question about who are the enlightened monks. What a subtle and gentle way of pointing out the double benightedness of the monk!

亲见作家来

师参南院①，入门不礼拜。院曰："入门须辨主。"师曰："端的请师分。"院于左膝拍一拍，师便喝。院于右膝拍一拍，师又喝。院曰："左边一拍且置，右边一拍作么生？"师曰："瞎！"院便拈棒。师曰："莫盲枷瞎棒，夺打和尚，莫言不道。"院掷下棒曰："今日被黄面浙子钝置一场。"师曰："和尚大似持钵不得，诈道不饥。"院曰："阇黎曾到此间么？"师曰："是何言欤？"院曰："老僧好好相借问。"师曰："也不得放过。"便下参众了，却上堂头礼谢。院曰："阇黎曾见什么来？"师曰："在襄州华严与廓侍者②同夏③。"院曰："亲见作家④来。"

——延沼语录，引自《五灯会元》卷十一

Excerpts from
Zen Buddhist Texts

You've met a veteran

When the monk Yanzhao went to pay his respects to Zen Master Huiyong of the Nanyuan Monastery, he did not bow on entering the monastery. The Master said, "When one enters a house, one should identify the host." Yanzhao replied, "Who is the host? Please identify." The Master slapped his left knee once, and Yanzhao gave a shout. Then the Master slapped his right knee once, and again Yanzhao gave a shout. The Master demanded, "We won't refer to the slap on the left knee for the moment. But what do you say to the slap on the right knee?" Yanzhao snorted, "Huh! What blindness!" The Master seized his staff. Yanzhao said, "Don't use your staff so freely, I will take it from you and hit you with it. You have been warned." The Master threw down his staff and said, "This pale-faced kid from Zhejiang has made a fool of me today!" Yanzhao said, "You look as though you're saying you're not hungry just because you can't get a bowl of rice." The Master asked, "Have you been here before?" Yanzhao replied, "What kind of a question is that?" The Master said, "I'm asking you a courteous question." Yanzhao replied, "I can't even let that pass." Then Yanzhao went to pay his respects to the monks in

白话翻译

亲眼见过行家

延沼参见南院禅师，进门不礼拜。南院说："进门应该先辨认主人。"延沼说："究竟谁是主请师分辨。"南院在左膝上拍了一拍，延沼就吆喝一声。南院在右膝上拍了一拍，延沼又吆喝一声。南院问："左边一拍暂且不说，右边一拍怎么样？"延沼说："瞎！"南院就抄起拄杖。延沼说："别盲目地上枷施棒，我会夺过棒来反打和尚，别怪我事先不说。"南院丢下拄杖说："今天被这黄面孔的浙江小子折腾了一场。"延沼说："和尚真像不能拿钵盂却谎称不饿。"南院问："你曾经到过这里吗？"延沼回答："这是什么话！"南院说："老僧我好好地问你。"延沼答："也不能放过。"于是下去参见了众僧，又到方丈来向南院礼拜道歉。南院问："你曾经见过什么人？"延沼答："曾在襄州华严寺和守廓侍者一同坐夏来着。"南院说："你原来亲眼见过行家！"

注释

① 南院：南院慧颙禅师。

② 廓侍者：南院禅师的侍者守廓。

③ 同夏：指同时同地坐夏。僧人于夏季三个月中安居不出，坐禅静修，称坐夏。

④ 作家：见第162页注②。

Excerpts from Zen Buddhist Texts

the monastery, and returned to Zen Master Huiyong, bowed and apologised to him. The Master asked, "Whom have you met?" Yanzhao replied, "When I was in Xiangzhou, I was at a summer retreat in Huayan Monastery with your attendant Shoukuo." The Master said, "Oh, you've met a veteran."

— Recorded Dialogues of Yanzhao,
from *Amalgamation of the Sources of the Five Lamps*, vol. 11

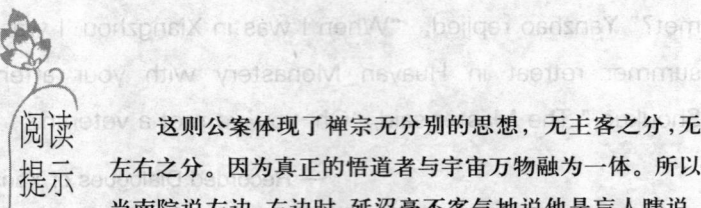

阅读提示　这则公案体现了禅宗无分别的思想,无主客之分,无左右之分。因为真正的悟道者与宇宙万物融为一体。所以当南院说左边、右边时,延沼毫不客气地说他是盲人瞎说,延沼禅师的非凡表现使南院禅师十分惊异,打听后才知道延沼曾经受到高明僧人的熏陶。

Excerpts from Zen Buddhist Texts

Observations

☆ This excerpt highlights that aspect of Zen which does away with distinctions: between host and guest, between left and right. To the truly enlightened, all are one in the universe. That is why when Huiyong referred to the left and to the right, Yanzhao said, "What blindness!" The unusual behaviour of Yanzhao amazed Huiyong, only later did he discover that Yanzhao had been briefed by a veteran.

★ Although the game played between Yanzhao and Zen Master Huiyong does bring out the crucial point of Zen about oneness and obliteration of distinctions, and Yanzhao has indeed won the game handsomely — a fact the Zen Master himself acknowledges when he laments that he has been made a fool of by Yanzhao — it must be said that on the level of etiquette, Yanzhao's behaviour is arrogant and exasperating. Could it be that the Zen Master's attendant, having seen how great an emphasis his Master places on this same Zen point in his teaching, wants to see how well the Master is able to practise this point in his ordinary everyday life and so arranges for Yanzhao to put his master to the test?

佛法见成

雪霁辞去,地藏门送之,问云:"上座寻常说三界唯心,万法唯识。"乃指庭下片石云:"且道此石在心内在心外?"师云:"在心内。"地藏云:"行脚人[①],着什么来由安片石在心头!"师窘无以对,即放包依席下,求决择。近一月余,日呈见解说道理,地藏语之云:"佛法不恁么。"师云:"某甲词穷理绝也。"地藏云:"若论佛法,一切见成。"师于言下大悟。

——引自《文益语录》

Excerpts from Zen Buddhist Texts

Buddhism is about what is here

When it stopped snowing, the monk Wenyi took his leave and Zen Master Dicang saw him to the gate of the monastery. Dicang said to Wenyi, "Your reverence often say that the three realms[1] arise from the mind, and all things come from perception and knowledge." Then he pointed at a rock in the courtyard and went on, "This rock. Is it inside the mind, or outside it?" Wenyi replied, "Inside the mind." Dicang said, "Why would a travelling monk want to carry a rock in his mind! " Wenyi was speechless. So he put down his luggage, and stayed under Dicang's tutelage for a review. For over a month, Wenyi explained his views and presented his arguments to Dicang every day. But Dicang would tell him, "Buddhist doctrine isn't like this." In the end Wenyi said, "I have exhausted my arguments and my words." Dicang said, "If you want to talk about Buddha's Way, you deal with what is here." It was a revelation for Wenyi.

— From *Recorded Dialogues of Wenyi*

佛法现成

白话翻译

雪停之后,文益告辞离去,地藏禅师送到寺门口,问道:"上座经常说三界都因心生,万物皆由识起。"他指着庭院中的一块石头说:"这块石头在心内还是在心外?"文益回答:"在心内。"地藏说:"行脚之人有什么必要把一块石头安放在心中!"文益语塞,无法回答,就放下行李,留在地藏禅师法席下,请求鉴别。一个多月时间内,文益每天表述见解,讲说道理。地藏对他说:"佛法不是这样的。"最后,文益说:"我词穷理尽啦!"地藏说:"如果要谈佛法,一切都是现成的。"文益一听,立刻大悟。

注释

① 行脚人:指外出寻访师友、步行修习的僧人。

阅读提示

关于片石的发问,按禅宗说法,既不在心内,也不在心外,既不肯定,也不否定。若说在心内或说在心外,就是执着两边,都是偏差。石头在它该在的地方,万物都是现成的,本无好坏善恶等差别。文益大悟,悟的是他四处寻找的佛法,原来就现现成成地在他自己身边。

Excerpts from Zen Buddhist Texts

Note

① the three realms: In Buddhism, the three realms are the world of sensuous desires, form, and the formless world of pure spirit.

Observation

☆ To the question about the stone, a Zen reply would be that the stone is neither inside the mind nor outside it, for the stone is where it is, and that is also where it should be. In his moment of revelation, Wenyi realises that Buddha's Way, which he has been searching for, is in fact right before him, is where he is.

长连床上稳坐地

……后江南国主请师居章义道场①，示众曰："总来这里立作什么？善知识如何沙数，常与汝为伴，行住坐卧不相舍离。但长连床②上稳坐地，十方善知识自来参。上座何不信取，作得如许多难易？他古圣嗟见今时人不奈何了，乃曰：'伤夫人情之惑久矣，目对真而不觉。'此乃嗟汝诸人看却不知。且道看却什么不知？何不体察古人方便？只为信之不及，致得如此。诸上座，但于佛法中留心，无不得者。无事体道去。"便下座。

——道钦语录，引自《五灯会元》卷十

Excerpts from Zen Buddhist Texts

Go sit on the bench

The Emperor of the South Tang Dynasty invited Zen Master Daoqin to be the abbot of Zhangyi Monastery. The Zen Master said to the gathering at a class he gave, "Why are you all standing here? So many enlightened masters live in your midst, keeping you company in all you do, whether you are walking, resting, sitting or lying down. You only have to go and sit on the bench for meditation and rest, and all the enlightened masters will come to see you. Why don't your reverences put more faith in them and not make so much trouble for yourselves? The ancient sages watch our people and sigh, 'Too long have these people been befuddled by worldly desires, even when their eyes see reality they don't know it.' These sages feel sorry for you because you see but do not know it. What is it that you see but do not know? Why is it that you don't learn much from the help the ancients have left you? Well, you are in this state because you don't have enough faith. Your reverences, if you attend to the Way, you will not fail. There is

在长连床上稳坐着

白话翻译

后来南唐国主请道钦禅师主持章义寺院,禅师上堂对大众说:"都来这儿站着干什么?无数位得道禅师,一直和你们作伴,行、住、坐、卧从不分离。只须在长连床上稳稳地坐着,天下得道禅师自会来参见。上座为什么不相信,弄出这么多麻烦来?那些古代圣人看到今时人无可奈何,就感叹地说:'这些人被俗情迷惑折磨得太久了,眼睛对着真实而不察觉。'这是感叹你们各位看见了却不知道。你们说看见了什么却不知道?为什么不体察古人的教说?只因为不相信,才弄成这样。诸位上座,只要在佛法中留心,不会得不到的。没事啦,悟道去吧。"说完就下座了。

注释

① 道场:禅师演法的场所,多指寺院。
② 长连床:寺院僧堂里的大床,可供多名僧人坐禅和休息。

Excerpts from Zen Buddhist Texts

nothing else. Go and experience the Way." Then he left.

—Recorded Dialogues of Daoqin,
from *Amalgamation of the Sources of the Five Lamps,* vol. 10

不惧生死和尚

大将军曹翰部曲①渡江入寺，禅者惊走，师淡坐如平日。翰至，不起不揖。翰怒诃曰："长老不闻杀人不眨眼将军乎？"师熟视曰："汝安知有不惧生死和尚邪！"翰大奇，增敬而已。曰："禅者何为而散？"师曰："击鼓自集。"翰遣裨校②击之，禅无至者。翰曰："不至，何也？"师曰："公有杀心故尔。"师自起击之，禅者乃集。翰再拜，问决胜之策③，师曰："非禅者所知也。"

——圆通缘德禅师语录，引自《五灯会元》卷八

Excerpts from
Zen Buddhist Texts

The monk who fears not death

The army of General Caohan crossed the river and charged into Zen Master Yuande's monastery. All the monks fled except the Zen Master, who sat in meditation as usual. When the General came before him, Yuande did not get up nor did he bow in greeting. The General was furious, and he shouted at Yuande, "Have you not heard that this general kills without batting an eyelid?" The Master took a long look at the General and replied, "Have you not heard of monks who fear not death?" The General was astonished and felt a surge of respect for Yuande. He asked, "Then why have the monks scattered?" The Master said, "Beat the drum and they will assemble." The General ordered his officers to beat the drum. but none of the monks came back. The General asked, "Why don't they come back?" The Master replied, "Because you have bloodshed on your mind." Then the Master beat the drum himself, and the monks returned to the monastery. The General bowed to the Master again and again, and asked the Master to teach him the ways to win victory in battle. The Master replied, "That is not

白话翻译

不怕死的和尚

大将军曹翰的部下渡江进入寺中,坐禅的众僧人吓得逃走,只有圆通禅师跟平日一样神情自若地坐着。一会儿曹翰到,禅师坐着不起,也不行礼。曹翰怒声喝斥说:"你没听说杀人不眨眼的将军吗?"禅师久视后说:"你可知道有不怕死的和尚吗?"曹翰听后十分惊异,增加了敬意,问道:"坐禅僧为什么都跑了?"禅师说:"一敲鼓就会聚来。"曹翰命副官击鼓,却没有僧人回来。曹问:"为什么没人回来?"禅师说:"因为你有杀心。"禅师起身亲自击鼓,众僧果然都回来了。曹翰对禅师拜了两拜,请教作战取胜的策略,禅师说:"这不是禅僧所能知道的。"

注释

① 部曲:部属、部下。
② 裨校:副官。指武官。
③ 决胜之策:指作战取胜的谋略。

Excerpts from Zen Buddhist Texts

what Zen Masters know."

— Recorded Dialogues of Yuande,
from *Amalgamation of the Sources of the Five Lamps,* vol. 8

禅宗语录　中华传统文化精粹

夜放乌鸡带雪飞

初到梁山，问："如何是无相道场？"山指观音，曰："这个是吴处士画。"师拟进语，山急索曰："这个是有相底，那个是无相①底？"师遂有省，便礼拜。山曰："何不道取一句？"师曰："道即不辞，恐上纸笔。"山笑曰："此语上碑去在！"师献偈曰："我昔初机学道迷，万水千山觅见知。明今辨古终难会，直说无心转更迷。蒙师点出秦时镜，照见父母未生时。如今觉了何所得？夜放乌鸡带雪飞②。"山谓"洞山③之宗可倚"，一时声价籍籍。

——警玄语录，引自《五灯会元》卷十四

Excerpts from Zen Buddhist Texts

A blackbird flying in snow in the dark of night

When Jingxuan first called on Zen Master Yuanguan of Liangshan, he asked the Master, "A place of enlightenment that is yet without form — what is it? Could you tell me?" The Master pointed at a painting of the Goddess of Mercy and said, "This one was painted by the artist Wu." Just as Jingxuan was about to ask another question, the Master added, "This one has a form. Which one has no form[①]?" Jingxuan saw the point and he bowed to the Master. The Master asked, "Why don't you say something?" Jingxuan replied, "I could say something, but it might be committed to form, to pen and paper." The Master smiled and said, "What you say may even be committed to a tablet in stone." Jingxuan offered a verse:

> My search for the Way has been so benighted:
> Over mountains and rivers knowledge to seek,
> Of times ancient and new, I knew but did not feel,
> 'Twas an obsession to dismiss.
> Thank you, my mentor, for a mirror to reflect.

361

白话翻译

夜放乌鸡带雪飞

警玄初到梁山(缘观)禅师处,问:"什么是无相道场?"梁山指着观音像说:"这是吴处士画的。"警玄刚想再问,梁山紧接着追问:"这个是有相的,哪个是无相的?"警玄于是省悟了,连忙礼拜。梁山问:"何不说上一句?"警玄答:"说说倒没什么,恐怕落纸笔。"梁山笑着说:"这句话要刻上碑石的哩!"警玄奉献偈诗一首:"当初学道法我真是痴迷,跋涉万水千山寻觅见知。明辨古今终究难以领会,直说没有妄念反更痴迷。幸蒙老师点出秦时古镜,照见我未生时本来面目。如今觉悟之后有何心得?夜半放出乌鸡带雪飞舞。"梁山说"洞山的宗法有了指望",一时间,警玄名声大盛。

注释

① 有相……无相:指事物的形象状态。佛教主张万有皆空,心体本寂,称造作的相或虚假的相都是"有相";凡有相者,全是虚妄。"无相"与"有相"相对,指摆脱世俗有相观而得到的真如实相。观音的画像是"有相",而观音本身是"无相"。

② 夜放乌鸡带雪飞:此句形容人一旦彻悟后那种自由自在的感觉和意境。

③ 洞山:原作"洞上",今改。

Excerpts from Zen Buddhist Texts

My formless nature ere I my form beget.

This moment my heart is alight:

A blackbird flying in snow in the dark of night.

Yuanguan exclaimed, "A worthy successor of the Dongshan sect is here!" Jingxuan's reputation spread.

— *Recorded Dialogues of Jingxuan*,
from *Amalgamation of the Sources of the Five Lamps*, vol. 14

Note

① no form: Buddhism stresses the doctrine that all phenomena and all things have no reality, but are composed of elements which disintegrate. Anything that is artificial, or false, is said to have a form. "Form" is contrasted with "no form", which means the attainment of absolute truth, or *nirvana*, by freeing oneself from the world of forms. The painting of the Goddess of Mercy has a form, but the Goddess of Mercy has no form.

美食不中饱人吃

令依圆通秀禅师,师至彼无所参问,唯嗜睡而已。执事白通曰:"堂中有僧日睡,当行规法。"通曰:"是谁?"曰:"青上座。"通曰:"未可,待与按过。"通即曳杖入堂。见师正睡,乃击床呵曰:"我这里无闲饭与上座吃了打眠。"师曰:"和尚教某何为?"通曰:"不参禅去?"师曰:"美食不中饱人吃。"通曰:"争奈大有人不肯上座。"师曰:"待肯,堪作什么?"通曰:"上座曾见什么人来?"师曰:"浮山①。"通曰:"怪得恁么顽赖!"遂握手相笑,归方丈。由是道声籍甚。

——义青语录,引自《五灯会元》卷十四

**Excerpts from
Zen Buddhist Texts**

Food has no attraction for a man who is full

Zen Master Fayuan of Fushan ordered Yiqing to seek tutelage and patronage from Zen Master Faxiu of Yuantong. When Yiqing arrived there, he did not attend the lectures nor asked any questions, but slept much of the time. The monk in charge of discipline reported to Faxiu, "There is a monk here who sleeps through the day. We should discipline him according to the rules." Faxiu asked, "Who is it?" The monk replied, "It's the Reverend Yiqing." Faxiu said, "Wait a little. I'll go and talk to him." Faxiu took his staff and went to the dormitory of the monks. He found Yiqing sleeping, so he struck the bed with his staff and shouted, "We have no food to spare for a reverend lie-abed!" Yiqing asked, "What would you have me do, Abbot?" Faxiu demanded, "Why don't you do your Zen meditation?" Yiqing replied, "The food may be nice, but it has no attraction for a man who is full." Faxiu said, "There are many who do not agree with you." Yiqing replied, "And when they do, what is the use?" Faxiu then asked, "With whom have you discoursed, Reverend?" Yiqing answered, "Fayuan of Fushan." Faxiu exclaimed, "No wonder you are so cheeky!" And the two laughed and shook hands and went to the abbot's

白话翻译

美食饱汉吃着不香

　　(法远禅师)让义青去投靠圆通法秀禅师,义青到了那儿并不参问,只是贪睡而已。执事僧告诉圆通说:"堂中有个僧人总是白天睡觉,应当按规法处理。"圆通问:"是谁?"执事僧回答:"是义青上座。"圆通说:"别忙处理,让我去问一问。"圆通就带着拄杖走进僧堂。见义青正在睡觉,就敲击禅床呵斥道:"我这里没有闲饭让上座吃了睡大觉。"义青问:"和尚教我干什么?"圆通说:"为何不参禅去?"义青答:"食物虽然味美,饱汉吃着不香。"圆通说:"无奈不同意上座的大有人在哩!"义青答:"等到同意了,还有什么用?"圆通问:"上座曾见过什么人?"义青答:"浮山。"圆通说:"难怪这样顽赖!"于是两人握手对笑,一同回方丈。从此义青名声远扬。

注释

① 浮山:指法远禅师。

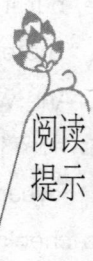

阅读提示

　　义青每日昏睡不去参禅,实际是设下机缘,等待圆通禅师来接应,以求印证。"美食不中饱人吃"一方面表明义青并非为吃闲饭而来,另一方面暗示自己在等待应接禅机,"待肯,堪作什么"(等到同意,还有什么用)意思是自性自知自用,按本性行事。如果按他人意愿行事,就丧失了自性。文中二人应对默契,心投意合,所以"握手相笑"。

Excerpts from Zen Buddhist Texts

study. Since then Yiqing's reputation spread far and wide.

— *Recorded Dialogues of Yiqing,*
from *Amalgamation of the Sources of the Five Lamps,* vol. 14

Observations

☆ Yiqing sleeps all day instead of practising meditation because he believes that when one is enlightened about one's true nature, it can be manifested in everything one does, and formal practice is unnecessary. With the remark, "Food has no attraction for a man who is full", Yiqing tells the abbot that he is not there for the food (the Zen meditation) but is waiting for an opportunity to discuss Zen with the abbot. Yiqing's other remark, "When they all agree, what use is it?" means that self-knowledge is for the self to attain, and for the self to use, so that a person can act according to his nature. To act according to the wishes of others would be to lose oneself. When the two men find themselves talking on the same wave-length, they shake hands and laugh.

★ This story is the disciplinarian's nightmare. Here is a person who breaks the rules which keep order in monastery life, and he does so with impunity. But the crucial point is implied in Yiqing's rejoinder about good food/Zen meditation: when a monk has achieved enlightenment, what is the point of making him sit there in meditation? The second part of Yiqing's rejoinder, "And when they do, what is the use?" can be taken as a dismissive rhetorical question. But it can also be taken as a serious challenge to Faxiu to think about the nature and uses of enlightenment, to think about how tutelage of the monks should be conducted, too. It is this challenge which changes Faxiu's attitude to Yiqing from contempt to admiration. But alas! How easy it is to miss this point and come to the conclusion that Yiqing has escaped punishment because he is the disciple of the abbot's friend, that he has connection!

为汝正之

有旨赐官舟南归。中途石霜楚圆谓侍者曰："我忽得风痹疾①。"视之口吻已㖞斜②。侍者以足顿地曰："当奈何！平生呵佛骂祖③，今乃尔。"师曰："无忧，为汝正之。"以手整之如故，曰："而今而后，不钝置④汝。"

——石霜楚圆禅师语录，
引自《五灯会元》卷十二

白话翻译

我把嘴扳正给你看

皇帝赐官船送石霜楚圆禅师南归。途中楚圆对侍僧说："我突然中了风。"侍僧一看，楚圆的嘴已歪斜，急得跺脚说："这可怎么办呢？谁让您平时呵佛骂祖，今天变成这副模样。"楚圆说："别耽心，我正过来给你看。"于是用手把嘴扳正了，说："从今以后，再也不跟你开玩笑了。"

Excerpts from
Zen Buddhist Texts

Look, I'll straighten it

One day, as Zen Master Chuyuan of Shishuang was sailing home southwards in a royal barge by the special favour of the Emperor, he suddenly said to the monk attending on him, "I've had a stroke." The monk looked at him and found that the Master's mouth was all awry. In panic the monk stamped his foot and shouted, "What do we do now? And you would blaspheme against Buddha and the saints! Look where that's got you!" The Master said, "Don't panic. I'll straighten it." So he straightened his face, and said to the monk, "All right. I won't play this trick on you again."

— Recorded Dialogues of Zen Master Chuyuan of Shishuang,
from *Amalgamation of the Sources of the Five Lamps*, vol. 12

注释

① 风痹疾：中风病。
② 㖞斜：歪斜。㖞：wāi 音同"歪"。
③ 呵佛骂祖：斥骂佛祖，对佛祖不恭敬。
④ 钝置：作弄，折腾。这里指开玩笑。

阅读提示

石霜楚圆禅师跟侍僧开玩笑是为了说明：没有什么因果报应，自性掌握在自己手中，我要它正它就正。这里体现了悟透自性、把握自我的禅家风度。

Excerpts from Zen Buddhist Texts

Observations

☆ The Zen Master plays this trick on the monk to teach him a lesson: there is no need to get too obsessed with the idea of cause and effect, one has complete control over one's own nature; if one wants it to be just, it will be just; if one wants it to go awry, it will go awry.

★ The trick that the Master plays on the monk brings out the point about the importance of the individual's effort in practising the Way of Buddha, and ridicules the superstitious element in religion. It is not difficult to imagine this episode as the culminating point of a long and exasperating experience of superstitious nagging by the attendant monk about punishment and reward.

主要梵语词汇表

三乘：指小乘、中乘、大乘三种超度众生，使之从生死轮回之道进入涅槃境界的方法。也泛指佛法。

大迦叶：释迦牟尼的高徒。传说佛祖释迦当初曾摘花给大迦叶以传授佛道，大迦叶微笑表示领悟。中国禅宗认为他是传承佛法的第一代祖师，西土二十八祖之始祖。释迦死后他召集僧人编辑佛祖讲义并为首座。

大乘：梵语 Mahayana 的意译。公元一世纪左右在印度形成的佛教派别。大乘强调以慈悲为怀、自度度人、普度众生的利他精神。

小乘：梵语 Hinayana 的意译。公元一世纪左右，印度佛教中出现了主张普度众生的新教派，自称"大乘"，而称原有的教派为"小乘"。小乘佛教看重自我修身，苦行持戒，以求自我解脱，往往被评为只顾自度，不度他人。小乘佛教更近于原始教义。

文殊：菩萨名。梵语 Manjusri 音译"文殊师利"的省称。意译为"妙吉祥"。他骑金狮持剑，是智慧与威猛的象征。他的像经常供奉在佛堂内，位在佛祖左侧，与右侧的普贤相对。

佛/佛陀：梵语 buddha 的音译，意思是"觉者"。佛是最高的果位，往往是

Excerpts from Zen Buddhist Texts

佛教始祖释迦牟尼的尊称,也泛指三世十方一切佛。(另见释迦牟尼)

(佛)法:梵语 *dharma* 的意译,指佛道、佛教教义。不少禅师认为佛道在佛陀之前已存在,佛陀乃佛道的化身。

佛经:有时特指佛祖的语录。

涅槃:梵语 *nirvana* 的音译,意为"灭"、"寂灭"、"圆寂"等。指彻底断灭俗世的生死烦恼,是佛家修习所要达到的最高理想。

梵王/大梵天王:指色界初禅天的大梵天王,也泛指色界诸天之王。

普贤:菩萨名。梵名 *Samantabhadra*。常骑白象,与文殊共为佛祖的左右侍士。他用"理"超度众生,以"大行"(高尚的品行)著称。

菩提:梵语 *bodhi* 的音译。意为对佛教真理的觉悟。

菩萨:佛教指上求佛法、下化众生的圣者,其地位高于罗汉而次于佛。菩萨大慈大悲,普度众生,是大乘精神的象征。我国民间熟悉的菩萨有观世音、文殊、普贤、弥勒、地藏等。菩萨往往变现各种化身来普度众生,比如观世音有三十三种化身。

达摩:菩提达摩的省称。天竺高僧,为佛教二十八祖,又是中华禅宗的始祖。他于公元 520 年(南朝梁普通元年)入中国传道,后止嵩山少林寺,面壁九年而化。法传于慧可。

僧：一般指出家修行的男性佛教徒，通称和尚。僧人入教时要参加剃发、披袈裟、诵经的仪式。

羯磨：梵语 karma 的音译，意译为"业"。指因人的身（行为）、口（言语）、意（思想）三方面的活动而引起的生死轮回，因果报应。能从轮回中解脱出来才能得到心灵的自由。

罗汉：梵语"阿罗汉" arhat 的省称。佛教小乘的最高果位，指已断除烦恼，超出三界轮回，承受人天供养的尊者。佛典有十六罗汉之说，民间则流行十八罗汉。

释迦牟尼：梵语 Sakyamuni 的音译。是佛教徒对佛教始祖悉达多的尊称，意为释迦族的圣人。相传他是王子，婚后入雪山刻苦修行，三十五岁时坐在菩提树下忽然醒悟得道。明白要超脱生死轮回不在于苦行，而在于意念上的纯净。此后说法凡四十余年，年八十示寂。（另见佛／佛陀）

A Glossary of Selected Sanskrit Terms

Arhat: A Buddhist monk who has attained *nirvana*, regarded as a sage and a saint in *Hinayana* Buddhism. Buddhist literature often talks about a group of sixteen *arhats*, while Chinese folk legend often makes reference to a group of eighteen *arhats*.

Bodhi: The state of enlightenment; the illuminated or enlightened mind.

Bodhidharma: Or *Bodhitara*, is commonly known as Damo in Pinyin transliteration, regarded as the Twenty-eighth Patriarch of Buddhism, and reputed as the founder, the First Patriarch, of Zen Buddhism in China. He arrived in China from India in AD 520, and after many years spreading the teachings of Buddha, he stayed in the Shaolin Monastery in Songshan and went into retreat in a cave for nine years before he passed away. His disciple was Huike.

Bodhisattva: In Buddhism, a *bodhisattva* refers to a saint who seeks the enlightenment of Buddha, and also seeks to help save others. A *bodhisattva*'s attainment is higher than that of an *arhat*, and just below that of Buddha. *Bodhisattvas* are known for their boundless compassion and their will to save and help all sentient beings, and they embody the spirit of *Mahayana* Buddhism. In Chinese Buddhism, among the best known of *bodhisattvas* are the Goddess of Mercy (Guan Yin), Manjusri, Samantabhadra, Maitreya, and Titsang (or Ksitigarbha). *Bodhisattvas* appear in different manifestations to help people. Guan Yin, for instance, has thirty-three different manifestations.

Brahma: The father of all living things, the first god of the Hindu triad of deities, recognised by Buddhism as a deity.

Buddha: The term means "the Enlightened One". It is also a title given to Gautama Siddhartha, an Indian philosopher who reputedly founded Buddhism. The same word, with a small letter "b" (*buddha*) refers to a being who has attained Buddhahood, i.e. a state of enlightenment or religious salvation characterised negatively as release from the earthly fetters of suffering, sorrow and illusion, and positively as the state of perfect spiritual fulfilment. See also **Sakyamuni**.

Dharma: Derived from the Sanskrit root "dhr", which has a large number of meanings including "bearing", "upholding", "supporting", "that which forms a foundation". The primary meanings in Buddhist usage are "doctrine", "righteousness", "condition", and "phenomenon". Of these, "doctrine" is the meaning most frequently referred to. In this usage, *dharma* means the Way of Buddha, the universal and ultimate truth proclaimed by Buddha. Many Buddhist masters are of the view

Excerpts from Zen Buddhist Texts

that in itself, the *dharma* is ontologically anterior even to Buddha, who is also the expression or historical manifestation of the *dharma*. Buddhas appear at intervals in the course of time; they come and go, but the *dharma* goes on for ever. The discourses of Buddha are referred to collectively as the *dharma*, since they expound on this ultimate reality. A life lived in accordance with this truth, or doctrine, or teaching, is a life characterised by *dharma*, or righteousness.

Hinayana: Literally, "Small Vehicle", it is the orthodox school of Buddhism and, according to historians of religion, more in direct line with the Buddhist succession than *Mahayanism*, which developed in India around AD 1 on fundamentally different lines. *Hinayana* is sometimes described, some would say unfairly, as an endeavour to seek *nirvana* through solitariness, the destruction of the body, and an extinguished intellect. Its followers are criticised for striving merely for their own deliverance through asceticism and therefore lacking in compassion for others.

Karma: The force generated by a person's actions — comprising thoughts, words, and deeds — that is held in Buddhism to be the motive power for the rounds of rebirths and deaths which the person has to endure until he achieves spiritual liberation and freed himself from the effects of such a force.

Mahakashyapa: Also known as, in short form, *Kashyapa* (*Kasyapa*). An outstanding disciple of *Sakyamuni*, the historical Buddha. It is said that Buddha imparted to *Mahakashyapa* the secret of Zen by plucking a flower without further explanation, and *Mahakashyapa* smiled in appreciation of his meaning. He is considered the First Patriarch of Zen Buddhism in India. He took over leadership of the *sangha* after the death of Buddha and was credited with supervising the first compilation of Buddha's sermons.

Mahayana: Literally, "Big Vehicle", it is a branch of Buddhism established in India around AD 1 and teaches the *bodhisattva* ideal of compassion and salvation for all. The essence of its teachings is sometimes described as unlimited altruism and pity; its followers are said to seek self-benefit for the benefit of others, with the ultimate goal of universal Buddhahood.

Manjusri: The *bodhisattva* representing wisdom and bravery, often depicted as riding on a golden lion and holding a sword. *Manjusri's* image is the conventional main icon in Zen meditation halls and usually placed on Buddha's left, with *Samantabhadra* on Buddha's right.

nirvana: A state of supreme liberation and bliss as a contrast to bondage in the repeating cycle of death and rebirth.

Sakyamuni: Literally the saint of the Sakya tribe. As the story goes, he was born the son of the ruler of Kapilavastu. In due course he

Excerpts from Zen Buddhist Texts

got married, but he left home in search of spiritual truth, became an ascetic, severely disciplined himself, and finally, at the age of thirty-five, he realised, while sitting under a tree, that release from the chain of rebirth and death lay not in asceticism but in moral purity. He founded a community on the basis of poverty, chastity, and insight or meditation, and it became known as Buddhism, as he became known as Buddha, the Enlightened One. His death was probably in or near 487 BC, a few years before that of Confucius in 479 BC. The sacerdotal name of his family was Gautama, said to be the original name of the whole clan, Sakya being that of his branch. His personal name was Siddhartha, or Sarvarthasiddha. See also **Buddha**.

Samantabhadra: The *bodhisattva* representing the ultimate principle of union of knowledge and deeds for the enlightenment of all beings. *Samantabhadra* is depicted as riding on a white elephant. He and Manjusri are the right-and left-hand assistants of Buddha. He is reputed for his ability to save the benighted with reason and noble deeds.

Sangha: An assembly. The term is used to refer to the monastic order founded by Buddha. The community consists of monks (*bhikshu*), nuns (*bhikshuni*), and novices (*shramanera*). Those who join the Order have to perform an act by which they indicate their willingness to renounce the world. This includes shaving of hair and beard, donning the yellow robe and reciting the *Tisarana*. The person is then a novice. The ordination ceremony takes place before a chapter of at least ten senior monks. No oaths are taken, and the monk is free to leave the Order at any time if he desires to do so. In a wider sense, the term *sangha* refers to the entire community of followers of the *dharma* in the world, rather than an exclusive few who retire from the world.

Sutra: One of the narrative parts of the Buddhist canonical literature, especially the dialogues attributed to Buddha.

Triyana: The three vehicles, or conveyances, which carry living beings across mortality (births and deaths) to the shores of *nirvana*; the three methods advocated by Buddhism for deliverance from all the trammels of life.

致选译者

"中华传统文化精粹"丛书,是根据我公司20世纪90年代出版的"一百丛书"重新编选、修订的。与本丛书有关的各项版权事宜,包括选译者的稿酬等,我公司已委托中华版权代理总公司代为办理。

中华版权代理总公司电话:010-68003549;联系人:赵秀清。

中国对外翻译出版公司
2007年11月